The Enforcer's Mark

Ashlynn Carter

Copyright © 2024 by Ashlynn Carter

All rights reserved.

No part of this publication may be reproduced, distributed, or transmitted in any form or by any means, including photocopying, recording, or other electronic or mechanical methods, without the prior written permission of the publisher, except as permitted by U.S. copyright law. For permission requests, contact Ashlynn Carter at ashlynn.carter@proton.me.

The story, all names, characters, and incidents portrayed in this production are fictitious. No identification with actual persons (living or deceased), places, buildings, and products is intended or should be inferred.

Book Cover by Ashlynn Carter

First edition 2024

Chapter 1

Beep. Beep. Beep. The sound of my alarm had me scrambling, in my half-asleep state, to shut it off. Once I finally silenced it, I lay flat on my back for a moment listening. I was relieved when I didn't hear anyone moving around.

I quietly got to my feet and folded the toddler sized blanket I used during the night to keep warm before stuffing it into my backpack. I glanced at the towel that I called a bed as I yanked the alarm clock's cord out of the wall. It was better to reset the clock each night than it was to come home after work to find that I had accidentally hit the snooze instead of the off button. I only had to learn that lesson once.

Holding my breath, I pulled open my door and winced as the hinges creaked. I paused and listened. All was quiet. I moved silently down the stairs and out the front door before I let out a sigh of relief.

The crisp morning air caused my breath to puff out in white clouds and I shivered. Winter was beginning to give way to spring, but the mornings were still freezing. I pulled my hoodie out of my bag and slipped it on before heading down the long driveway.

The sun was just starting to peak over the mountains as I reached the main road. I loved early mornings. It didn't matter if it was summer, fall, winter, or spring. The world seemed at peace during this time of day. Most people were still in bed and traffic was practically nonexistent. Lucky for me, my aunts usually were asleep, so I didn't have to interact with them much. They hated me and did not hide that fact.

I moved in with them shortly after my parents died in a fire, leaving me an orphan at the age of eight. Being my father's sisters, they were my next of kin and the state turned me over to them. That was nearly ten years ago. Aunt Grace and Aunt Lucy took me in only to save face with the community. They blamed my mother for taking away their brother as a young man and told me, often, how much I looked like her. Usually that statement preceded a "punishment" of some sort.

At first, they yelled at me or gave me an occasional slap, but they became harsher and more creative over the years. When I was close to ten, they had discovered that I was deathly afraid of basements and the dark, so they started chaining me up in their basement for certain periods of time to punish me.

I also hated to be touched. If they were really angry with me, not only would they chain me up in the dark, but they would also grab my arms and legs. A shiver ran down my spine just thinking about it.

I gave myself a mental shake as the little diner I worked at came into view at the end of the street. I needed to put on my game face. It was hard to switch from being scared all the time to pretending that everything was okay. After being at work for a little while, it would be easier to keep a smile on my face. It always was.

The diner was small and not terribly busy. The owner, Murphy, was so much fun and reminded me a lot of my dad. He was in his late forties and loved to laugh. His black hair was starting to grey at his temples, but he said it made him look distinguished.

Besides him, there were only a few other workers; his nephew, Matt, and a couple of girls who attended the local high school. The other girls only worked on the weekends and during school breaks. They weren't terrible to work with. They did tend to avoid me whenever possible. They seemed to hate my close relationship with Matt.

Matt was only a couple of years older than me and was just as much of a jokester as Murphy was. Matt had quickly become a brother figure to me and had, on several occasions, scared off a few customers who wouldn't take 'no' for an answer.

Unlike most kids my age who went to school, I went to work. The moment my aunts brought me back to their house, they put me to use cleaning the house while they told everyone I was homeschooled. When I turned sixteen, they had me find a job to pay for my living expenses. I had been working at Murphy's Diner for almost two years now and loved it.

As I walked across the diner's empty parking lot, headlights flashed across me. I ignored them and continued to the door. "Hey Trinity, how many times do I have to tell you, if you need a ride into work, all you have to do is ask." Murphy called out as a car door closed.

I turned around with a smile on my face. "And I have told you that if I needed a ride, I would call you." That was not entirely true. I didn't have a phone and I wasn't allowed to use the one at the house. Even if I could call him, I wouldn't. There was no way I was going to have Murphy or Matt see where or how I lived.

"Your cheeks and nose are bright red, Trin. You must be freezing with only a hoodie on." Matt jogged over to the door. He unlocked it quickly and held it open for me.

I stepped inside and flipped on the lights as I headed for the kitchen to hang my stuff up on the coat rack by the employee lockers. "It really isn't that bad, Matt. Plus, the cool morning air is refreshing and helps me wake up." I said over my shoulder.

"If Uncle Murphy would just push back the time he opened, neither of us would have to be up at this unholy hour." Matt grumbled as he followed me, and I forced a laugh. Any later and I might have to deal with my aunts in the mornings. He took off his coat and hung it up next to my bag.

"Are you bickering about having to be here by 5:00 am again?" Murphy rolled his eyes as he smiled. "Do we have to go through this every morning, Matt? If you hadn't hurt your arm, you would be training with the others at this time of day, anyway."

I laughed at their banter as I moved out into the small hallway that led to the restrooms. I entered the women's bathroom and opened the cleaning closet to pull out a small bag from the back.

I stashed my toiletries I bought with my tip money in there because if my aunts knew I had a hairbrush they would smack me with it. I brushed my teeth and pulled my hair up into a high ponytail before putting my stuff back into its hiding place.

When I got back to the kitchen, Matt had run off somewhere and Murphy was starting up the grills. Murphy gave me a fatherly smile. "How are classes going, kid?"

I let out a huff of frustration. "Math is still killing me, but I think I'm slowly getting it. I have finals in a few days."

When Murphy found out I had only a third-grade education at the age of sixteen, he had been livid. He managed to coax me to tell him about my aunts' refusal to allow me to go to school. The next week he had scheduled me a double shift, but when 7:00 pm rolled around, he took me into the breakroom off of the kitchen and sat me down. He placed his laptop in front of me and told me he was enrolling me in an online school.

That day had been the happiest day of my life. Well, the happiest day since my parents' deaths. The day they died, so did my happiness. I had genuinely smiled while we completed the forms instead of giving the practiced smile I used to make everyone think everything was okay. From that day on, I worked from 5:00 am to 7:00 pm before going to the breakroom to study until 11:30 pm.

In just two years I had managed to go from a third-grade education to finishing my eighth-grade year. My aunts, thankfully, hadn't found out because Murphy gave me a raise so that the money matched the time I worked.

"Keep at it, Trin. You'll get it." Murphy gave me an encouraging smile before turning back to opening the diner for the day.

Like always, the day passed quickly. When I wasn't taking people's orders, I was joking around with Murphy or Matt. It sure beat having to stay at my aunts' house all day. 7:00 pm rolled around and I spread my books and the old laptop on the table and began my schoolwork.

A soft knock on the door frame pulled my head up from trying to work out a word problem. "I'm closing early tonight because my nephews are back in town from training, and we are celebrating their return." Murphy said while beaming ear to ear.

I had heard a lot about Murphy's nephews. They had come into the diner several times since I started working but I was usually doing schoolwork when they did so I hadn't met them. The only reason I knew Matt was because he had an injury and started working at the diner six months ago while the other three left for training of some kind.

I glanced at the clock at the corner of the computer screen. It was 9:30 pm and I still had ten more problems to do before I could start on my writing assignment.

"Do you mind if I make cookies for a snack?" I asked. Baking was not all that fun for me, but I had a wicked sweet tooth, and I was stressed. I needed a little pick me up to hopefully finish everything I needed to tonight.

"I just locked the front door, so the kitchen is all yours." Murphy left and I jumped from my seat.

After looking at the ingredients in the pantry, I decided that a cinnamon swirl cake sounded way better than chocolate chip cookies. I kicked off my shoes and turned on the radio as I gathered the ingredients.

Fifteen minutes later, I slipped the glass cake pan full of deliciousness into the oven. I set the timer for forty minutes and went back to the breakroom. I grabbed my math book and scratch paper before moving back into the kitchen. I set my stuff on the metal prep table that was near the door to the dining room and the oven. I began working on my math again.

'Hero' by Skillet filled the room and I sang along. I sometimes felt like this song was written for me. If only there was a hero that could save me from my aunts. I was humming along to the music as my hips swayed.

Music always put me at ease. Before my parents died, there was always music in the house. I shook myself from the thoughts of my parents and focused back on my math problems.

'Stitches' by Shawn Mendes came on the radio, and I turned it up. I loved this song! I started singing aloud and dancing, forgetting about my homework. I grabbed the spatula I used earlier and started using it as a microphone, getting lost in the music. I was out of breath by the time the song was over, but I smiled as I stepped back to the prep table.

My back was facing the oven as I started to reread the word problem but 'Trying To Find Atlantis' by Jamie O'Neal came on next. I again ignored my dreaded math and started to sing. The music was so loud that I barely heard the oven timer go off behind me. I was still singing at the top of my lungs as I pulled the cake pan out of the oven.

"Ala..." As I turned to place the pan on the prep table, my singing ended in a scream.

Five men were standing just inside the kitchen door watching me with amused expressions on their faces not five feet away. How had I not noticed them? The pan slipped from my hands. One of the guys reached out and grabbed it as it began to fall.

He let out a hiss of pain and he too, let go of it. The pan shattered when it hit the floor at our feet. Glass was everywhere and silence filled the room. Someone must have turned the music off. No one moved for a long moment.

My heart was beating so fast, I was certain everyone could hear it. I hadn't expected an audience to my impromptu dance number. I slowly lifted my gaze from my ruined cake and came face to face with a gorgeous blue-eyed man with dark brown hair. He blinked several times before looking down at his hands. They were bright red from grabbing the hot pan.

"I'm so sorry." I said as I rushed across the room and grabbed the first-aid kit off of the wall.

The man was burned because of my clumsiness, and I felt guilty. I knew from experience that there was a burn relief gel inside the kit. I could use the bright blue color of the gel to mask my magic as I healed him. It was the least I could do.

As I was running back to him, I stepped on a piece of broken glass. I cried out in pain as a shard sliced the bottom of my foot. A startled gasp escaped my lips as Mr. Blue Eyes wrapped his arms around my waist and lifted me up before he carefully deposited me on the prep table.

Murphy was at my side in a moment and lifted up my foot. "Where are your shoes, Trinity?" Murphy growled out as he pulled a piece of glass out of my foot.

"Ouch!" I yanked my foot from his hand and glared at him. He knew I did not like to be touched. "I think better without shoes on, and I wasn't expecting people to come into the kitchen unannounced." I snapped back.

"I called your name twice, Trin." Matt moved closer to the table, and I could hear the glass crunch under his boots. "You were too absorbed in your music to hear me." He reached out to pat my shoulder, but I slapped his hand away.

I opened the first-aid box, pulled out the gel and squirted it out onto my hand. "Here." I said as I grabbed Blue Eyes' hand and began to smear the gel over the red and blistering skin.

I felt my magic swirl inside me as a faint, almost unnoticeable glow came from my hand. I repeated the action on his other hand before wiping the leftover gel off on a hot pad that was sitting next to me.

I pulled my foot up and rested it against my other leg. I reached back into the first-aid box and grabbed tweezers. "So, why were you all in here anyway?" I asked. The silence in the room was beginning to unnerve me.

I picked three pieces of glass out of my foot before anyone spoke. "Trinity, let me help you." Murphy reached for the tweezers, but I shook my head. He let out a frustrated sigh. "We heard you turn on music a while ago, but when you cranked it up and started singing with it, Matt was curious to see what you were doing. We stuck our heads in, and you were owning the stage."

"Well, for future reference, I prefer to 'own the stage' without an audience, okay?" I said as I smeared triple-antibiotic ointment on the bottom of both feet. "Matt, can you grab my shoes and socks please?" When he brought them over, I quickly grabbed my socks and slipped them on. I glanced over at the clock as I put my shoes on. "I am going to leave you guys in charge of cleaning up, I am heading home." I picked up my textbook and put it into my locker before slipping my hoodie on. I grabbed my backpack and headed for the door with a slight limp.

"Let me at least drive you home, Trin." Matt followed behind me. The other three guys just watched me, and it made me feel uneasy.

"I am in no rush to get home Matt, but I am definitely not staying here. My walk back to the house will be blissfully quiet and I can try to forget this," I wave my hand around the kitchen. "...ever happened. He started to protest so I interrupted him. "I said no, Matt. I will see you tomorrow."

I turned and walked out the door, but paused just outside and took a deep breath. I was just about to start walking when Matt's excited voice came through the cracked door. "Did you see that? She touched someone! Like, willingly touched someone!"

"I saw." Murphy said, sounding tired.

"Why is that significant?" One of the other men asked.

"Trinity has had a difficult life from what I can gather. She has a..." Murphy's voice trailed off as if he were trying to find the right words.

"Trinity never touches people. Well, almost never. It has taken me six months to get an occasional high-five." Matt explained. "But she grabbed your hand and put that gel on it. That's huge!" Matt sounded so proud, and I rolled my eyes.

"Did you see it glow?" The unknown man spoke again, and I tensed. I had hoped he hadn't seen anything.

"It looked like light glinting off it." Another man said.

"If she doesn't like touching, does that mean she doesn't have a boyfriend?" The third unknown man asked.

"You try anything with her, and you will be sipping soup through a straw." Matt growled out. I covered my mouth as I tried not to laugh. Matt had gone from kid in a candy store excited to overprotective brother in seconds. Shaking my head, I began my walk back to my aunts' house.

It was just after 11:30pm when I approached the house. I usually didn't get in until after midnight, so I hoped my aunts didn't notice the difference. They were unpredictable when their routine was interrupted. All the lights were off, and I prayed that they were sleeping. As I closed the door quietly behind me, the hall light clicked on. I gasped in surprise as I whirled around.

Both Aunt Lucy and Aunt Grace stood on the stairs glaring down at me. My hopes plummeted and I began to feel sick. The looks they were giving me usually preceded some sort of painful punishment. Aunt Grace slowly moved down the stairs as I took a few small steps toward the sitting room.

The entry hall wasn't very big and had a wide archway that led to the sitting room. There was a small step up into the room and I stopped moving a good two feet from it. I did not want Aunt Grace to think I was trying to run from her.

"Where have you been?" Aunt Grace sneered at me.

"Mr. Murphy closed the diner a little early today and I came straight home." I stammered out while staring at the ground.

"If that is so, then where is our money?" Aunt Lucy stepped down two steps before stopping again.

"I-I don't get paid until tomorrow." I answered.

As quick as lightning, Aunt Grace's hand flew through the air and hit me with such force that I lost my balance. On the way down to the floor, my head cracked against the edge of something, and pain exploded through my head. I blinked several times trying to stop the world from spinning, but instead, my vision began to fade.

"That will teach the stupid girl to sass you, sister." Aunt Lucy's voice sounded like it was far away. "And we better have the money tomorrow or it will be a full twenty-four hours in the basement." That was the last thing I heard before the blackness completely overtook me.

*   *   *

I groaned softly as I blinked several times. There was light coming through the window and I bolted upright as I realized it was morning. What time was it? I tried to stand but stumbled into the wall.

I looked around as memories from the night before came rushing back to me. I touched my head gingerly and winced. When I pulled my hand away, there was blood all over my fingers. I made my way to the bathroom and looked in the mirror.

Aunt Grace must have been wearing rings and hit me with the back of her hand or her fist. The left side of my face was puffy, and I had a black eye that was partially swollen closed. The right side of my face and head were covered in blood.

On closer examination, I found a gash along my hairline near my temple. What had I hit and what was I going to do? I was already late for work, and I needed to get cleaned up before getting there. Unfortunately, today was not the day I was permitted to shower. That was not for another three days.

Footsteps on the stairs caused me to freeze. "At least she is gone." Aunt Lucy said. "I was afraid she would have died in the night, and we would be blamed for it."

"She left her blood all over the floor. Well, when she gets back, she is going to clean that up. It is positively disgusting that she leaves that stuff all over the place." Aunt Grace said angrily.

The sound of footsteps against the wood floor in the entryway were loud in my ears. The front door slammed shut followed by the sound of squealing tires as a car drove away.

Relief flooded my body, and I stripped off my clothes. As quickly as possible, I took a shower to wash the blood out of my hair, wincing as the water ran over the cut on my forehead.

I didn't want my aunts to come home and see me there, so I dressed quickly and put a wad of toilet paper against the gash to stop it from bleeding. It had started up again in the shower.

As I was heading to the door, I saw the puddle of blood on the wood floor next to the step going into the living room. Well, that explained what I hit. I left, walking fast. Halfway down the driveway I had to slow down. I was starting to get dizzy, but I pushed on. I couldn't afford to miss work. I had to get that paycheck.

Too bad I couldn't heal myself. Mother was the one who always healed me. As a magic user, she could use her magic to heal others, but not herself. When I was three, my powers started to appear. Mom started teaching me little things immediately and both her and my father were extremely proud of me. The first thing mother taught me was how to heal. It worked out great because I would heal her, and she healed me whenever either one of us was hurt.

Oh, how I missed her now.

There were only three cars in the parking lot when I arrived. Before stepping through the back door to the kitchen, I made sure that my hood was pulled low over my face to hide my bruises as much as possible. Taking a deep breath, I opened the door and stepped in. Matt was standing at the sink whistling as he washed dishes. At the sound of the door opening, he looked over at me. I kept my head down and hung up my bag.

"Hey, Trin. I am so glad to see you." He said with relief in his voice. "Look, I'm sorry for last night." He apologized as he turned the water off and faced me.

"Don't worry about it, Matt." I shrugged while keeping my head down. "But hey, I have a headache. Would you mind if I wash the dishes today while you work the tables?" I asked and mentally crossed my fingers. I really wasn't in the mood to interact with people and my head really was pounding.

"Sure thing. I'll let Murphy know you are here. He's been ready to send a search party out for you." Matt laughed and left the kitchen.

Murphy peeked in on me and expressed his own apologies for scaring me last night. I accepted his apology and was left to my own devices. Which was great because I couldn't bring myself to pretend today. All my energy was going into staying upright. The day felt so long as I attempted to stay on my feet.

My headache had been steadily getting worse and I suspected that I had a concussion. I jumped when the kitchen door slammed open, and Murphy stormed in while talking on the phone.

"What do you mean there is no way to get the stubs here tonight?" Murphy yelled. He was definitely angry. Murphy never yelled. "My employees rely on that money to live." He paused his yelling to listen to the person on the other end of the line as he paced. I finished rinsing the last dish in the load and turned to watch him as the pit in my stomach began to grow. "Next week is not good enough! I don't care if the truck had mechanical issues. You will have all my paychecks here by eight tomorrow morning or I am taking my business elsewhere." I watched as Murphy slammed the phone down on the counter and cursed.

"Is everything okay, Murphy?" I asked tentatively. If I didn't have my paycheck to give to my aunts tonight, then I would be chained in the basement again. My heart rate accelerated and the pounding in my head increased with it.

"There was a problem with the truck that was supposed to deliver the paychecks today." He ran his hand through his hair in agitation. "I'm sorry, Trin. I am hoping that I can get it for you by tomorrow morning."

The rushing in my ears drowned out whatever he said next. My hands began to shake, and my breathing became uneven. The basement. A Full twenty-four hours. What was I going to do?

A hand lightly touched my shoulder and I dropped to the floor. I heard myself whimper as I pulled my knees to my chest and threw my arms over my head. Even though I knew my aunts weren't there, my mind conjured up images of them stalking toward me with a belt and the chains.

"Trinity? What's wrong, honey?" I heard Murphy's worried voice, but I was too scared to respond. "Matt! Get in here!" I jumped, and a soft cry escaped my lips at the sudden loud noise.

"What is it Mur...What's wrong with Trinity?" Matt's voice went from curious to worried as soon as he walked into the kitchen.

"I don't know. Sit with her while I close the diner." Murphy sounded panicked as his hurried footsteps left the kitchen.

The basement. It had been two weeks since I did something that warranted me being chained in the basement. I didn't look up as I felt Matt sit on the floor next to me. His arm brushed mine, and I scooted a little away as I whimpered again. I laid my right cheek against my knees as I faced away from him. Every touch over the last ten years was followed by pain. I couldn't handle it right now. I was going to be enduring who knows what for the next twenty-four hours in that dark, damp torture cell my aunts called a basement.

Suddenly, I was back in the basement of my home. My father sat me down before kneeling in front of me. His face was smeared with ash, and he looked worried. I was crying and shaking with fear. The day had started out great but had taken a terrifying turn as soon as the man showed up.

"I need you to stay here. Okay, Princess?" He said urgently while looking at me intensely. I had never seen my father look so scared. "I am going to go get your mother and then I will be right back." I nodded my understanding as he pressed a kiss to my forehead before rushing up the stairs.

After several minutes, I heard my mother scream my father's name before she cried out in pain. A man's voice reached me, and it made my blood run cold.

"I want the girl!" He yelled. "I will get her one way or another and when I do, I will pull every drop of magic from each and every last cell of hers!" The roof collapsed with a loud crack, and I was sealed underground in complete darkness. The last thing I heard was my mother's screams.

The kitchen door crashed open again and I screamed. "Hey, it's okay. Trin, can you tell me what's wrong?" Matt's voice was soft, but I shook my head. The action caused the cut on my forehead to brush my pant leg and I winced at the sharp pain. The area around it was really tender. "What happened, Uncle Murphy? Why is she like this?" He sounded upset but I didn't look at him.

"I don't know. I told her about the truck and the paychecks being delayed, then she just...broke." I started to cry. I didn't mean to worry Murphy and Matt. Maybe I should have just stayed at the house. "Is that blood?" Murphy whispered. "Trinity, look at me." He commanded but I didn't respond to him.

I felt my hood being tugged back and I gasped as I looked up into Murphy's horrified face. Matt sucked in a sharp breath as he rotated to see me better. "Who did this to you?" Matt asked furiously. "Someone, grab the first-aid kit!" He demanded as he reached out a hand to touch me.

I shoved away from him and scrambled to my feet. I ran to my bag and grabbed it. I needed to get away, needed to find some place safe. When I turned around, I saw the three men from last night also in the kitchen.

The blue-eyed one was standing next to a worried Murphy. Matt had moved to block the door that led to the diner. The other two were to my left, blocking the back entrance. One was a redhead with brown eyes and freckles. The other had reddish brown hair, brown eyes and last night when he smiled, he had a dimple.

Blood dripped onto my shoulder, and I knew I needed to suture the cut soon. I took a step to my right, away from Freckles and Dimples. Blue Eyes and Murphy took a cautious step toward me. I didn't want them to touch me, I couldn't have them touch me. If I could get past Matt, I could run to the bathroom and use the suture kit in my bag.

I took another step to my right. Taking a deep breath, I sprinted forward. As Matt reached out to grab me, I twisted and used his forward momentum to push him to the ground. I pushed through the door, but only made it a couple of steps before I felt the hood of my hoodie being tugged back. I dropped my bag and twisted to face the person that grabbed me. Bending forward, I let my hoodie get pulled off.

A thump sounded as something heavy hit the wall. I grabbed my bag and continued to the restroom. Once inside, I slammed the door and threw the lock into place. I stumbled to the sink as tears threatened to fall. I blinked them back, now was not the time. If I started crying now, then I wouldn't be able to see well enough to stitch up the wound on my head.

A banging on the door caused me to jump. Murphy's anxious voice called through the door. "Trinity, please open the door. We are just trying to help you, sweetheart. I know you are scared but we can protect you."

"No." I called back in a weak voice. My hands were shaking so badly that I struggled to grasp the needle from my small kit. I grabbed several paper towels and blotted most of the blood away. I had done this before; I can do it again.

Taking a deep breath, I pushed the needle through the tender skin next to the cut. I had to bite my lip to keep from crying out at the pain. Forty minutes passed in agony, and I was near to collapsing. I had given up a while ago on trying to keep quiet, the tenderness of the wound combined with trying to stitch it closed was excruciating. I threw up twice from the pain, but I pushed through it. I tried to put my stuff away, but my legs gave out and I started crying again.

"M-murphy?" I called through my sobs.

"Trinity. Open the door, honey." He sounded desperate for me to comply.

"I can't." I cried as I lay on the floor.

"Why not?" Matt asked.

"I can't get to the lock." I mumbled as I started to feel heavy, and I knew I was close to passing out. I didn't know if I was even loud enough for them to hear me.

There was a muffled conversation before Murphy spoke again. "I need you to move into one of the stalls and close the door, okay?"

I didn't respond to him, instead I focused on pulling myself towards the corner near the cleaning closet. If they were going to kick the door in, it would be safer over there. I pulled the mop bucket out of the corner and moved into its place before pulling it back to me.

"Trinity? Did you move into a stall?" Murphy sounded even more panicked and slightly farther away.

"Murphy." I tried to respond but my voice barely reached my own ears.

"We can't wait any longer. She could be bleeding to death, Murphy. She can heal if she is hurt by us blowing the door open." Matt said angrily.

I screamed as the door splintered inward. Men's frightened voices and then hands. I tried to open my eyes, but my eyelids were too heavy. I pushed at the hands that grabbed me, but they did not let go and I was too weak to fight them off. By the time I was able to open my eyes I was being laid in the backseat of a car.

"No." I tried to get up. "I need to get back to the house."

"Trin, you're not going anywhere until you are better, and you tell me who did this to you." Murphy's stern voice sounded from the driver's seat.

I reached for the door only for strong arms to pull me back. I struggled as best I could as I began to cry. I couldn't break the grip of whoever had me and I finally gave up and sank back against them. The arms that had held me firmly in place relaxed slightly as I heard someone telling me everything was going to be okay. Then the darkness consumed me once again.

Chapter 2

I groaned as I rolled over and blinked my eyes open. The light in the room was incredibly bright. I looked around and gave a startled squeak when I realized I was in a super soft bed with a thick comforter. I wasn't allowed on the furniture.

I leapt out of the bed and fell to the floor as my foot got caught in the blankets. I looked around the room trying to figure out where I was. This was definitely not my aunts' house, and it definitely wasn't a hospital.

Cautiously I got to my feet and gasped. Where were my clothes? My work uniform had been replaced with a man's shirt that reached just below my rear end. I moved to the nearest closed door and yanked it open hoping to find my things.

Instead, I found a large walk-in closet filled with men's clothing. Whose clothes were these? Well, whoever this room belonged to was going to have to deal with me borrowing some things. And once I was decent, I was going to find them and give them a piece of my mind. Who did they think they were? You can't just change someone into different clothes while they are unconscious.

I sighed in relief as I pulled the second drawer open and found several pairs of basketball shorts. I quickly slid them on and tied them as tight as I could. However, they still slipped off my hips. Being five foot three and barely over a hundred pounds, my waist was narrow making it impossible for the shorts to stay on. Whoever this guy was, he was quite a bit bigger than me. I rolled the waistband several times, and to my relief, the shorts stayed on. Barely.

Hey, I'll take it.

I spotted a hoodie on the floor and picked it up. I pulled it over my head and felt much better about confronting my captors. As I walked out of the closet, I spotted another door right next to it. I slowly opened it and walked into an ensuite.

It was a really nice bathroom with a large tub just left of the entrance. A closet was right behind the door. Next to the closet was a sink and large counter. The toilet room was on the same wall as the bathtub. Across from that was a medium sized walk-in shower.

The towels were navy blue and looked thick and soft. I moved farther in and looked in the mirror. A strangled gasp escaped my lips. The bruising on the left side of my face had deepened in color, but at least the swelling had decreased. I leaned closer to get a better look at the stitches I did. They weren't the prettiest, but they did the job.

It looked like someone had tried to wipe away the blood but missed several spots. I did not want to ruin any of the expensive-looking washcloths or towels, so I decided to wait and shower after I went to see who owned this house.

I pulled open the door and cautiously stepped out into the hallway. The hall had at least three doors on each wall and the floor was a lush carpet. I looked to my left and spied the stairs leading down to the main level. I slowly moved down each step. A wave of dizziness came over me, and the pounding in my head increased. I wobbled, caught myself, and took a deep breath before continuing.

With a hand on the wall to steady myself, I moved down the hall. I heard voices coming from an open door on the left. I peeked inside and saw Murphy, Matt, Blue Eyes, Freckles, and Dimples sitting at a rectangular table eating bowls of cereal.

At least this was Murphy's house and not some random person's place. I no longer felt threatened being here. Murphy would never hurt me, but I was still mad that they had brought me here. I needed to get this confrontation over with so that I could go lay back down. I stepped into the room as I crossed my arms over my chest and leaned a shoulder against the doorframe. "Where are my clothes?" I demanded.

"Trinity! You're awake!" Matt jumped to his feet and looked like he was ready to run to me. I held up my hand to tell him to stop.

"I want my clothes, where are they?" I asked again.

Murphy leaned back in his chair as he watched me closely. "Trinity, your clothes were ruined."

"What?" I uncrossed my arms. What was I going to do now? I couldn't leave and go back to my aunts' house in some guy's clothes. "And whose are these?" I tugged on the sweatshirt as I glared at the occupants of the table.

Matt, Dimples, and Freckles all pointed to Blue Eyes in unison. His eyes went wide at their gesture before he glared at them.

"It is not what you think, Trinity. You were covered in blood, and we had my niece get you cleaned up and in clean clothes." Murphy explained calmly. I squeezed my eyes shut. How mortifying. Not to mention the fact that someone touched me without my permission. "Why don't you sit down and eat something? Then we can talk about the other day." My eyes popped open as I glared at him.

I was so mad and mortified that I yelled. "It is exactly what I think it is, Murphy! Someone, I don't know, touched me while I was unconscious! Not only did they touch me, but they also undressed me and put me in some guy's T-shirt!"

Tears started to burn my eyes as I turned around and stomped out of the room. Matt called after me. I broke into a run and ran back to the room I woke up in. I moved to the window seat and pulled my knees to my chest.

I finally let the tears fall. How was I going to face my aunts when I eventually went back? What were they going to do when I did show back up? Memories of the last time I tried to run away when I was ten flooded into my mind.

I had just spent an hour in the basement, and I was in a complete panic. I climbed through my window and ran into the forest. I was gone for only six hours before the police picked me up and took me back to my aunts' house. They pretended to be concerned about me while the officers were there but as soon as they left, I was dragged back down to the basement by my hair.

Aunt Lucy was so angry that she ripped off my shirt and dragged a needle across the skin on my back. She put just enough pressure for the needle to barely break my skin. She did it several more times before Aunt Grace scrubbed my back with rubbing alcohol and a rough brush. What would happen this time when they found me?

A soft knock sounded at the door, and I stifled a scream. The sudden sound had scared me, but to my relief it pulled me from my terrible memories. I kept my face toward the window. A second later I heard the soft click of the door as it closed. I turned my head to see who was there and my eyes met those of Blue Eyes.

He held a bowl with a spoon in one hand and a gallon of milk in the other. He stood awkwardly by the door. He cleared his throat and moved in my direction. He set his offering on the bench next to me and took a small step back.

"I brought you up some Fruit Loops since that is the only thing we have. Murphy says it is an addiction of ours." He paused before continuing. "You know, Murphy has been beside himself with worry over you. He nearly sent for a doctor after you hadn't woken up in the last two days, but Matt said you would just get angry if a doctor came." Blue Eyes said softly.

I rotated forward to face Blue Eyes fully and put my feet on the ground. "Days?" I asked in a strangled whisper. "How long have I been here?"

"Three days." Blue Eyes answered, keeping his voice soft.

My breathing became ragged as my anxiety rose. Three days? Aunt Lucy and Aunt Grace would definitely be livid when they found me. I couldn't go back. There was no way I would be able to handle whatever they would do.

"Hey." Blue Eyes crouched down in front of me. He was careful not to touch me as he placed his hands on either side of me on the bench. "It's okay. You're safe here."

I shook my head as my tears started again. "No, it is not okay. Nothing has been okay for the last ten years. I can't go back to them now. Three days? They...they..." A sob escaped and I buried my face in my hands, ignoring the pain from the bruises. A moment later I felt the thick comforter wrap around me before I was pulled gently off the bench. "W-what are you doing?" I asked.

"You do not like to be touched, right? So, I'm not touching you." I looked up and noticed that I was sitting in his lap and his arms were around me. I waited for the familiar panic of being touched to surface but it didn't. Probably because I couldn't feel him through the thickness of the blanket. We fell into silence as my tears continued to fall.

My eyes began to droop. A little while later, I felt myself being lifted before I was placed back on the bed. "Everything really is going to be okay. You are safe here from whoever hurt you, Trinity. Just remember that." Blue Eyes whispered before he turned and left the room.

I lay there for several minutes thinking about what Blue Eyes had said. If I truly were safe here, then maybe I could stay until my birthday next week. Once I was eighteen, my aunts wouldn't be able to hurt me anymore. I could leave and not have to ever see them again. I sat up and wiped my tears. A small smile turned up my lips as I thought about the possibility of never having to go back to live with my aunts.

I spied the bowl and milk on the window bench that Blue Eyes had brought in. I picked them up and poured the milk. I ate quickly and rinsed my bowl out in the bathroom sink. Knowing I couldn't hide in this room forever, I decided to go to the kitchen to put the milk and dishes away.

I retraced my path from earlier that morning and easily found the dining room. I moved one more door down and found the kitchen. The room was amazing. In the center of the white marble tiled floor was a large island. The countertops were white granite, and a black farmhouse sink was in the center of the island.

There was a large fridge against the wall, and I walked over to it to put the milk away. Everything was so clean and organized. Not at all what I expected from a bunch of bachelors.

A tall door labeled PANTRY caught my eye and I opened it. I gave a short laugh as I stared in disbelief. At least fifteen boxes of Fruit Loops were lined up on a shelf. A smile tugged at my lips. Blue Eyes wasn't kidding about Fruit Loops being the only option. I wondered what would happen if they poured a bowl of cereal, only for it to be Grape Nuts instead of their precious Fruit Loops.

I started to feel the once familiar sensation of magic flowing through me. I had rarely used my magic since moving in with my aunts. I closed my eyes as a memory of my parents resurfaced. I was close to six and my mother was whispering in my ear. Father loved mashed potatoes and had a large serving on his plate. Mother asked me to try to change the potatoes on dad's fork to green beans. I giggled because dad hated the vegetable. It took me several tries but on his fifth bite he spit green beans all over the table. He looked over at us with wide eyes before chasing us around the room as we laughed.

I blinked several times, and the memory was gone. I left the pantry and went to explore the rest of the house. Hopefully, I could find Murphy so that I could ask about the possibility of staying here for another week.

After thirty minutes of peeking into rooms without seeing anyone, I decided to go back to the lounge I had come across earlier and see if I could find something to watch. I didn't think Murphy would mind me using his TV since I watched the one at the diner throughout the day without him getting angry.

The lounge was different from all the other rooms in the house. It had mismatched furniture and a side bar that was probably used to hold snacks. Everywhere else in the house had matching furniture and a color scheme. There was a love seat couch in the center of the room with two lazy boy chairs on either side of it. They all faced the largest TV I have ever seen in my life.

I grabbed the remote off the side bar and made my way to the far side of the room. I hesitated before sitting in the lazy boy recliner nearest the wall. No one was around so I figured why not sit on the soft looking chair. If I heard anyone coming, I would move to the floor so no one would know I was on the furniture.

Flipping through the channels I came across a sportscaster announcing the women's soccer game that would be starting in an hour and a half. He continued talking about different sports news and I quickly lost interest. I continued flipping through the channels until The Bachelorette came on.

I had never seen it before, but I had heard several of the customers at the diner talking about it frequently. I settled back in the chair. I decided to watch this until the soccer game came on. Twenty minutes in, I made up my mind; even though most of the guys were hot, this had to be the dumbest show I had ever seen. Listening to the sportscaster would be better than this.

I reached for the remote I had put on the arm of the couch. It wasn't there. I started feeling in the creases of my chair when I heard a sound from the door. My head snapped up only to see all five men walking into the room. I struggled to keep my panic in check.

"Mind if we join you, Trin?" Matt asked as he took a seat.

"Um... Sure." I said as I slid off the couch and scooted to rest my back against the wall before turning my attention back to the TV. The contestants were shirtless on a beach as they flirted with the girl. I desperately hoped they didn't notice that I was on the couch. Maybe if I pretended to be into the show, they would leave me alone.

"What are you doing, Trinity?" Matt asked in confusion. My breath caught in my lungs as dread started to freeze my limbs. They had noticed. I smiled over at Matt, trying not to show how scared I was.

"I'm watching smoking hot guys as they play on a beach. I mean have you seen anyone as hot as Brad." I said, trying to distract him. I knew Matt thought of himself as attractive and liked flirting with all the girls that came to the diner. In truth Matt, Dimples, Freckles, and Blue Eyes were way more attractive than the contestants, but I wasn't going to tell them that.

"No, on the floor. Why did you move to the floor?" Matt clarified. He glanced at the TV briefly with a scowl.

My brow furrowed in confusion. I didn't understand his question. "I'm never allowed on the furniture." I said slowly. Murphy looked angry and I scooted farther back against the wall. Was he mad that I was sitting on the couch when they got here? A quick glance at the others and all had various degrees of anger written on their faces. "I'm sorry. I know I shouldn't have sat in the chair; it won't happen again." I rushed on to say. I started shaking as fear began to spread through my veins.

"Trinity, stop." Murphy's voice was clipped. He moved over to me and sat down on the floor in front of me. I whimpered and tried to scoot away but got trapped between the chair and the wall. Hurt flashed in his eyes. "You can sit on whatever you want, Trinity. You do not ever have to give up your spot on the couch to any of us. If there are not enough seats, one of the boys will give it up for you. Do you understand?" Murphy said softly as he stared at me.

I shook my head. "That's not how it works, Murphy." I said quickly. "Those kinds of things weren't meant for me." My aunts had beaten that lesson into me from the moment I stepped into their house. They had repeatedly told me that my parents had spoiled me. Given into my selfish desires. Furniture was for those who earned it. Those kinds of lessons were hard to forget. Especially when you have a scar on your chest reminding you of them.

"What do you mean by 'those kinds of things'?" Freckles asked softly from the couch.

I kept my eyes cast down even though I watched all of them out the corners of my eyes. I wanted to see any potential threat coming. This was so humiliating. I know they knew what I was talking about, so why were they forcing me to say this? Was this some sort of trap? "Couches, beds, blankets, you know this. Why are you making me say it aloud?" I mumbled as I looked over at Murphy.

"You weren't allowed a bed or blankets?" Dimples growled, sounding upset. "Where the heck did you live? Who doesn't allow someone to sleep in a bed or have a blanket?"

I looked over at him in surprise before looking back at Murphy. "Trinity, you are a human being. Every human being deserves to be able to sit on a couch or sleep in a bed. And if you are cold, you have every right to have a blanket. I don't care what lies those people told you. From now on, you don't live by their rules. Do you hear me? You get to sleep in a bed with as many blankets as you want, and you get to sit on the couches." Murphy said firmly.

"Thank you." Was the only thing I was able to get out. Murphy kept eye contact with me for several moments before standing back up and moving back to his chair. The room was uncomfortably quiet.

Giggling and squealing came from the TV as Brad picked up the Bachelorette girl and ran with her into the waves. I heard a scoff come from the couch. How funny would it be if the guys got stuck watching this ridiculous show? I felt my magic flow through my veins as I got to my feet. I walked toward the door. "I'll be back, I need to use the restroom." I called over my shoulder.

As soon as I was out of sight, I heard Dimples laugh. "Now that Trinity is gone, let's watch the game."

"As soon as she gets back, you will switch it back to whatever this is." Murphy said firmly.

A mumbled chorus of "Yes, sir." Reached me and I smiled.

I opened the next door down the hall, hoping it was a bathroom, but it was an office. I spotted an intercom system on the wall and moved to it to get a better look. A button was labeled as "Servants Quarters". Curious, I pressed the button. A light started to flash near the button and a moment later a voice came through the intercom asking if I needed anything.

"Oh...Um...Yes. Mr. Murphy asked that snacks and some tissues be brought up to the lounge as quickly as possible. He and the boys are watching a tear-jerker of a movie, I guess." I said smiling.

"Right away." The woman said, and the intercom went dead.

I moved out of the office and continued looking for the bathroom. I finally found it at the end of the hall. I finished and was just opening the door to head back to the lounge when I saw a woman around my age. She was coming out of the lounge with a bewildered look on her face.

As we passed in the hall, she gave me a friendly wave before she continued on her way. I paused outside the lounge and listened to Freckles, Dimples, and Matt arguing about the remote that didn't seem to work and the other ways to change the channel that didn't seem to work either. I decided that since I really didn't want to watch The Bachelorette anyway, I would go to the kitchen for a snack. I was going to make my cinnamon swirl cake, since I wasn't able to enjoy it the last time I made it.

I sat quietly on the counter and swung my legs as the cake baked. Did Murphy really mean what he said about couches and beds? Was I going to be able to sleep in a bed tonight? It had been nine years since I had that luxury. Not since I left the hospital. I glanced around and saw a radio by the window. I moved to it and turned it on.

Country music filled the room. Mom loved country music. I turned it up. 'All of It' by Cole Swindell came on and I started singing. I returned to the counter and sat down, closing my eyes. Several songs played as I sang along softly. I felt eyes on me again as the timer went off. I hopped off the counter, keeping my gaze down and away from the door.

"Can I help you with something?" I asked as I searched through the drawers for hot pads.

"You never came back, and we sat there for nearly an hour watching your stupid show." Matt grumbled.

"That's not my fault." I smiled as I glanced over at him.

"You were the one watching it in the first place." Blue Eyes said as he moved to a drawer I hadn't checked yet and pulled two hot pads out.

I grabbed them from him and gave him a smirk. "I couldn't find the remote to change the channel, otherwise I would have been watching the pregame talk for the women's soccer game." I opened up the oven to get the cake out, but Blue Eyes grabbed the hot pads from me. I shot him a glare as I ripped them out of his hands. "Oh no you don't, Blue Eyes. When I am cooking, no one encroaches on my space. Especially, when it comes to my Cinnamon Swirl Cake." I grabbed my cake out of the oven and moved it to cool on the stove. I went back to the oven and turned it and the timer off.

"Blue Eyes?" Matt laughed out loud. "Wow Trin, when did you start giving out nicknames?"

I grabbed a plate and dished up a large serving before turning around to see all the guys there watching me with amusement on their faces. "Well, Matt. I only know two out of five of you so instead of assigning numbers to those I don't know, I decided to give them names." I walked to the door and started for the lounge again. I could hear them all following me.

Deciding to test what Murphy said, I moved back to the chair I had been on earlier and tentatively sat down. The guys filed in after me and each took a seat. Blue Eyes moved to the spot on the floor where I had sat and leaned against the wall.

"I guess that is fair. So, what is my name?" Freckles gave me a smile as he played with the remote that didn't seem to be working, except it did adjust the volume.

"Can you please pass me the remote, Freckles?" I lifted a brow, and his smile grew.

"Freckles? You call Axel 'Blue Eyes' and I get 'Freckles'?" He put a hand over his heart as if I had wounded him as he passed the remote to me.

"If you don't like the names I give, you could always introduce yourself like a normal human." I commented as I pressed the button to change the channel and flipped through them until I reached the soccer game. I put the remote on the arm of the couch and took a bite of my cake.

"How did you do that?" Dimples asked with wide eyes.

"I pressed the button on the remote." I answered as I took another bite.

"We have been trying that since you left to go to the bathroom." Dimples shook his head.

"Can I ask you something, Dimples?" I said while keeping my eyes on the TV. Matt's laughter filled the room. "Can you smack the back of Matt's head for me?"

A few seconds later I heard a loud smack. "Hey!" Matt yelled. "What was that for, Trin?"

"I am currently staying with five men and don't know three of their names and would feel more comfortable if I did." I said while shooting him a glare.

"Okay kids, calm down." Murphy laughed. "Trinity, these are my nephews. Axel is the one on the floor. Freckles' real name is Noah and Liam is the one with a dimple."

I gave each one a nod as they were introduced before turning back to the game. Everyone began to relax, and I found I liked watching the teasing between the boys as they watched the game. The game was nearly over when the doorbell rang. Murphy pulled his phone out of his pocket and frowned at it. He got to his feet and looked over at me and my stomach tightened with anxiety. They were here. My aunts had found me.

Chapter 3

"Axel, take Trinity back to your room; use the back stairs. Noah, Liam, and Matt, stay here and watch the game." Murphy called out orders and the atmosphere became tense instantly.

Axel got to his feet, grabbed my hand and pulled me from the room. My fear of my aunts finding me over-shadowed Axel touching me. He led me up a second set of stairs and down the hall to his room. As he closed the door, I heard Murphy answer the front door.

Axel continued pulling me to the bathroom before he locked us in. He finally let go of my hand as he moved to the shower and turned on the water, making sure it was nice and hot. He didn't say anything as he moved back to the door and listened. He finally looked at me as I stood in the center of the room trembling with fear.

"Take off the hoodie." He whispered.

When I just stood there, he moved over to me. He grabbed the hem of the hoodie with one hand and the hem of my shirt with the other as he tugged the hoodie over my head. I gasped in surprise before wrapping my arms around myself. He took a step back and pulled his shirt off as he moved back to the door. I started at his bare chest with wide eyes. What was he doing?

Steam started to fill the room as we waited. A few minutes later, Axel cursed under his breath. He undid his belt and slipped his jeans off, leaving him only in his boxers. My heart rate accelerated as a different fear started to take hold of me. He grabbed me around my waist as he stepped into the shower.

I whimpered as panic took over my brain and I pushed against his chest, trying to get away from him. The shower door closed, and he let go of me. I stepped back as far as I could go, which still didn't put much distance between us. What was he planning to do with me?

He stepped close, his body nearly pressing me into the wall as he leaned his head down and whispered close to my ear. "I need you to sit in the corner and stay quiet."

I looked into his blue eyes. There was no hint of a threat or hunger I had seen in other men's eyes. Just worry. My eyes shifted to the shower door, but Axel's large frame was blocking the way out. Not seeing any other choice, I did as he said. I took a step to the side and slid down the wall until I was sitting on the wet floor. I watched as Axel wet his hair and squirted shampoo into his palm. Then he just stood there. What was he doing?

A minute later a knock came at the bathroom door, and he scrubbed the shampoo into his thick brown hair. Another knock sounded and I felt like I couldn't breathe. My heart was beating so fast I was sure a hummingbird wouldn't be able to keep up with it. My aunts were going to kill me for sure if they saw me in a shower with a man, even if I was fully dressed.

"What do you need?" Axel called out loudly. I jumped at the sudden noise, and I covered my mouth to prevent my startled squeak. Axel's eyes shifted to me.

"Axel, I need you to open the door." Murphy called through the closed door.

"I'm a little busy, Uncle. Can't this wait until I'm done?" Axel called back, his eyes never leaving mine.

"Afraid not." Murphy said.

Axel's jaw ticked as he half rinsed off. He stepped out of the shower and wrapped a towel around his waist before stomping over to the door. "What?" He growled out as he yanked it open.

"My word!" Aunt Lucy gasped. I began to shake even more.

My aunts really were here, and they would definitely punish me for this. A memory came back to me. I wasn't totally helpless. Mother had taught me several things that I could use now in order to defend myself.

I thought back to when we played hide and seek. Mother had taught me to think of a blanket being placed over me, one that would keep me hidden from the seeker. Warmth from my magic began to course through my veins and I closed my eyes.

"Can you put some clothes on, sir." A male voice asked as he cleared his throat.

"I am in the middle of a shower, and you are the one banging on my bathroom door. So, no. I won't be getting dressed. What is it that you need, officer?" Axel's steely voice sounded dangerous.

"Oh, well. We are looking for a runaway. She is seventeen and her aunts are worried for her safety." The man said after clearing his throat again.

"And you think that I have an underaged girl in my shower." Axel asked dryly.

"No, sir. But your uncle gave us permission to walk through the house to see if she is here." The officer sounded uncomfortable.

"Please, we only want what's best for her. She is sick and must take her medications, otherwise she can be a danger to herself." Aunt Grace sniffled.

I wrapped my arms around my knees and squeezed my eyes closed tighter. Maybe this was all just a bad dream. If my aunts convinced Murphy that I was a danger to myself, would he hand me back over to them? I had to believe he wouldn't. My life very well depended on it.

"Go ahead and take a look but hurry up so I can finish my shower before all the hot water is gone." Axel snapped out with irritation.

There was a hint of worry in his voice that caused my heart to race even faster. My eyes flew open, and I watched a short balding man step into the bathroom. He checked the linen closet before he walked all the way to the shower. I held my breath and prayed I was cloaked. The man barely glanced in my direction before turning around and walking out.

"Great. Am I free to finish my shower now?" There was a small pause before the door slammed closed and I heard the lock turn. I uncloaked as my eyes focused on the floor in front of me.

A blast of cold air surrounded me, and I looked up to see Axel stepping back into the shower. He didn't say anything as he finished rinsing the shampoo from his hair and body. When he was done, he turned around and sat on the floor next to me.

He didn't look comfortable at all. His six-foot muscular frame was way too big to fit comfortably on the floor with me. He didn't complain and he did his best to give me as much space as possible.

I could feel myself trembling still. He reached up and turned the knob causing the water to become warmer. I turned away from him as tears fell from my eyes.

Murphy and Axel had protected me from my aunts. But my aunts had gotten the police involved. Would me being here endanger Murphy and his nephews? I sniffled and the water temperature increased again. It was borderline scalding, and I wasn't sure if I could stay in it much longer.

After a few minutes, I felt Axel shift again as he started to reach up. I grabbed his arm quickly and he looked over at me. "If you turn up the temperature anymore, I am going to be boiled alive." I whispered.

"You're shivering. I thought you were cold." he said quietly as he studied me.

I shook my head and looked down. I realized I was still holding his arm, but I couldn't seem to let go. "I'm not cold, Axel. I am terrified." I whispered as I tried to curl more into a ball but because I still held his arm, I ended up hugging it tighter.

He slowly removed his arm from my grasp before putting it around my back and his other hand gently grabbed mine. He gave my hand a gentle squeeze and silence fell between us again. We sat there for a long time before there was a patterned knock at the door and Axel stood up. He pulled me up beside him, not letting go of my hand, and turned the water off.

He opened the shower door and grabbed a towel before letting my hand go and wrapping it around me. Sitting in the shower had eventually started to calm my fears and my trembling had gone away. I still felt worried about my aunts looking for me, but I wasn't crying from the thought of them dragging me away.

Axel grabbed a second towel before wrapping it around himself. He walked to the door and opened it to show a very angry-looking Murphy.

"Are you okay, Trinity?" Murphy asked with thin lips. I gave a small nod and Axel walked past his uncle. "Who were those women?"

And just like that, my anxiety and fear were back in full swing. My bottom lip started to tremble, and tears stung my eyes as I stood there soaking wet and wrapped in a towel.

"Murphy, leave her alone." Axel's voice was stern as he came back into the bathroom with a stack of dry clothes. "Let her get dressed before you cause her to have another panic attack." He handed me the clothes as he gave me a small smile. He turned back to his uncle and this time when he walked out of the bathroom, he closed the door, leaving me standing there alone.

I stood there for several minutes before finally drying off. I ran into a problem when I went to get dressed. My only underwear and bra were completely soaked through. I bit my lip as I thought about my options. I really didn't want to go walking around the house with no underwear on, but I couldn't stay in my wet ones. I hesitantly threw them into the shower before I pulled on the dry shorts and T-shirt, feeling exposed. I slipped the hoodie back on and used the comb on the counter to untangle my hair.

With nothing else to do, I squared my shoulders ready to face Murphy and his questions. Despite telling myself that I was brave, my hand was trembling as I reached for the door handle. As I opened the door, I saw Noah, Liam, Matt, Axel, and Murphy all sitting around the room waiting for me. I moved quickly to the bed and climbed under the covers and pulled the blanket up to my chin.

"Trinity, I'm sorry for being so angry earlier." Murphy's voice was gentler than a few minutes ago. "Can you please tell us who those women are?"

I took a deep breath and squeezed my eyes closed trying to convince myself to answer. I was shaking so much that you would think that I was standing outside in the snow in nothing but shorts and a tank top. "They are my father's sisters." I managed to answer quietly as I opened my eyes and looked down at my hands.

"Your aunts?" Noah asked in disbelief.

"Only for the last ten years." I muttered.

"Are they the ones who did that to you?" Matt asked, gesturing to my face.

I looked over at him and his anger was shining in his eyes. "Yes, and no." I looked back down.

"Be more specific." Liam growled out.

I threw the blanket over my head as I laid down. Maybe they would all go away, and I could cry myself to sleep. My hopes were dashed when the blanket was pulled back slowly. Axel was standing there with an unreadable expression on his face. He didn't say anything as he kept me from pulling the blanket back over my head when I tried to hide again.

"Fine!" I yelled and sat up as hot tears rolled down my face. "When I got back to the house that night when you all showed up in the kitchen, they demanded my paycheck. When I reminded them that I didn't get paid until the next day, my Aunt Grace struck me with the back of her hand, I think. Maybe her fist?" I pointed to the left side of my face. "I fell, and I think I hit my head on the step because I woke up in a puddle of blood on the floor the next morning."

I covered my face with my hands as I continued to cry. Now that I was finally talking about what happened everything seemed to just tumble out. "They told me that if I didn't bring them the money the next evening, I was going back to the basement." It took a few minutes for me to find my voice again as my shaking increased. "The chains and the dark. I can't handle it. The memories. The needles. I can't…" I was sure I wasn't making any sense as I started gasping for air.

"Trinity?" A worried voice called to me, but I was so lost in my terror filled memories I barely registered it. Suddenly, I was lifted up and sat down in an upright position instead of the ball I had been curled up in. "Look at me." I shook my head as I continued to struggle to breathe.

"She is going to pass out if we can't get her to calm down." Someone commented.

"Do something, Axel!" Another voice yelled out.

"Matt, help me." That voice seemed closer than the others. Hands touched my face, and I cried out and tried to shove them away but someone else grabbed my hands and held them down. "Trinity, look at me." The voice said calmly. The hands on my face wiped the tears gently off my cheeks. I opened my eyes, but everything was blurry from the tears. "Take some slow breaths for me. Come on, Trinity. Please." I tried but couldn't seem to breathe in slowly enough. My vision started to fade, and I blacked out.

Chapter 4

Voices broke through the dark fog of my brain. I moved my head to the side, and I felt a gentle touch brush hair off my forehead. "Don't." I swatted the hand away and I heard a low chuckle.

I opened my eyes and saw four pairs of eyes watching me with concern. Murphy had a small smile on his face even with his worry. "There you are. Feeling better?" he asked softly.

"No, as a matter of fact, my head is pounding." I grumbled as I tried to sit up. A hand settled on my shoulder. "Please, stop touching me." I said stiffly as I closed my eyes and leaned back.

Something shifted behind me, and I turned to see Matt sitting there. I was leaning against him. I jumped off the bed so fast, I stumbled. Axel caught me before I hit the floor.

"What the heck, Matt?" I yelled angrily as I shoved Axel away.

"Hey easy, Trin." Matt put his hands up to show he meant no harm. "Axel was the one to pick you up and tried to calm you down, but then you passed out a few minutes ago. He needed to go do something and you woke up as he passed you over to me. You didn't seem to mind sitting with him."

"I was unconscious, Matt!" I screamed at him. I was burning with fury. I was tired of being on the verge of panic attacks all the time even if people didn't know. I was tired of living my life from sunup to sundown in constant fear of being trapped in my nightmares. I was tired of reliving the day my parents died. And I was tired of not having clothes. I grabbed the waistband of the shorts as they started to slip.

Matt got off the bed and moved to stand next to his cousins. He kept his movements slow as if he was dealing with a wild, unpredictable animal. Matt, Liam, Noah, and Axel all stood in a line as they watched me with wide eyes.

"Now listen up, because I am only going to say this once." I growled out. "I better have clothes that fit me sitting on this bed in the next two hours or I swear I will end up killing one of you." I threatened and I could feel my magic start to spread through my veins. I turned around and walked into the bathroom and slammed the door.

I gave them several minutes to leave before I walked back out into the bedroom only to find Murphy sitting in a chair. "You are just like your mother." He gave me a sad smile as I walked back to sit on the bed. "She had a temper on her too. I remember when your father and I refused to let her practice with us. Her eyes glowed the way yours just did. We could feel her anger all the way to our bones." He gave a small chuckle. "Needless to say, she ended up sparring with us and gave your father a black eye."

"You knew my parents?" I asked in surprise. I had no idea that Murphy and my parents even knew each other.

"Why don't you come with me to the library." Murphy stood and led the way to the library on the ground floor.

He pointed to a chair, and I sat. He moved to a picture on the wall and pulled on the frame. It swung out to reveal a wall safe. After opening the safe, he pulled out a book. He made sure to close the safe and put the picture back.

"I didn't realize who you were until your eyes glowed." He shook his head. "What do you know about your parents?" He finally asked me.

"My mother and father didn't get along at first, but after her family was attacked, my father saved her life. They went into hiding together and over the following year my dad convinced my mom to marry him. I came along a year later. My parents adored each other." I said as I shrugged my shoulders. I didn't see how any of this explained how Murphy knew my parents.

He was flipping through the book and finally stopped on a page. He passed it over to me and I looked at it. I ran my fingers lightly over the image of a shield with a sword diagonally through it. The hilt of the sword was at the top right of the shield and the tip of the blade came out the bottom left. Vines swirled around the edges of the image.

"Do you know what that is?" he asked curiously.

"My father had a tattoo on his left shoulder blade that was almost exactly like this. His tattoo had a rose on the bottom right and top left corners." I said as I continued to trace the shield.

"This is the mark of the royal guard, Trinity." Murphy said. I looked up and met his intense brown eyes with a look of confusion. "Your father and I were members of the royal guard from the time we were two. Our parents took us to the castle the day the princess was presented as an infant. She was born a magic user. And during her presentation, magic rose from her and claimed five boys as royal guards. This tattoo was the magic's way of stamping the new guards. Your father and I were among them. We moved to the castle and began training for our duties to protect the princess when we turned six. Your father and I became fast friends.

"As young teenagers, your father was attracted to the princess, but she refused to give him the time of day. We ended up playing jokes on her in order to draw her attention." Murphy smiled as he got lost in the memory. "On the princess's eighteenth birthday, the King and Queen had another presentation for their daughter. This one was to introduce her to potential suitors. Your father struggled that night watching the woman he had been in love with for years being presented to several men."

"If my father was in love with the princess, why did he not present himself to the king and queen?" I asked, totally absorbed in the story.

Murphy completely ignored my question and continued his story. "It was getting late, and your father and I were asked to escort the princess back to her room. Your father touched her back lightly as he guided her through the crowd. A light arched between them, and your father hissed in pain. The moment his hand left the princess the light was gone.

"Everyone had seen it and whispers started to flow through the crowd. Your father fell to his knees as the crowd backed away from him. Several royal guards rushed forward and created a protective circle around him and the royal family. All he was able to say was 'my shoulder'. I helped him remove his armor and shirt. His mark was glowing the same blue as the blue light that had connected him to the princess. A rose had appeared on the bottom right of the shield. The king and queen were ecstatic. The changed mark was the magic's way of claiming your father as the princess's Enforcer."

"What is an Enforcer?" I asked in confusion. My parents had never told me any of this.

"An Enforcer is a specialized bodyguard. All the royal princesses who are magic users, are given one. They are connected through magic so that the Enforcer can know when the princess is in danger or needs help. An Enforcer is only chosen once the princess turns eighteen. A week after the princess's presentation, the castle was attacked. Your father was able to get the princess out safely, but the rest of the royal family was killed. Your father and the princess disappeared. About two years after the tragedy, a knock sounded at my door. Your father and the princess stood on my doorstep holding an infant girl."

"My father and the princess?" I asked completely confused. Where was my mother?

Again, Murphy ignored my question. "My sisters were visiting, and their boys took an instant liking to the baby girl, especially Axel and Matt. They were about three at the time. The twins were two, but still seemed to gravitate towards the baby. Your parents asked me to take care of you if anything were to happen to them. I, of course, said yes. They left shortly after. That was the last time I saw or heard from them. That night my sisters were bathing the boys and I heard them scream. When I ran into the bathroom, all four boys had the mark of the royal guard on their left shoulder blades."

Murphy had to be wrong. I was not some princess, and neither was my mom. We were magic users, but not royals. "I think you have made a mistake. My mother wasn't a princess and my father had two roses on his tattoo. My mother said the bottom right meant he would protect her from harm and the top left one meant he would protect her heart. There is no way that we are talking about the same people. My mother even had a matching rose on her left shoulder blade." I looked back down at the image. If my mom was a princess, could that be the reason my parents were killed?

"Your parents had matching marks?" Murphy asked, surprise lacing his voice.

"My father said he had the second rose since the day they ran away together. And my mother told me that she got her rose the day she fell in love with him." I said distractedly. My mind was still trying to wrap around the fact that my mother could be a princess and killed because of it.

Murphy chuckled as he leaned back in his chair and shook his head. "Who would have thought that the fiery princess and the man she was constantly butting heads with, would end up married, and a bonded pair to boot?" When I didn't say anything, he studied me. "Trinity, you look pale, what's wrong?"

"Why was the royal family attacked?" I asked, looking at him.

"Rumor has it that Jason Monroe wanted to harness the magic from your mother. She was the first female royal magic user to be born in nearly fifty years. Royal magic users tend to be more powerful than the average magic user who can only do one or two things like heal, transfiguration, teleport, or cloaking. But a female royal can do most, if not all of them.

"The Monroe family has sought power for a long time. They felt wronged for being turned down by the royal family as a potential husband for the princess. After the attack, word spread that Jason was working with a magic user that could strip the magic from another. He planned on stripping your mother of her magic." Murphy told me with a sad smile. "Magic is embedded in every cell of a magic user and stripping them of their magic would be a long painful way to kill them."

"Mom was scared and told me to hide. I was lying in a field by the house. Suddenly, it felt like the long grass I was laying in, was reaching up and grabbing me. It felt like hands with long dagger-like claws scratching along my skin. My father found me screaming and rolling around on the ground in pain. The hands wouldn't let go of me. It hurt so bad but there weren't any marks visible. When dad picked me up, the hands finally let go. I was crying in his arms all the way back to the house." I said quietly.

I wasn't sure why I felt the need to explain, but I did. "Once we got there, the whole place burst into flames. Dad held me tight as he took me to the basement. He set me down and told me to stay there so that he could go find momma. He kissed my forehead for a long moment before he ran back upstairs and closed the hatch door." A tear slipped off my cheek and fell onto the book.

"It was so dark. I found my way to a corner before I sat on the ground. I cried as I waited for mom and dad to come and get me. That is when I heard my mom yell my dad's name. She continued screaming and then a man asked where the girl was. He said he was going to get the girl's magic one way or another. My mom screamed again as I heard a loud crack. The roof above me collapsed. It took three days for the emergency responders to find me in the basement." That was the day I couldn't handle people touching me or the dark or basements. However, talking about it was freeing in a way. I missed my parents so much. I needed their love and comfort right now.

A hand touched my shoulder, and I looked up and saw tears in Murphy's eyes. I didn't pull away from him this time. I had felt so alone for so long and I just wanted my parents back. Murphy pulled me slowly to him as he gave me a light hug. The flood gates on ten years of suppressed emotions finally broke. I wrapped my arms around his waist as I sobbed into his chest. His arms tightened around me.

"Oh, my dear girl. I am so sorry." Murphy whispered; his own voice was thick with emotion. After several minutes, my crying finally slowed down. "Would you like to go watch something while we wait for the boys to get back?" he asked gently.

I nodded my head but was hesitant to let him go. He really did remind me of my dad. I could almost imagine Murphy was him comforting me in that moment. He kept his arm around me as we walked a couple of doors down to the lounge.

We sat on the couch, and I leaned on him. I felt like a little girl desperately needing comfort from her parental figure. Murphy turned on a soccer game and put a blanket over me. I was so emotionally exhausted that it didn't take long before I fell asleep.

Chapter 5

"Do you think they are dead?" I heard Matt ask with uncertainty.

"I think we just walked into the twilight zone." Liam added.

"If you boys wake Trinity up, I will murder you myself." Murphy's voice rumbled through his chest. I stayed quiet, hoping that I could fall back to sleep.

"I don't understand what I am seeing, Uncle Murphy. What happened between the two of you?" Noah loudly whispered.

"What part of 'don't wake up Trinity', did you not understand?" I grumbled as I pulled the blanket over my head. I felt Murphy chuckle as he gave my shoulder a squeeze. "Tell them that if they can sit down and be quiet, they can stay."

Only the sound of the TV filled the room as the guys sat on the chairs. I was just about to fall asleep again when I remembered that the boys had gone out to get me clothes. I sat up abruptly, causing everyone to jump.

"What is the matter?" Murphy asked in alarm.

I looked around at all the guys as they stared at me with wide eyes. "You're all back." I stated dumbly.

"Yes." Matt said slowly.

I jumped to my feet holding the blanket around me as I ran from the room. I was vaguely aware that the basketball shorts fell off as I sprinted down the hall. I made it to my room and slammed the door closed. There were ten bags on the bed. I rushed over to them, allowing the blanket to drop to the floor. I dug through the bags hoping to find underwear but found none.

"Great." I mumbled to myself as I went back into the bathroom to see if my underwear was dry yet. To my horror, my underwear and bra were gone! *No. no. no.* Where were my clothes?

I looked around the bathroom and noticed that all the dirty laundry was gone, and fresh towels were hanging up. Did the maids come and clean up? *Shoot!* I went back to the bed and started pulling items out of the bags, praying I had just missed them my first time through. A knock at the door caused me to squeak in surprise. I was so focused on trying to find something to wear that the sudden noise scared me.

"Miss?" A female voice called. "Mr. Murphy sent me up here to help put your things away. May I come in?"

I panicked. Here I was standing with just a hoodie on, and a maid wanted to come in. I pulled on a pair of pajama pants that I just took out of a bag and moved to the door. I opened it and I felt my cheeks heat. I nearly choked when I saw Axel standing just behind the young maid.

The maid walked past me. Axel extended out his hand and offered me the shorts I had been wearing minutes ago. "I think you dropped these." He said with a crooked smile.

"Thanks." I said dryly. "The real owner of these shorts is much fatter than I am." Axel's crooked grin only grew at my comment.

I wasn't going to stand there holding onto his shorts, so I started to close the door. Just before it shut, Axel's hand touched mine and I froze. "I'm glad you are feeling better." I gave him a small nod. "And I'm not fat, baby. This is all muscle." He patted his flat stomach, and I rolled my eyes at him. An image of Axel without his shirt on when we were in the bathroom earlier came to mind. He was right, even though I would never admit it to him. He was all well-defined, solid muscle.

"Whatever helps you sleep at night." I said, fighting my blush. I quickly closed and locked the door.

I turned back toward the bed and the maid gave me a friendly smile. She was the same one that had left the lounge earlier that day. "Hi. I'm Sara."

"I'm Trinity. So, Mr. Murphy sent you to help me?" I asked her hesitantly. I had never had anyone help me with anything lately and I certainly hadn't had this many clothes before.

"Yeah. If you would like, we can pull everything out and sort through it before putting it away?" Sara smiled at me.

I gave her a nod and a smile. I was amazed at how thorough the guys had been, but at the same time how many crucial items they missed. I had pants, shorts, tank tops, T-shirts, blouses, skirts, pajamas, a few dresses, swimsuits, socks, and several pairs of shoes.

But they didn't get any bras or underwear and most of the clothing they got me required them. I stared hopelessly at all the clothes that I was no longer excited to see. I didn't have any hygiene items either. No deodorant. No toothbrush. No hairbrush. Nothing.

"It seems that you are missing a few important items of clothing and other necessities. I think I have an extra toothbrush you can have at least." Sara tried hard not to smile.

"What am I supposed to do? The only pair of underwear I had was in the bathroom earlier and now they are gone." I sat down heavily on the bed and looked at Sara hoping she had the answer.

"That is my fault. I cleaned up and took them down to get washed. As for the time being, you could always wear this." She held up the skimpiest bikini I had ever seen in my life.

"Did they honestly think I would wear that in a pool?" I felt my face going bright red. I grabbed it and a tank top from her before I headed for the bathroom. I slipped the swimsuit on before I put back on my pajama pants and pulled the tank top on. I still felt exposed, so I put Axel's sweatshirt back on and went back out to help Sara put the clothes away.

We finally finished twenty minutes later, and Sara turned to me with a conspiratorial smile. "What are you doing tomorrow morning?" I gave her a shrug and she clapped her hands with excitement. "My friends and I are going shopping at nine. You should join us."

I hesitated at first, but a smile slowly spread across my face. "That sounds great." For the first time ever, I was going to go hang out with some girls my age. I didn't have any money, but it would still be fun to hang out. At least, I hoped it would.

"Perfect. I will meet you in the entryway at 8:50 so we can walk out to the road." Sara said good night and I made my way back down to the lounge.

Everyone was sitting where they had been when I left an hour ago, except for Axel, he was sitting in my seat next to Murphy. Seeing me enter the room, Murphy got to his feet. He said goodnight to everyone, gave me a hug, and kissed the top of my head before he left.

I sat on the couch and curled up against the arm. I was getting into the game that was on when the doorbell rang, and I jumped. Matt got to his feet and left. My heart rate increase and my breaths started to come faster. My hands started shaking and I felt the need to hide, to escape. Axel touched my hand and I turned to look at him. I am sure he saw the fear in my eyes because he put an arm over my shoulders and pulled me close.

"It's only the pizza we ordered. Just breathe, Trinity." He whispered softly in my ear.

I nodded and closed my eyes as I tried to focus on my breathing. He removed his arm from around my shoulders and I kept my eyes closed. *In. out. In. out.* I kept telling myself. It wasn't helping.

A blanket was draped over my lap. I jumped again when Axel grabbed my trembling hand. His thumb started to gently rub the back of mine. The movement was as unexpected as it was unfamiliar. I wasn't used to such a soft and gentle touch. It was distracting to the point that it was hard to focus on anything else.

By the time Matt got back with four pizzas, I felt nearly back to normal. I pulled my hand from Axel's and rubbed my arms to try to rid the sensation of his hand around mine. I glanced at him out of the corner of my eye. He didn't seem to be at all affected by what had happened.

I took a single slice of the pepperoni pizza when it was offered to me, and I settled in to watch another football game. The guys were relaxed and teasing each other over the two teams playing. For the first time in a long time, I felt warm and safe. My eyes started to droop, and I heard the guys start whispering.

"What do you think happened while we were gone? Trin and Murphy are crazy close all of a sudden. I mean they were acting like father and daughter or something." Liam asked.

"They have been close for a while now. Trinity has been working at the diner for two years. She just has never allowed us to touch her before." Matt corrected.

"Whatever happened, I am glad it did. Trinity seems more at peace now than she did when we first met her." Axel commented as he shifted on the couch.

"I agree. She seems so much lighter." Matt whispered.

"Now that she has fallen asleep, what are we going to do? Should we leave her here on the couch or draw straws to see who carries her up to bed?" Noah asked.

"We should probably take her up. She has had a crazy day." Matt said. "But I'm not carrying her. Last time I tried that I thought she was going to cause my head to explode."

"I'll do it." Axel stood from the couch and in the next second, I was lifted into his arms.

I squeaked in surprise and grabbed Axel's shirt. "Put me down. I can walk." My feet touched the ground and I immediately jumped away from Axel. "Next time just wake me up and I can walk up to bed on my own. You gave me a heart attack." I said as I wrapped my arms around myself and looked between the guys.

"We thought you were asleep." Matt commented after a moment.

"I was." I rubbed my eyes. "When you sleep in a house where your caretakers would dump scalding hot or ice-cold water on you if you weren't up before them, or lock you in the basement and send men..." I cut myself off. I can't believe I almost told them that my aunts would send men in to touch me. I shook my head. "I learned to be a light sleeper." I said quickly and headed for the door, but I heard them following me.

I made it to the bedroom before any of them got the courage to ask what I knew was on all their minds. "Men to do what, Trinity?" Liam asked.

"Don't ask questions you don't want to know the answers to, Liam." I said as I reached for the door.

Noah stepped in the way and crossed his arms over his chest. "We want to know the answer."

"No, you don't." I whispered as I tightened my arms around my torso and shook my head. Tears stung my eyes, but I refused to let them fall.

"We need to know, Trinity." Matt was tense as he stared intently at me. "Please."

They weren't going to drop this, and I needed to get to sleep so I could go shopping with Sara. I let out a huff, pushed Noah to the side, and opened the door. "Come on in. Let's get this over with." I muttered as I walked in.

All four of them were stiff and looked like they were ready to go destroy something. They stood around the room, and I could tell they weren't going to sit. I started to pace. I didn't even tell Murphy this and I had planned on taking it to my grave. But here I was about to tell my overprotective watch dogs. I couldn't even look at them. The tears I had tried so hard to keep from falling spilled down my cheeks.

I took a deep breath and kept my eyes on the ground as I explained in a quiet voice. "I was thirteen when this punishment happened the first time. Aunt Lucy got mad at me for not being up before her. She was having company over and wanted me to clean the house. Aunt Grace dragged me down to the basement by my hair and put the chains on my wrists. That part was nothing new. They had left me there for hours. I was terrified. Whenever they did this, I would go into a panic mode. All I could think about was getting out of there. I was a complete mess when they finally came back. At first, I was relieved to see them, but then six men followed my aunts down the stairs. Aunt Grace told them the rules and they paid up." I shrugged as I swallowed hard.

"What rules?" Matt asked through barely restrained anger.

"No touching below the waist. Only hands can touch my skin. Lips can only touch the neck." I squeezed my eyes closed and took a deep breath. "Then Aunt Grace stepped back and one by one they got to touch me for ten minutes." I stopped pacing and clasped my trembling hands together. "That punishment stopped when I turned sixteen. I was forced to get a job and Aunt Lucy said I couldn't have marks on my neck when I went to work."

"The first time you came to the diner looking for a job, you had hickeys all over your neck. Like five or more." Matt said as the realization dawned, and I turned away from him. I felt so ashamed even if I couldn't have done anything to stop it. "I thought you had a boyfriend!" He yelled.

I flinched at the sudden volume before I shook my head quickly. Suddenly, I was pulled into a tight embrace. I squeezed my eyes shut, willing my tears to stop falling as I tentatively returned his hug. He pulled back and looked me in the eye.

"Why didn't you say anything to me?" He sounded hurt.

"Yeah, because I am going to go around telling everyone that I get chained up in the basement and I sleep on a ratty towel on the tile floor. Get real Matt, there are some things that are better left not said." I stepped away from him and headed for the bed. Hopefully they got the hint that I wanted to be left alone.

I was nearly tackled to the ground by Liam and Noah as they gave me a tight group hug. "If any guy tries to touch you again without your permission, I will break his hands." Noah said as he stepped away.

"Or his fingers, one by one." Liam added. "And don't worry Trinity, you aren't alone anymore. We will fight your battles alongside you."

I watched as Matt, Liam, and Noah headed for the door. I turned toward the bed again when a hand touched my arm gently. I looked up at Axel as he studied me carefully. He reached up and tucked my hair behind my ear.

"Trinity, is that everything? You're not hiding anything else that those men did to you?" The pain and regret in his eyes tore at my heart.

"I promise that was all those guys ever did." I said while staring into his deep blue eyes that looked like a stormy ocean.

"But that isn't everything your aunts did, is it?" he asked as he took a small step closer.

I shook my head and gave him a small smile. "Sorry, Axel. I don't plan on spilling what ten years of living with my aunts was like in a single night." I broke eye contact and looked down. "There is not nearly enough time to even get through a year."

He put his arms around me, and I wrapped my arms around him. He held me for several minutes before pulling back. "If you ever want to talk, I'm willing to listen." I nodded and he turned toward the closet. I climbed into bed and watched as he walked toward the door with a stack of clothes in his hands. "Sweet dreams, Trinity." He whispered before turning off the light and stepping out the door. I quickly rolled over and turned the bedside lamp on. I still had a hard time sleeping in the dark.

Chapter 6

Morning came quickly and I took a quick shower. It was amazing what a nice warm shower can do to one's outlook on the day. I was excited to get dressed in clean clothes. The jeans felt weird while wearing the super tiny bikini. After thinking over and considering my options for several minutes, I decided to go with running shorts, a tank top and one of Axel's hoodies. I slipped on a pair of tennis shoes and headed down the stairs. It was nearly 8:45 am and I wanted to eat before heading out.

I heard the guys talking in the dining room, so I made my way there. They were just setting out bowls and the milk. Two boxes of Fruit Loops were already on the table.

"Morning, Trinity." Liam smiled at me as I sat down at the table. "Here, you can polish off this box." He passed me a box of cereal and Matt pushed a bowl over to me.

"Thanks." I said as I poured the Fruit Loops in my bowl and Noah passed me the milk.

"What the heck?!" Matt yelled just as I was taking a bite.

I looked up to see what was wrong, and I choked on my mouthful of cereal. His bowl was filled with Grape Nuts. I coughed as I tried to clear my throat. Noah patted my back as he tried to assist me as I struggled to breathe normally again. At first the unexpected touch caused my panic to tighten my muscles, making me cough harder. My eyes were a bit watery when I finally stopped coughing.

Axel came in with another unopened box of Fruit Loops and sat on his chair. I took a drink of the water Liam had gotten for me when the same thing happened to Axel; his bowl was filled with Grape Nuts. The mouthful of water I was attempting to drink sprayed out of my mouth as I started to laugh. I couldn't stop. The looks of shock on the guys' faces were too much.

All eyes turned to me as I started to hyperventilate from laughing so hard. Tears were streaming from my eyes. Every time I thought I was getting control over my laughter, I would look up to see the surprised looks on their faces and my laughter would start up again.

"Excuse me." I wheezed out and I tried to get to my feet but tripped and fell to the ground as I continued to laugh.

A few minutes later, I was able to stop laughing. I lay on my back, and I looked up at the ceiling as I grabbed my ribs. I blinked a few times before I started crying. Murphy beat the others to me and scooped me up off the floor. I threw my arms around his neck as I struggled to get control of my emotions. I finally pulled back and smiled at him as I wiped my tears on the sleeve of the hoodie. I turned to face the bewildered Liam, Noah, Matt, and Axel.

"Thank you." I said to them, "That was the first time since my parents died that I have truly laughed."

"You did this?" Murphy began laughing and I smiled at him. "You are definitely your mother's daughter."

"I will take that as a compliment." I laughed.

"What just happened?" Noah asked, completely lost.

"I may have accidentally on purpose swapped your Fruit Loops for Grape Nuts. I was thinking about how my mom and I used to change my father's mashed potatoes to green beans, just as he would take a bite. Then I thought how funny it would be if the crazy amount of Fruit Loops was actually Grape Nuts. I didn't really mean to." I rushed to explain. "I'll change it back." I closed my eyes and felt the magic swirling through me as I thought about the Grape Nuts transforming back into Fruit Loops. I opened my eyes and Murphy still had an amused expression on his face. The clock just over his head caught my eye. I was late. "Well, I'm going to go study." I scrambled to my feet and rushed from the room.

As I came around the corner, I saw Sara standing there in the front foyer. We greeted each other and headed out the door. I pulled the hood over my head to try to hide my face the best I could while we walked down the lane. As we approached the large metal gates, I saw a car parked just on the other side. I nearly panicked until I heard Sara call out to the occupants as she waved at them.

She introduced me as a new maid in the household. The driver had shoulder length, raven black hair with purple tips. Her name was Maggie. She was full of energy and talked the whole time. The other passenger was Ruth. She had blonde hair and was much quieter. They were both super nice and I quickly felt comfortable around them. Before I knew it, I had agreed to allow them to help me with my hair and purchases. I tried to use the argument that I didn't have money, but they just waved it off.

We were only on the road for fifteen minutes before Maggie pulled up to a beauty salon. The three girls ushered me inside and told the stylist that I needed a complete makeover. The stylist was super excited as she studied my waist long black hair. I hadn't had it cut since I was eight and it showed. I heard multiple comments about how unhealthy my hair was and how the number of dead ends was astounding.

Maggie and Ruth sat me in a chair before picking up several magazines. They chose a hairstyle they thought would look amazing on me, and Sara refused to let me see any of the progress. I was nervous but I trusted them. I had no idea what would look good or not. Mom had always been the one to trim my hair when I was young. Back then I didn't care what my hair looked like as long as it was out of my face.

Several hours later, Sara spun me around to see the mirror. My normally drab, excessively long hair now hung just below my shoulders. I had side bangs and layers that gave my hair volume and movement. Instead of hanging straight down and hiding my face, my hair framed my face and bounced when I moved. My hair had a shine to it as well. The color was dark brown, almost black instead of jet black with grease and grime. I was completely speechless.

My hair looked amazing. I never thought that I would ever feel like I was pretty. My eyes dropped to my face. My olive skin tone was hidden by the bruising. The stylist, Kristin, gave me a smile. She led me over to another station where she spent the next two hours teaching me about makeup and how to conceal the bruising.

Before we left, Sara purchased every single product Kristin had used on my makeup and hair and led the way out. The girls were chatting excitedly, but I was still in shock. I followed slowly behind them with my arms wrapped around myself.

"You okay, hun?" Maggie asked as she draped her arm over my shoulders. I flinched slightly but fought the urge to shrink from the contact. I was really trying to be better with physical touch. Pain wasn't the result of every touch now that I was away from my aunts.

"I just didn't think I could look like this." I said as I ran a hand through my silky hair.

"You mean, smoking hot?" Ruth laughed. "Just wait until you are out of your boyfriend's clothes. I have a feeling you are hiding an amazing figure underneath that baggy thing." She gestured toward Axel's hoodie. "He won't be able to keep up with chasing all the other guys away."

My cheeks flamed. I could tell I was as red as a beet. "Oh, he isn't my boyfriend. He is just a friend." I stammered out.

"Well, he will definitely regret being in the friend zone when he sees you next." Ruth smiled at me. "Let's grab a bite to eat before we head to the mall."

We ate at a burger place, and I was so full by the end. I usually just snacked throughout my shift at the diner. Eating a full meal was new to me and my stomach didn't have much room. The trip to the salon had been exhausting and I wanted a nap, but the day was only half over. The girls didn't show any signs of stopping as they talked excitedly about all the stores they wanted to stop by.

We went from store to store as they helped me pick out everything from a hairbrush to deodorant to a purse. They even picked out shampoo, conditioner, and body wash. I was shushed every time I told them I didn't have money. I tried to say I could just use what was already at the house, but they all gave me a look and I let them buy the items.

The last stop was Victoria's Secret. Maggie claimed it was the only place to purchase proper underwear. We spent a small fortune there, but Sara kept reassuring me that everything was fine. She handed the woman behind the counter a shiny card as she winked at me. I caught the name on the card. Axel Brooks.

As we drove back to Murphy's, I was amazed at how fun the day had been. I felt like I had made three friends and I felt like a completely new person. The car came to a stop in front of the gate. Sara and I quickly unloaded our shopping bags. Sara had purchased way more stuff for me than I first realized.

We were laughing as we got to the front door. It was yanked open, and Liam was standing there. He looked like he was headed out but when he saw us, he froze. He blinked several times before his shock turned into relief then frustration. He grabbed my arm and yanked me inside causing a startled squeak to escape my lips.

Sara followed quickly and Liam slammed the door shut behind us causing both Sara and I to jump. I pulled away from Liam and turned to face Sara to see if she was okay. She looked just as confused as I felt. What had gotten into Liam?

"I got her!" Liam yelled so loud that it echoed around the house.

I rolled my eyes and whispered to Sara. "We still on for later tonight?" I really hoped she was still up for it.

"Absolutely." She gave me a wink as she whispered back. Talking in her normal voice she said. "I'm going to put my stuff away. See you later, Trin."

I gave her a little wave, grabbed several of my bags and moved toward the stairs. Running feet filled the quiet. "Where is she?" Murphy's anxious voice asked. I stopped and looked up at him. He took a step back as a look of surprise crossed his face.

"Trin?" Matt let out a low whistle. "Dang girl. Where is your fairy godmother?"

"Shut up, Matt." I rolled my eyes at him, but I could feel the blush creep up my neck.

"Where did you go?" Murphy found his voice again.

"I needed some things and while I was out, I got a trim." I said as I shrugged my shoulders. After the shock wore off, both of them looked as frustrated as Liam was. I bit my lip as I grew nervous. Had I done something wrong? No, I needed a few things, and I went and got them.

"What did you need? I thought we got everything for you yesterday." Matt asked, confused.

I heard two more people approaching and glanced in that direction. Axel's eyes were shining with an emotion I couldn't place while Noah's jaw dropped open. I turned back to Matt as I ran my hand through my hair nervously.

"Look, Matt, I really appreciate you all getting me everything you did, but there were some crucial items that were overlooked. But that's okay. It was probably better that I went and got them anyway."

"Like what?" Liam asked with his brow furrowed.

Seriously? Did I have to spell out everything to them? Irritation sparked to life within me. Why did they need to know, anyway? After several long moments of silence, I relented. Making it as awkward as I could. "Underwear, Liam. And Bras. Hygiene products like tampons, a hairbrush, deodorant. Should I go on?" I asked as I crossed my arms over my chest. "Better yet, would you like to look through my bags?"

Matt, at least, had the decency to look embarrassed for a second before his face turned hard. "You went out shopping all day, looking like that, wearing no underwear?" I bit the inside of my cheek to keep from laughing. They didn't give me much of a choice.

"What's wrong with the way I am dressed?" I asked innocently, knowing full well that the shorts were pretty short, and Axel's hoodie dwarfed me. It's their fault really. They were the ones that bought me these short shorts in the first place.

"Trin, I think what Matt is trying to say is that with the hoodie and shorts, it makes it look like you do not have any pants on. And well, you aren't exactly a chore to look at." Liam tried to explain, turning as red as his hair.

"I don't understand." I said as I looked each of them in the eye. If they wanted to push me about my purchases, then I could make them uncomfortable too.

"Trinity, you are beautiful." Axel said and I looked over at him. He cleared his throat. "We are just concerned about any unwanted male attention that you might have experienced while you were shopping today."

"Everyone was really nice. The guys at Victoria's Secret were really helpful in picking out the best fit and styles for me." They didn't need to know that 'the guys' were Maggie, Ruth, and Sara. I watched a muscle tick in Axel's jaw as he watched me. His face started to go red, and I could almost see steam coming out of his ears. When I turned back to Matt, he was the same way.

Sara was standing in the hall by Murphy covering her mouth as she tried to hold in her laughter. Murphy cleared his throat as he stepped over to me and picked up the bags on the floor. "Let me help you get these to your room, Trin." He followed me up to the room and set the bags just inside the door. "You should be nicer to them, young lady." Murphy's voice was firm, but his eyes sparkled with laughter.

"Oh, come on, Murphy. They started it. I had to tell them I went to purchase pads and tampons and underwear. Plus 'the guys' were some female friends I made. So, there is nothing for them to worry about. I'm rarely paid any attention and I don't see why that would change now." I rolled my eyes and sat on the bottom of the bed.

"You were an attractive young woman before, but your little makeover with Sara has made you stunning. As your guards, we are very protective of you. It is ingrained into the very fiber of our beings to protect you. They still are new to these big brother feelings and don't know where to draw the line yet." Murphy explained with a smile.

"Big brothers, huh? More like a bit smothering. How did you and my father figure out where to draw the line?" I asked. Maybe Murphy could help the boys figure it out.

Murphy laughed. "It wasn't hard for me. I had sisters and I knew my boundaries. Your father never did, and he fell hard for your mother. Now, get your stuff put away and come down so we can figure out dinner." Murphy turned and walked away still chuckling.

I closed the door and went to my bags. I pulled out a pair of underwear and bra before moving to the closet and finding a cute shirt and jeans. I dressed quickly and skipped downstairs. I found everyone in the kitchen. I grabbed an apple and began eating it. I could feel eyes on me, but I didn't look at them.

"What would you like to eat, Trinity?" Axel asked into the silence.

I finally glanced up and saw everyone watching me. "I already ate. Plus, I'm meeting up with Sara in a few minutes. She promised to introduce me to someone. I should be back by 1:00 am at the latest." I smiled at Murphy who covered his laugh with a cough. I walked over to the trash and threw away my apple core and gave Murphey a hug. "Good night boys." I called over my shoulder before making my way to the door. As I was slipping out the back door, I heard men's raised voices and paused to listen.

"You are just going to let her go?" Liam yelled.

"She is not a prisoner, Liam. I can't keep her locked in the house." Murphy's voice was much quieter and calmer than Liam's was.

"Did you see the way she was dressed? She looks way too cute to be going out without a chaperone and you didn't even ask who she was meeting!" Matt accused.

"You boys are the ones that bought her those clothes." Murphy laughed. "And I am not her father. I have no right to butt into her affairs. If you want to know who she is seeing, you can ask her when she gets back." Murphy said firmly and I left the house, not wanting to be late meeting Sara.

Chapter 7

I walked across the lawn to a small shed-like barn just out of sight of the house. Sara was already inside and smiled when I walked in. "This is my she-shed. Murphy gave it to me. The guys rarely, if ever, come out here." She smiled proudly as she gestured around. "You ready to meet the cutest boys you have ever seen in your life?" She giggled.

"Absolutely." I smiled back at her. She led me over to a stall and opened the door. Five balls of golden fur came rushing out the open door and I dropped to my knees. They were seriously the cutest things I had ever seen. I laughed as all five puppies climbed on me and began trying to lick my face.

"Come on, Trin. Let's get them back into their pen and then we can play with them for a while." Sara laughed as she helped gather up the puppies.

We closed ourselves into the stall with them and settled into the straw. There was a bigger dog lying in the corner watching us but didn't seem to mind us being there.

"Did Axel tell you to use his card today?" I asked.

"He has told me multiple times that if I needed anything, I should use his card. I figured that extended to you." Sara shrugged her shoulders.

"Why would that extend to me?" I was so confused as to why she would think that Axel would pay for anything of mine.

"He called you 'Baby'." Sara looked at me confused. "Aren't you guys like a thing?"

"We are most definitely not a thing." I shook my head.

"Oh." Sara mouthed. "Well, don't worry about it. Axel has more than enough in that account. I doubt he will even notice."

The smallest of the puppies climbed up into my lap and settled down to watch its siblings run around. I gently ran my hand down the little guy's back and played with his ears. His fur was impossibly soft.

"You look like this is the first time you have ever played with a puppy." Sara laughed as she tossed a toy and several of the puppies ran after it.

"It is." I replied as I continued to pet the puppy in my lap.

"What?" Sara was clearly shocked as she scooted closer to me. "You're what, eighteen and you have never held a puppy before?"

I looked over at my new friend and saw a guarded interest in her eyes. I gave her a sad smile. "I turn eighteen in a few days. My parents and I lived in a very remote part of the country and never had a dog. I was eight years old when they died. I ended up living with my aunts who were very controlling." I gave a small shrug as I picked up the puppy and cuddled him to my chest.

"Trinity?" Sara asked hesitantly. I looked over at her and she watched me carefully. "I was the one who cleaned you up the night you got here. I saw what I at first thought was hair or something, but realized they were thin scars all over your back. There is also a large scar along your collar bone. Did your aunts do that to you?" Her voice was soft and full of concern.

I buried my face into the puppy's fur as silent tears began to fall. I felt Sara's arms come around me as she tried to comfort me. I tensed at the contact before telling myself to relax. We sat like that for a long time. The puppy was calm and would periodically lick the tears off my face.

Once my tears were all spent, I told Sara a watered-down version of what living at my aunts' house was like. I told her about most of the treatment I received from when I first moved in with them to when I locked myself in the bathroom at the diner, including my lack of schooling. Sara looked sick to her stomach as she listened, but she didn't interrupt. When I was done retelling my terrifying history, we sat in silence.

"Is that why you kept trying to fight me while you were unconscious? You were afraid I was going to hurt you?" she asked quietly as tears ran down her own cheeks. "I am so sorry, Trin. But now that you are here, you don't ever have to go back to them. Murphy will never allow it." She gave me a watery smile, which I returned.

We went back to sitting in the quiet and watched as one by one the puppies curled up and fell asleep. The puppy in my arms settled more against me and I placed a kiss on his head. "His name is Duncan. He was the runt. He is the only puppy not spoken for. Next week, all the others go to their new homes." Sara said as she patted the puppy's back. She yawned and stretched. "It is getting late. We should probably head back so that you can get some rest before having to take your finals in the morning."

I nodded and reluctantly put Duncan with his littermates. As we left the stall, he began to whine and howl. I looked back at him, not wanting to leave him there. If it was up to me, I would take him back up to my room with me. I was going to have to ask Murphy if I could.

We walked across the grass and back into the house. All was quiet and Sara gave me one last hug before turning toward the servants' quarters. I tiptoed up the stairs trying not to wake anyone and slipped into the room, closing the door slowly to be as quiet as possible. I screamed when the light behind me flipped on suddenly. There were four very angry men standing with their arms crossed and one very amused one reclining in a chair.

"What the heck, guys? You seriously scared me half to death." I placed a hand over my racing heart as I glared at them.

"Where have you been? You said you would be back by 1:00 and it is close to 3:30!" Matt was clearly trying to keep his anger under control, but his voice was still nearly a yell.

"What?" I asked as I glanced over at the clock. Crap it was 3:30 am. Telling my life story must have taken longer than we thought. "Sorry, I must have lost track of time." I shrugged and walked over to the closet and grabbed some pajamas before locking myself into the bathroom. I was surprised to see that everyone was still in the room when I walked back out.

"How was your evening, Trin?" Murphy asked with a smile.

My earlier excitement about seeing the puppies returned and I beamed at him. "It was amazing! It was the first time I had ever experienced something like that. He was seriously the cutest thing I have ever seen! His brown eyes saw right into my soul, and he cuddled with me all night as we talked." I couldn't wait to see the cat Sara said was around the property. I had never pet a cat before either and I was curious to know if cats were as soft as the puppies.

"You were out with a boy?" Noah asked as he crossed his arms over his chest.

"I went out with Sara, and she introduced me to him." I turned my attention back to Murphy. "I was wondering, could I bring Duncan up here tomorrow night to sleep with me?" I asked hopefully and a spark of understanding flashed in Murphy's eyes.

"No." Axel stated firmly. When I turned to look at him, he looked ready to kill someone.

"Do you have an allergy or something?" I was confused.

"No, I don't have an allergy." Axel's hands were in fists, and he was glaring at me.

"Then I don't see what the problem is." I said, crossing my arms over my chest and glaring back at him.

"I said, no, Trinity. You're not bringing a boy over here and sleeping with him in my bed." Axel growled out.

"Kids, let's all calm down." Murphy tried to deescalate the situation, but I ignored him.

Who did Axel think he was? "Since you don't have an allergy and since you aren't sleeping in here, I don't see where the problem is!" I yelled at him. "Do you hate dogs or something?"

"What do dogs have to do with sleeping with a boy?" Axel had stepped threateningly toward me.

I was seeing red, and my anger bubbled close to the surface. Did Axel think I was going to bring a *human* boy here to sleep with? Is that what he thought of me? "Duncan isn't just some boy, Axel." I began to explain but he cut me off.

"I don't care if you think you love him, you aren't bringing him here!" Axel's booming voice shook the walls.

"That's it. I'm done." I said as I grabbed the blanket off the bed and headed for the door. Noah moved to block the exit. He too looked angry and a bit worried. I was so mad. If he didn't move out of my way, I was going to hit him.

"Where are you going?" Matt asked with irritation in his voice.

"Since you all think I'm sleeping around, I might as well go find another bed to sleep in." I said angrily. "Now, move Noah." I demanded.

He didn't move. He glanced over my shoulder at something. I took the opportunity and grabbed the handle of the door, yanking it open with such force that Noah jumped out of the way before it hit him. With my hand still on the knob, I slowly locked the door, praying no one noticed the small movement.

"I'm sure Duncan and his littermates won't mind me crashing with them, slut that I am." I commented as I stepped over the threshold and out into the hallway before turning around.

"Littermates? Do you mean siblings or roommates?" Noah asked with a furrowed brow.

"No, I mean littermates. Duncan is a puppy." I slammed the door closed and ran down the stairs. I dropped the blanket by the front door before opening it and slamming it quickly. I heard a crash come from upstairs and I cloaked myself before moving to the opposite wall. My heart was beating erratically as I slowly started to walk down the hallway toward Sara's room. All four guys came running down the stairs and I paused to see what they were going to do.

"A puppy? She made it sound like a freaking boy." Matt grumbled.

Axel picked up the comforter and looked around the entryway. "Noah, Liam. You two go out front and see if you can find her. Matt, check the house and I will go out to the barn to see if she went there." Axel took charge. "We owe her a huge apology." I could hear the regret in his voice. I didn't want to hear an apology right now. I was so angry with them. He dropped the blanket before jogging past me as I pressed myself against the wall. Matt ran back upstairs while Noah and Liam ran outside.

I waited until they were all out of sight before I grabbed my blanket and continued towards Sara's room. I reached a short hallway with two doors on each side. I paused, trying to figure out how I was going to find out what door belonged to Sara. A light suddenly shone out from under the door on the far left. I knocked softly and waited anxiously. I glanced over my shoulder and uncloaked. I prayed Sara would open the door before someone saw me.

A moment later, the door cracked open, and Sara peeked around it. Her eyes widened in surprise when she saw me standing there. "Trinity? What's wrong? I thought you were going to bed." She pulled the door open the rest of the way and yanked me inside. She closed the door and turned to look at me with concern written all over her face.

I locked the door before I sat on the edge of the bed. Sara sat next to me but kept quiet as she waited for me to say something. "They pretty much called me a slut." I seethed.

I told her what had happened, and she was just as mad as I was. After explaining everything I can see the miscommunication about Duncan being a human boy. I had tried to tell them, but Axel had interrupted me.

"I can understand that they didn't realize Duncan was a puppy, but what makes me mad is that they think they can control where I go and who I see. They have no sense of boundaries when it comes to what I do. Not only that but they thought I would sleep with someone after just meeting them. Is that how I come across to people? That I would do that?"

"Not at all, Trin. If anything, you are quite innocent when it comes to boys." Sara reassured me. "You are a woman, they are men. They need to respect your privacy. Just like they wouldn't go into the girls' bathroom at the store, they shouldn't just be coming into your room without permission, Trinity. What would have happened if you walked out of the bathroom in a towel and they were all in there hanging out?" Sara said and I nodded my agreement. They needed to start respecting me. I wasn't used to being able to set boundaries. I was glad Sara was here to help me navigate these new waters. I was a private person. I liked keeping things to myself. They needed to understand that I needed my space. "Let's go to sleep, Trin. You look exhausted and your test starts in four hours."

"Thanks Sara. You are the best." I gave her a smile as I settled on the floor. "I'll take the floor."

She protested, but I insisted. The thick comforter provided enough cushion that I was comfortable. Sara turned out the lights and climbed into bed. I had a moment of panic but concentrated on my breathing and calmed down. It didn't take long until I started to fall asleep.

Chapter 8

A knock sounded at the door and my heart began to race as panic set in. Did I oversleep? Were my aunts coming? Sara shot upright in bed and looked around. When our eyes met, she put a finger to her mouth to tell me to be quiet.

"Who is it?" She called.

"Sara, it's me." Axel's voice sounded through the door. "I need your help."

"Just a sec." Sara called as she pointed under the bed, and I wiggled under it with my blanket. She made sure that I was completely hidden before opening the door. "What is it, Axel? Hey!" Sara started to ask but he shoved past her and sat heavily on her bed. His legs were right in front of my face.

"I screwed up." Axel groaned.

"That is a bit of an understatement, don't you think?" Sara said dryly as she closed the door.

"Geez, thanks sis. Rub salt in the wound, why don't ya?" Axel muttered. Sis? Axel and Sara were brother and sister? "Wait? You know?" He sounded perplexed.

"Axel, you called my friend a slut because you jumped to conclusions. What were you thinking?" Sara started to yell, and I covered my mouth to keep from laughing. "Do you honestly think that I would take her out to hook up with guys or that Trinity is the type of girl that sleeps around? Seriously Axel, the girl flinches whenever anyone touches her!"

"No. But you should have seen her, Sara. She was so excited about her evening and then she asked Uncle Murphy if she could have Duncan come over to sleep with her. I would have flipped if you had asked the same question." Axel defended himself.

"You have a problem, Axel. And inferring that Trinity is a lightskirt is the least of your issues." Sara crossed to the bed and sat down.

"What do you mean?" Axel asked, confused.

"What did you do when you came to my room?"

"I knocked to..." Axel was cut off.

"Exactly. You knocked. Since Trinity has been here, have you ever knocked on your bedroom door and waited to be invited in?" Sara asked. Silence followed her question. "That's what I thought." Sara sounded smug. "You, Matt, Liam, and Noah invade her privacy and demand to know everything about her. You have no respect for her or her feelings. What would have happened if you guys walked into your room, and she was walking around in her underwear? You can't keep doing this, big brother." Sara's voice had softened slightly.

"Do you know where she is?" Axel asked hopefully.

"Yes." Sara said slowly. My heart began to race. I wasn't ready to talk with them right now. I needed to focus on my test before I could even start thinking about what I wanted to do about the whole boundaries thing.

"Great!" He jumped to his feet. "Where is she?"

"She is safe, Axel, and that is all that I am going to tell you." Sara said firmly as she got to her feet as well. "Don't give me that look. You guys hurt her, Axel. And I am not going to allow you guys to bully responses from her. She will talk with you when she is ready to and not because you give her no choice. Now, if you don't mind, I need to get dressed for the day." I watched Sara's legs move to the door as she opened it and waited. Axel hesitated before walking towards the door too.

He paused just before leaving. "Please, Sara. Ask her to come back to the house. We have been looking for her all night." He sounded exhausted and I felt slightly guilty for causing them to worry so much.

"You can tell the rest of the gang that Trinity is safe, but she will not be coming back until she starts getting the respect she deserves. Heaven knows that girl has had very little of it since moving in with her aunts." Sara pushed Axel the rest of the way out of her room and closed the door in his face. She locked it and moved to her desk. I slowly crawled out from under the bed, and she gave me a smile. She motioned me over as she turned on her laptop. "You can take your tests here." She whispered.

"Thank you." I whispered back. Sara was truly becoming a great friend. "Why didn't you tell me Axel was your brother?" I asked her. I was still trying to puzzle through the familial connections between Murphy, the guys and Sara.

"Yeah, Axel is my older brother. Our mother and Murphy's sisters are great friends. Our father was gone a lot for work, and we spent a lot of time with Liam, Noah, and Matt's families. They adopted us in a way." Sara explained as she signed into the computer.

"I thought Axel was Murphy's nephew? If he is your uncle, why are you working for him?" I sat down on the computer chair but turned to look at Sara.

"Liam, Noah, and Matt are his nephews by blood from his two sisters. Axel and I are more like his honorary niece and nephew. I work here because I hate sitting around and not doing anything. I do what I can until I go to college. And I earn some money for the next semester. Axel pays for all my necessities, but I like having spending money." Sara became excited. "Where are you applying to? How fun would it be if we were roommates?"

"Oh, I'm not applying to colleges right now. Remember, I am hoping to finish my eighth-grade finals today. I will take my high school placement test in two days, so college is still a few years out." I gave her a sad smile. Going to college with Sara would have been so much fun.

"Why don't you take the GED test? That way you could skip having to go grade by grade through high school." Sara asked as she grabbed a change of clothes before moving to the bathroom.

When she got back out, I was just starting my first test. She locked the door on her way out with a promise to bring food in a little bit. I got lost in my tests and before I knew it, I was done with three of the four finals. I sat back and rubbed my eyes. I was so tired. Just one more test and I could take a nap.

Two hours later, I pressed the submit button as I let out a sigh. I turned around and nearly screamed when I saw Murphy sitting on the bed. "How do you feel now that you are all done with your tests?" he asked as he smiled at me.

"How did you know I was here?" I asked without smiling back at him. Now the only place I felt safe was compromised. How long until the watch dogs showed up?

"Sara asked me to bring you some food. She said the boys are watching her every move and she was afraid that if she brought the food here herself, they would find you." Murphy's smile fell as his lips pulled into a thin line. "You need to talk with them."

"I really don't feel like I am ready to, Murphy. Not yet anyway. I am far too exhausted and upset with them to have a calm conversation." I crossed my arms over my chest.

Murphy gave me a sad smile. "I understand. Eat your sandwich and get some rest." He got to his feet and headed for the door. He hesitated just before opening it. "Please come to dinner tonight. You and Sara both should be there." I started to protest but he cut me off. "Just think about it." He opened the door and left.

I blinked several times as I stared at the closed door. I looked at the clock and saw that it was just past 2:00 pm. If I went to sleep now, I could get a few hours of sleep before dinner.

I looked over at the sandwich and my stomach knotted. I tried to take a bite, but my stomach just wasn't having it. Deciding to forgo forcing lunch, I climbed onto the bed with my comforter and quickly fell asleep.

I was awakened by Sara shaking my shoulder. "Hey girl. Wake up. It's almost time for dinner." I sat up and yawned. I rubbed my eyes as she continued talking. "Here, I brought you some clothes. Go ahead and take a shower if you want, but we should hurry."

I took the clothes without saying a word and headed for the bathroom. I felt like a zombie. I took a hot shower trying to wake myself up, but it didn't really help. I dressed quickly and stepped out to find Sara, stern faced, with her hands on her hips.

"What?" I asked.

"You didn't eat lunch." She scolded me as she pointed to the sandwich still on its plate.

"I tried but I was so tired. It must be all the stress with finals and well, everything else." I said with an apologetic look.

"Fine. But you better eat something at dinner." Sara said as she pulled me out into the hall.

We made our way to the dining room quickly. When we walked in Liam, Noah, Matt, and Axel jumped to their feet as if they wanted to rush over but Murphy told them to sit. They grudgingly did as he commanded.

Matt, Liam, and Axel sat on one side of the table while Murphy sat at the head. Noah sat on the other side with two empty seats. I took the closest one letting Sara sit next to Noah. I looked up and met Axel's eyes across the table. I quickly lowered my gaze and focused on my plate. Murphy told everyone to start eating.

Conversations slowly started up around me, but I kept my gaze down as I pushed the food around on my plate. I still had no appetite.

We had been sitting there for half an hour when Sara kicked me under the table. I glared over at her, and her eyes darted over to Murphy. Everyone was looking at me as if expecting me to answer. "I'm sorry, what did you say?" I said with no emotion in my voice.

"I asked if you felt comfortable enough to move back to your room?" Murphy asked again.

I looked over at Sara and she patted my leg under the table. "She would if there were some rules in place."

"Trinity can speak for herself, Sara." Matt said. And I shot him a glare.

"When it comes to her room, you boys are not allowed to waltz in. You knock and wait to be invited in. And Axel." Sara turned her attention to fully look at her brother. "You may share a room with Trinity when it comes to your clothes but that doesn't give you free range either. You are allowed inside between eight and ten in the mornings and then seven and eight for the evenings. Trinity will make sure she is not there during those times to respect your privacy as well." Sara sat back and looked at everyone as she waited.

"I agree to the terms." Axel said. I looked over at him and he was watching me closely. I looked back at my plate and the other three boys murmured their agreements as well.

Silence fell around the room again. I began pushing my food around once more, giving up on trying to eat. I jumped when Sara touched my hand.

I looked back at her, and she had a concerned look on her face. "Are you okay?" she mouthed.

"What?" I asked, blinking quickly to refocus. "Oh, um...Yeah, I'm fine." I mumbled as Sara's question registered in my brain. I scooted my chair back and got to my feet. "I think I am going to go to bed. Good night." I stumbled once on my way up the stairs but made it to the room quickly. I climbed into bed without changing and fell asleep almost instantly.

A knock came at the door, but I ignored it. Another knock came, this time louder. I groaned as I got up. I shuffled to the door and opened it. Axel was standing in the hall wearing a sweaty T-shirt and basketball shorts. I stood there looking at him as I leaned on the door. I had a bad headache and just wanted to go back to bed. His expression turned from uncertainty to concern.

"Are you feeling, okay?" He took a step toward me.

"I think so. I Just have a headache. Did you need something?" I asked as I closed my eyes and rubbed my temple.

"Can I come in and grab my clothes? I promise not to be long and then you can go back to bed."

I nodded and stepped back to allow him room to enter. I walked back to the bed and crawled under the covers. I could hear Axel moving around in the closet for a few minutes before I heard the sink in the bathroom turn on.

A gentle hand brushed my hair back out of my face, and I opened my eyes. Axel was crouched next to the bed making him eye level with me. "I brought you some pain medication. Can you sit up so you can take it?"

I slowly sat up and Axel placed two white pills in one hand while putting a glass of water in my other. I swallowed the pills quickly before laying back down. Axel again smoothed my hair back as he crouched to my level.

"Thank you." I whispered as I closed my eyes. He kept stroking my hair and it soothed me back to sleep.

Chapter 9

"Trin, are you in there?" Sara's voice called through the closed door. I groaned as I rolled over. She knocked more urgently.

"Sara, I'm fine." I called back as I wiped my sweaty brow.

"Just checking on you. Axel said you had a headache last night." Sara said. I could hear the concern in her voice.

"All I need is some sleep. I was really stressed over my finals, and I must have made myself sick from it." It was quiet for a long time, but I knew she was still standing there. "I sound fine, don't I? Don't worry, I should be right as rain in a few hours." I lied. I was not feeling fine at all. I was beginning to feel hot and the pressure in my head was getting worse.

"Okay, fine. But I will be back tonight, young lady." Sara finally said before I heard her stomping down the hallway.

I dragged myself out of bed and made my way to the closet. I pulled out a pair of running shorts and a tank top. Maybe if I change out of my jeans, I will feel cooler. I climbed back into bed feeling only a little better. As much as I wanted to fall asleep, I couldn't get comfortable. I tossed and turned as my fever got worse.

A sound broke through the fog. I opened my eyes a sliver as it came again. I concentrated on it and words began to form. "Trinity, how are you feeling? Can I come in?" That sounded like Sara. Maybe she could bring Duncan. I would feel so much better if I had him to cuddle with.

"Only if you have Duncan." I called back as I tried to mask the pain I was feeling. I felt like I was in an oven and my breathing was heavy. I began to toss and turn again as I tried to get comfortable. A whimper sounded and I wasn't sure if it came from me or not. A cold nose touched my face, and I reached up. My hand found a furry body as it cuddled up to my chest. "Hey, handsome." I mumbled.

"Trinity? What's wrong?" I heard Sara's cry of concern but couldn't bring myself to answer. A cold hand touched my forehead before pulling back quickly. "Murphy! Murphy, come quick!" Sara screamed.

The next thing I knew Duncan was pulled away from me and I cried out in protest. Another hand touched my face and voices sounded all around.

"She is too hot." Matt's voice echoed in my head, and I whimpered. Why did everyone have to be so loud?

"We need to bring down her fever and quick." Murphy said.

"How do we do that?" Liam asked.

"I'll draw a lukewarm bath and we can have her sit in it. It should help bring her fever down." Sara's voice was moving away from me.

Why was everyone making a big deal about this? And where was Duncan? "Duncan." I mumbled.

A hand touched my head. "As soon as your fever is down, we will bring back your puppy." Axel's voice was soft but filled with worry. I slowly reached up, intent on pushing the hand away, but my strength was gone, and my hand fell back to the mattress. The hand moved from my head and grasped my hand. "Everything is going to be okay, Trinity." Axel whispered close to my head. Axel's hand tightened on mine when I jumped as a cold cloth was placed on my forehead.

"The tub is filled." Sara called from the direction of the bathroom.

Axel let go of my hand and then I was lifted off the mattress. I didn't even struggle as I was carried into the other room. I wanted to, but I was too drained of energy. My feet were lowered slowly. I screamed and wrapped my arms around the person carrying me as I tried to lift my feet out of the ice-cold water. I was lifted back up quickly.

"She isn't going to stay in there long enough for it to help if that is her reaction to just her toes touching the water." Sara said anxiously.

"Matt, hold Trinity." Axel's voice was just as anxious as Sara's but there was a determination to it too. A second pair of arms tried to grab me, but I whimpered and held on tighter. Strong hands grabbed my arms and broke my hold, and I was transferred from one person to another.

"No, please. I'm okay. I don't need to go in." I begged as I tried to get down.

"Okay, hand her back." Axel's voice was full of tension.

"What's the plan?" Matt asked as he transferred me back to Axel. I tried to get away but the two of them were too strong for me.

"Please, no." I whimpered out. No one seemed to be listening to me.

"She's not going to stay in the water on her own. I'm going to sit with her." Axel explained.

I began fighting to get out of his arms, but his hold only tightened. He started to sit down and a second later I was plunged into icy water. I screamed and tried to get out, but he held me to him. After a few minutes, I gave up and began to cry as I started shivering.

"I'm so sorry." Axel just kept whispering in my ear over and over again.

My tears eventually stopped, but my shivering increased. I leaned against Axel's chest as my strength completely drained from me. A cold cloth was laid across my forehead and I turned more into Axel. He was the only source of warmth I could get to at the moment and I was freezing. I curled more into him, desperate to get warm. His thumb started to rub up and down my arm.

I heard someone crying softly and opened my eyes. Sara was crying as she watched me. She knelt down by the tub and helped pull my hair into a bun at the top of my head to keep it out of the way. She stood back up and took several steps back. My eyes began to droop as Noah moved to her side and put his arms around her in a hug. Axel cradled me close. I closed my eyes as I gave up on trying to get out of this torture.

Pressure. That is all I could think about. There was so much pressure in my head. It felt like it was going to explode. I lifted my hands to my head and squeezed my skull hoping to find some kind of relief. Warm liquid started dripping from my nose as the pressure continued to build.

"Make it stop!" I screamed as I squeezed my eyes closed.

Hands grabbed my face and lifted it up so they could look at me. "Her nose is bleeding and I think her fever has only gotten worse." I couldn't even tell who was talking. The only thing I recognized about it was that it was male.

"Let's get her out. I think we need to take her to a hospital." Another male voice called out.

The pressure continued to build. I pushed the hands away that tried to grab me. My vision was blurry as I looked around. Shapes moved around chaotically as others reached for me. I squeezed my head again as I screamed. A large hand covered mine as I was pulled to Axel's chest. He held me tight as I continued to scream in pain.

"Don't fight it." A faint female voice called from far away. I knew that voice. Mother? "It is a part of you, Trinity. Let it come."

Another wave of pressure came, and I gritted my teeth against the pain. I imagined an eggshell cracking and suddenly a burst of energy filled my whole body. Axel groaned in pain as his arm tightened around me. There was a loud boom and the cold water around me started to drain away.

Axel's arms tightened even more around me as we fell. When we came to a stop, hands lifted me up and away from Axel. I opened my eyes and saw Sara's pale face as she followed after me and whoever was carrying me.

I wasn't as hot as I was before, and I started to feel stronger as well. I wiggled against the arms that carried me as I fought to get down. "Put me down!" I cried out. The person carrying me set me down and grabbed onto my upper arms to keep me steady. "What happened?" I asked as I looked around.

Water was coming out from under the bathroom door and Sara was shaking. I was soaking wet and dripping all over the carpet. Murphy stood before me with wide eyes.

"What do you mean 'what happened'? You have an insanely high fever, and you were screaming in pain." Murphy was flabbergasted. "What is going on?"

"I don't know. I felt like I was in an oven and my head was going to explode. Then mom's voice called to me and then it all went away." I stepped farther away from Murphy and my legs collapsed under me.

The bathroom door opened, and Noah came out helping a bare-chested Axel into the room. Noah was pressing a wadded-up shirt to Axel's back. "Can the car take one more to the hospital?" Noah asked. He froze when he saw me kneeling on the ground with Sara and Murphy kneeling next to me. "Why is Trin not being loaded in the car yet?"

"Hospital? I'm not going to any hospital." I felt the blood drain from my face. Hospitals were full of needles and people that touched you. I wasn't going to go.

"Trinity, we need to get you to a hospital to lower your fever and to help stop your pain." Axel grimaced as he stood up straight.

"You will have to kill me first." I growled out. His eyes widened in surprise at my declaration. "What happened to you?" I asked as I tried to divert attention from myself.

Axel laughed. "It's just a scratch. Don't worry about it."

"Just a scratch? Liam pulled a chunk of the tub out of your back." Noah scoffed. "He is going to need stitches and he'll probably have a wicked scar from it. We should probably get you two on your way."

I furrowed my brows. "What happened to the tub?" I asked as I slowly moved farther from the door.

"It exploded." Matt came out of the bathroom throwing a towel on the floor to mop up the water. "You screamed and light swirled around you. Then the tub exploded. Axel managed to turn his body so that he took the fall so you didn't get hurt." Matt smiled at me. "You look like you are feeling better. Not so pale."

I moved to the bathroom slowly and pushed the door open. The room was a complete disaster. The mirror and shower door were broken, and glass was everywhere. Matt was right, the tub looked like it had exploded. Blood was all over the broken shards. Water flooded the whole room. I put a hand over my mouth as I looked at the mess. What had I done? This was all because of me.

I closed my eyes and wished I could repair the damage. Warmth flooded through me, and I felt the magic spread through my veins. The magic felt different than it had before. It felt so much more...potent?

The magic slowly faded and with it my strength. I felt myself falling but I didn't hit the floor. "Dang it, Axel! Now there is blood all over the floor." Liam growled at him.

"What was I supposed to do, let her fall?" Axel said as I felt myself being carried. I was set on the bed. I blinked my eyes open and sat up with a start. I still felt a bit weak but there was no way I was going to drop my guard and let them take me to the hospital. "Easy, Trinity. You just passed out." Axel looked down at me with worried eyes.

"How did you know she was going to pass out?" Murphy asked. I looked over at him as he watched Axel with a curious expression.

Axel shrugged. "I don't know. I could feel she was collapsing." He jumped and cursed. "Holy crap, Liam!" Axel growled.

"Sorry man, you're still bleeding like crazy." Liam apologized.

I scooted to the edge of the bed. Axel and Liam stepped back to allow me room to stand but I just hung my legs over the side. "Turn around." I said and both of them looked at me in confusion. "I'm cold and I'm tired and I'm not in the mood. Don't make me ask again."

They slowly turned around. I gently pushed Liam's hand off of the shirt and took over applying pressure. I pulled it back enough to take a look at the wound. It was a good five inches wide, and it was deep enough I could see torn muscle through the gap. Blood immediately began pouring from the opening, so I quickly returned the shirt to the wound and pressed firmly.

"I knew you were fat." I teased, trying to lighten the mood. "It's literally coming out of your 'scratch'." Axel chuckled but didn't say anything.

Dad had received a deep wound like this when I was six. Mother said she couldn't do it herself and asked if I could help her. We were able to heal him, but it had taken a lot of energy from us. I was out for two days, and mother was weak for nearly four days afterwards.

"Sara, get some towels and put them on the bed. Liam, Matt. I am going to have you help Axel lay down on top of them facing down. Noah, can I get some cold water please." I said in a tired voice. This was going to be exhausting. I would be surprised if I even stay conscious.

"Trinity, you don't have to." Axel began to protest.

"Just do as I ask." I pinched the bridge of my nose with one hand as I continued to apply pressure to Axel's wound. A hand gently touched my shoulder, and I looked up. Noah offered me a glass of water and I took it with a shaky hand. "Thank you." I whispered. Liam took back over applying pressure and I drained the whole cup. I watched as Axel lay face down on the bed. I scooted closer to him as I looked over at Murphy. He was watching me carefully. "Murphy, no matter what happens, you have to promise me that I will not go to a hospital."

Axel rolled halfway over and looked at me with a worried expression. "Whatever you are doing, it isn't worth it, Trinity." He said anxiously.

"I promise, kid. No hospitals. I trust you." Murphy gave me a nod and I swallowed hard.

I was really nervous about doing this without my mother, but I needed to. I took a deep breath as I turned back to Axel. He was still watching me closely and I gently pushed him back down. I pulled back his blood-soaked shirt and placed my hand over the wound.

Blood started to seep out around my palm and fingers. My hand was shaking. I closed my eyes as I focused. I felt the magic swirl through me with a strength that I had never felt before. The magic rushed to my hand. A gasp from behind me barely registered in my brain. I began to feel my energy slowly drain from me.

I wasn't sure how much time passed. I fell forward with my head landing on Axel's upper back and he tensed. Somehow, I managed to keep my hand on the wound just below his ribcage.

"No one move!" Murphy's booming voice commanded. I could feel myself weakening more and more until finally everything went black.

* * *

My body felt like it was being weighed down by sand. A small tail began to wag, hitting my hand as a wet nose nuzzled my throat. I cracked my eyes open, and Duncan's brown eyes looked up at me. "Good morning, handsome." I mumbled as I buried my face into his fur.

"Trinity?" Sara's excited voice sounded close to the bed. I looked up to see a relieved smile on her face. She screamed as she jumped on top of me. She wrapped her arms tightly around me. Duncan let out a startled yelp as he squirmed out from underneath us. "You scared the crap out of me. I thought you died, and Murphy refused to let us take you to the hospital." she cried.

I rolled so I could hug her back. She had become my best friend, and I don't know what I would do without her.

"What the…?" Murphy's breathless voice came from the doorway.

Pounding feet came running down the hall, but Sara was holding me so tightly that I couldn't turn and see who all was there. "You guys are going to have to wait your turn." Sara said sternly through her tears.

I laughed softly as she continued to squeeze me. "Hey, Sara?" I whispered.

"Shh. You're ruining the moment." She said to me, and I laughed harder. She finally released her hold on me but stayed on the bed. "You ever do that again and I will kill you myself, you hear me?"

"How long was I out?" I asked as I looked over at the five men standing at the edge of the bed.

"Just short of four days." Murphy said. All of them looked incredibly relieved to see me awake.

"You seemed to know this was going to happen." Liam commented. I nodded with a little shrug.

"Why did you do it then?" Axel asked. He looked furious.

"Why did you drop me into a bathtub full of water from Antarctica?" I shot back.

"Maybe because you were feverish, and we needed to get it down before you died." Axel threw his arms up in frustration.

"Now, now you two. Let's all settle down. The past several days has been stressful. Why don't we all go get some rest? Heaven knows none of us has really slept in a while." Murphy cut into our argument.

I got out of bed and moved to the closet. "What are you doing, Trinity?" Matt asked.

"As soon as you all leave, I am taking a shower." I commented as I gathered my clothing. As I was walking back out, I remembered the bathroom was destroyed. "Oh Sara, can I use your bathroom?" I hugged my clothes to my chest.

Everyone was watching me as I stood there. Axel bent down and picked up Duncan while Sara slowly got off the bed. Why were they all staring at me like that? "Trin, you can use this bathroom." Sara finally said.

"You got it fixed already?" I asked. How did they manage to get the bathroom redone in four days? I guess it could be possible if Murphy was able to find someone to come out immediately.

"*You* fixed it." Noah corrected.

"What? That's not...No..." I moved to the bathroom quickly. I stood in the doorway as I took in the room. The bathroom looked exactly how I remembered it the first time I saw it. "That's not possible." I breathed. "Unless...Oh no." Murphy was right. I was of royal blood then. My mother had said I was special and one day, when I was older, I would know why. All those lessons on the history of magic users. Mom was trying to prepare me for this. "What is today's date?" I asked without turning around.

"April 15." Liam answered.

"Murphy, the fever was…" I started to say as I turned around but couldn't finish. He nodded and I leaned against the wall. I slid down until I was sitting on the floor.

"The fever was what?" Sara asked anxiously as she looked between Murphy and me.

"The fever and the pain Trinity experienced were her full powers manifesting." He walked over to me and crouched down to my level. "Your mother went through the same thing the night before her birthday and when midnight hit, it all went away. Your father and I were stationed outside her door, and he was beside himself with worry as we listen for hours." Murphy gave me a sad smile. "I'm so sorry I didn't see the signs before."

I laughed softly. "You still wouldn't have been able to do anything. This way you worried for less time. And when we find my Enforcer, you all can be off the hook when it comes to watching out for me." Murphy laughed and the twinkle in his eyes sparked again.

"Go take your shower. We can talk when you are done. Sara can stay here just in case you need anything." Murphy patted my knee as he stood up. He ushered the guys out of the door and in seconds, I was left alone with Sara.

Sara helped me up but remained silent as I headed into the bathroom. I spent an hour enjoying the warmth of the water and the feeling of being clean. When I finally got out, I dressed in a pair of sweatpants, a T-shirt and one of my new hoodies. I brushed my wet hair and Sara helped me French braid it. We sat on the bed and Sara proceeded to tell me all about the night I got my powers.

"The water was actually quite warm, but you screamed as if we set you in a pool full of ice. You were burning up, so Axel picked you up and sat in the water with you. You completely freaked out for several minutes. You should have seen the pain on Axel's face having to force you to stay in the water.

"You eventually settled down though. We all were pretty shaken. You started trembling and your chin was chattering. You were like that for hours. Then you started screaming again and begging us to make it stop. Your nose started to bleed. We tried to get you out, but you fought us. Axel wrapped his arms around you as a light surrounded the two of you and then the tub exploded. Murphy lifted you off Axel so that he could get up. A large piece of the tub had stabbed Axel's back. You saved him, you know?" Sara gave me a smile. "Thank you for that. He can be a complete knucklehead at times, but I still love him."

I returned her smile. "I'm glad I could help. My mom and I healed my father once. It took both of us and the toll on us was great. I am surprised I feel as good as I do, especially since I healed such a deep wound by myself."

"Axel has been beating himself up these past four days. He blames himself since you passed out healing him. He has rarely left your side." Sara bumped my shoulder with hers. "But we should head downstairs. Murphy really wants to talk with you about something."

"Okay." I sighed and we both stood up.

"Oh, and happy belated birthday." Sara grinned. "I got you something, but it is downstairs."

"You didn't have to get me anything." I glanced at her. I hadn't received a birthday present since my parents were killed.

"I guess if you don't want Duncan, I can always find him a new home." Sara laughed when I squealed in delight and threw my arms around her.

Chapter 10

Everyone was inside the study when Sara and I walked in. There was an open seat on the couch next to Axel. I walked over and sat down. Duncan climbed out of Axel's lap and into mine. I scratched behind his ears as he tried to climb up my chest to get to my neck. He loved sticking his cold nose under my chin.

"How is my handsome boy doing?" I asked Duncan as I placed a kiss on his head. I was so excited that he was my puppy. When I looked up, Matt was trying to hide his laugh. "What?" I asked as our eyes met across the coffee table.

"For a second, I thought you were talking about Axel. Then I saw you kissing the pup." He said as he started to laugh, and I sent him a smirk.

"Yeah, because I would call a grown man 'handsome boy'." I said sarcastically as I rolled my eyes. "Not to mention none of you guys are cuter than Duncan." I kissed the puppy's head again causing his tail the wag faster.

Axel shifted slightly on the couch, but I didn't dare look over at him. Murphy stood up from his desk and moved over to the group of chairs. He looked uncertain but trudged ahead anyway. "We have found your Enforcers, Trinity." He stated.

"Uh, you mean Enforcer? You told me that only one Enforcer is chosen after the…person…turns eighteen." I couldn't bring myself to say princess when talking about myself. It felt so weird to think that my mother was one.

"No, Trinity, your magic has chosen more than one." Murphy said seriously. No one moved or said anything for several minutes. "You were sitting with Axel in the tub when your magic surfaced and well, he was marked. Over the several days that followed, Matt, Liam, and Noah all came in contact with you. They were marked as well."

I sat there waiting for the punchline. This had to be a joke. Murphy said only one Enforcer would be chosen. I got to my feet as I hugged Duncan closer. What does being an Enforcer even mean? Murphy made it seem like Enforcers were a lifelong assignment. If Liam, Noah, Matt, and Axel were my Enforcers, that would mean I was their responsibility. All their futures would be tied to mine. Constantly in danger. Not really being able to live a full life. All because of me.

Why would I have more than one? It didn't seem fair to trap four young men in a life of loneliness and danger. I needed to make sure they really did have the marks. Then I needed to see if there was a way to undo the magic tying them to me.

"Can I see the marks?" I asked tentatively. Murphy nodded and all five men pulled their shirts off. I blushed and looked away from their bare chests. They were all incredibly fit. They moved to stand in a line with their backs toward me. I walked over to Sara and handed Duncan over to her as I composed myself.

Taking a deep breath, I slowly moved over to the closest end of the line. Noah was first. He had the royal guards' symbol, but in the bottom right corner was a wolf's head instead of the rose that my father had had. I gently touched it before moving on to Liam. He too had the mark with the wolf's head. I ran my fingers over it as well. Murphy's mark was just the normal guard's mark and I moved onto Matt and then Axel. They both had the wolf's head next to the guards' mark. Why did the magic mark four? This wasn't right, I needed to free them from this obligation.

"Murphy, can I speak with you privately please?" I asked as my fingers traced the mark on Axel's shoulder. His muscles moved slightly under my touch as he shifted his weight and butterflies took flight in my stomach.

Axel turned around to face me with a strange emotion in his eyes as my hand fell back to my side. He blinked a few times, and it went away. Wordlessly he moved back to the couch and grabbed his shirt before leaving. Matt and Liam quickly followed suit. Noah stood close to Sara while they had a whispered conversation.

Noah was playing with the shirt in his hands as they smiled at each other. I bit the inside of my cheek to keep from saying something. Noah and Sara were obviously attracted to each other. Murphy cleared his throat, causing them both to jump. Sara looked over at Murphy before blushing. She quickly turned around and led the way out, Noah staying close to her side. They closed the door behind them as they left.

"What's on your mind, Trinity?" Murphy asked as he made his way back to the chair he had sat in before.

I followed him over and sat in an empty chair. "You told me that only one Enforcer was chosen for each…princess. Why did Liam, Noah, Matt, and Axel get marked? I don't understand." I looked at him, hoping he could explain it to me.

"I'm not sure, Trinity. I'm just not sure." He shook his head. "From everything we were taught, there has only ever been one."

"What do Enforcers even do? I shouldn't even need one." I complained.

"Enforcers are bonded with their princesses. They can sense when their charges are in distress or in danger. Your father described it as having a radar that would go off. Almost like a sixth sense. They are there as your personal bodyguard, the last line of defense. Versus a guard, who is just there to protect generally. I never felt when your mother was in danger like your father could. Your mother's family was assassinated, and your parents were killed. Someone is out there that wants to hurt your family, Trinity." Murphy had a pained look on his face.

"If Enforcers are bonded with their charges, can they have a normal life, like having a family?" I asked.

"Not to my knowledge. As an Enforcer, their first priority will always be the one they are protecting, regardless of them having feelings for another?" Murphy said matter-of-factly.

"Then how do I break the Enforcer's Bond?" I asked.

"I'm not sure. I can research it for you, but Trinity, Enforcers are chosen for a reason." Murphy stuttered out his response as he studied me.

"That would be great. The faster we get that information the better." I forced a faint smile.

For some reason, the thought of losing Axel and the others hurt. I gave myself a mental shake. I had only known them for a few short days, there was no way I had developed an attachment to them.

I stood up and walked from the room. Sara was waiting in the hall for me as she held Duncan. She gave me a smile as I walked up to her. "What was that about?" she asked curiously as she handed Duncan back to me.

"I just had a few questions for Murphy but I'm glad you waited. I was planning on asking you about the GED thing." I said changing the subject.

"I'll show you." She squealed as she grabbed my arm and pulled me down the hallway to her room.

She was practically bouncing with excitement and her enthusiasm was contagious. We spent the next hour going over the information on getting a GED. Sara scheduled the test in three weeks, and we started to study. Two hours later, my brain felt like mush.

"That's it, you need a break. Let's go take Duncan back outside and then we can watch a movie." Sara closed the lid of the laptop as she stood.

I stretched my arms over my head. Duncan had fallen asleep at my feet, and I scooped him up before I followed her from the room. We came across Noah on our way to the back door and his whole face lit up when he saw Sara.

"Where are you lovely ladies heading off to?" he asked as he smiled at us, but his main focus was on Sara.

"Trinity needs to learn how to relax. So, we are returning Duncan to his mom before watching a movie." Sara beamed at him as a light blush touched her cheeks.

"I'll take him for you if you want." Noah offered and I gratefully handed Duncan to him. I was ready to sit and not think about anything. "I'll even bring in some snacks for you guys when I get back."

"Thanks, Noah." Sara's blush deepened as they stood there staring at each other. I gently nudged her, and she blinked, breaking the spell between them. Noah cleared his throat before turning and heading outside. Sara watched him leave, then she let out a heavy sigh.

"What was that all about?" I asked her with a teasing smile.

Sara shrugged as we continued to the lounge. "I don't know what you are talking about?" Her face was red, and she avoided making eye contact with me. "What should we watch?" Sara clearly wanted to change the subject.

Giving her a moment to compose herself, I decided to help her pick a movie. "I haven't really seen much."

"What kind of movies do you like to watch?" I gave her a shrug. She stared at me like I was an alien from another planet. "Romance, comedy, horror, adventure, action, musicals?"

"Action sounds good." I responded. Hopefully that way I can stay awake to watch the full thing. I was starting to feel tired.

"Die Hard or Speed?" She asked me as I sat on the couch.

"Speed." I had never heard of either of them, but at this point I just wanted to stop having to make decisions.

Sara grabbed the remote and moved to the lazy boy to my right and settled in. We were five minutes into the movie when Noah showed up with an armful of snacks. Axel was right behind him with cans of soda and bottled waters.

"I thought you ladies would be watching a chick flick. Mind if we stay, I love this movie?" Noah asked hopefully.

"I don't mind if you don't, Sara." I shrugged and Sara blushed as she gave them her permission.

Noah settled in the chair next to Sara's. Axel handed Noah and Sara their drinks before taking a seat on the couch next to me. He passed me a water bottle and a bag of Skittles. I thanked him before turning my attention back to the movie.

Several minutes later, the light switched off and I jumped at the unexpected darkness. I turned to see Noah walking back to the couch. He settled in next to Sara on the oversized chair she was in. He spread a blanket over the top of them. I smiled as Noah put his arm around her and she laid her head on his shoulder.

I glanced over at Axel to see if he had noticed the two lovebirds, but he seemed to have fallen asleep. His legs were stretched out in front of him, and his head was resting on the hand that was propped up on the arm rest. His other arm lay along the back of the couch, and he was breathing deeply.

The movie was just about halfway over when I felt my eyelids growing heavy. I lost the battle to finish the movie. I sighed as I felt a blanket being draped over me. I rolled over and snuggled deeper under it and fell asleep.

* * *

"Mmm." I hummed as I tried to stretch but was wedged into a snug spot.

I sleepily blinked my eyes open. I was so comfortable, and I wasn't quite ready to get up. I ran my index finger over the design on the pillowcase. It was different than the one I remembered. I froze when I recognized the design I was tracing. It was the same one on Axel's shirt yesterday. I lifted my head quickly and his hand slipped off my shoulder. He was still asleep and snoring softly. How the heck did I end up sleeping on Axel?

I looked around trying to figure out what was going on. The lounge? Memories from last night came back to me. We must have fallen asleep during the movie. But I had no memories of snuggling up to Axel or ending up wedged between him and the back of the couch. Trying not to wake him, I slowly tried to untangle the blanket that was wrapped around us.

Axel shifted and he tightened his arm around my waist. I fell back onto his chest. His other arm went back around me, holding me tight. I gasped in surprise and my heart began to race. I held perfectly still and waited to see if he was awake or not.

Another snore answered that question. After a minute or two, Axel's arms relaxed again, and I was able to carefully extricate myself from the blanket and Axel's arms. I turned back to face him to make sure he was still asleep. Despite my earlier panic, I smiled.

He looked so peaceful and if I was to be totally honest with myself, Axel was downright gorgeous. I felt myself blush and I carefully placed the blanket over him. He was a complete pain in the butt. He was always pushing my buttons. Looks could definitely be deceiving. I couldn't get out of the lounge fast enough. Yes, Axel was attractive, but he was off limits. All men were. I was barely learning to trust others with my physical well-being. I didn't feel remotely ready to trust anyone with my heart.

I heard voices coming from the dining room, so I peeked in. Noah and Sara were eating bowls of cereal and talking. Still feeling a little off balance from waking up next to Axel, I hesitated in the doorway. They looked up at me and I had no choice but to walk in and join them.

"How did you sleep, Trin?" Noah asked with a big smile and a twinkle in his eye.

"Why didn't you wake me up last night?" I glared at them as I took a seat.

"We tried, but you just curled into a ball and mumbled for us to go away." Sara giggled. I covered my face with my hands. How embarrassing. Was I already cuddled up with Axel when they tried to wake me? "You two are kinda cute together. You know, when you are both unconscious and aren't trying to kill each other or arguing."

Noah laughed as my head snapped up and my mouth fell open in shock. "Don't get your hopes up, Sara, they can't spend their lives cuddled up and asleep."

"That's true. Trinity, you were tossing and turning like you were having a nightmare or something when you ended up with your head on Axel's shoulder. He was already asleep too, so I guess it doesn't really count towards you guys actually getting along." Sara pouted. "Even though that would be totally awesome." Sara added under her breath.

"Will you guys just stop? It's not like that and you know it." I stood up from the table. "I am going to go study." Just before walking out the door and my escape, I bumped into something hard. I looked up and saw Axel's startled face.

"Morning." He muttered. His voice was husky from sleep. He took a step to the side to put more space between us. "Where is your broom, Trinity? It's rare for the wicked witch to be seen without it." He smirked at me.

"You probably have it shoved up your..." I snapped at him.

"How did you sleep, Axel?" Noah called over interrupting me. I shot him a glare, which only made his smile bigger.

"Really good actually. Especially with sleeping on the couch." Axel shrugged as he took a seat and reached for a bowl. "Why didn't you wake me? It was my night for guard duty, and we can't have the flying monkeys escaping."

"Man, you have hardly slept in four days. Like I was going to wake you up and have you fall asleep at your post. Matt took your shift for you. So, don't sweat it."

"It's a good thing Matt took your shift, Axel. If you had been on the job, I'm sure the monkeys would have easily escaped." I crossed my arms over my chest.

"It's good to know you care about me getting rest. And here I thought you didn't like me." Axel placed his hand over his heart.

"You misunderstood but I guess that is common for a neanderthal. I was referring to your ability to do the job compared to Matt's."

Axel took a step towards me as his jaw tightened. I hit a nerve. Good. "Baby, I am a much better fighter than Matt is. Always have, always will."

"Awe, you actually believe that." I smiled at him. His face was growing red, and I could almost hear his teeth grinding. "Yup, my broom is definitely up your..."

"Do you two really need to be at each other's throats this early in the morning?" Noah interrupted me again.

"You really did need rest, Axel. Not to mention you looked pretty comfortable when we all left after the movie." Sara remarked with a straight face.

My hands were fisted at my sides as I glared at Axel for another moment. I turned away from the occupants of the table and continued walking to the door. "Honestly, I don't remember watching any of the movie last night. Just sitting down and then waking up a minute ago." Axel commented.

"Must have been all the sleepless nights recently. You looked ready to drop dead all day yesterday." Sara's voice barely reached me as I walked down the hall.

Chapter 11

"I'm never going to understand this, Sara, and the test is tomorrow." I whined as I dropped my head down on the small worktable we had set up in the kitchen. We had been at this for hours and I just couldn't seem to get it. Sara patted my shoulder comfortingly.

She jumped from her chair and ran to the radio. She cranked up the volume. "You need to dance with me." She yelled over the music. 'What If' by Kane Brown blared from the speakers. When I didn't move, Sara walked over to me and pulled me to my feet. "Come on, you need a break." She yelled.

Giving in, I smiled and started singing along. We danced around the kitchen singing at the top of our lungs. We were both laughing by the time the song was over. The next song that came on was 'Made' by Spencer Crandall. We were about halfway through the song when Sara screamed. I whirled around and there in the doorway stood Axel, Noah, and Liam. All three of them were grinning at us. Sara ran over to the radio and turned the music down.

"What the heck are you trying to do, give us a heart attack?" Sara yelled at them.

"We just got done working out and heard the music blaring." Liam said as he leaned against the wall with his smile still stretching from ear to ear.

"What are you ladies doing anyway?" Noah asked. "Sounded like you were clubbing." He was watching Sara.

"We were studying, and Trinity needed a break." Sara answered with a shrug. "Now would you guys please let us get back to our study session?" She put her hands on her hips as she glared at the guys.

"I can take a hint." Liam laughed as he turned and left the kitchen.

"Would you like to dance, Sara?" Noah stepped closer to her and extended his hand.

She hesitated as she looked over at me. I gave her a big smile and a small nod. She was blushing when she turned back to Noah and put her hand in his. He reached around her and turned the music back up before pulling her close.

I laughed as I walked back to my workstation and sat back down. I really did need to figure out how to do this math before my test tomorrow.

"What are you working on?" Axel asked from beside me.

I looked up at him and scowled. "Math." I made a disgusted face.

He laughed softly. "Mind if I...?" He pointed to Sara's chair on my right. I hesitated for a few seconds, not sure if this was going to end in an argument or not. I was not in the mood for a battle of wits right now.

"Knock yourself out." I finally said as I shoved the laptop over to him.

He took the seat and started to read through the information. I started to feel self-conscious about not knowing how to do basic high school math and began to fidget with my hands. A minute later he grabbed the scrap paper and pencil. He scooted closer to me and he put the paper in between us. His left arm went over the back of my chair as he angled toward me. I tensed, waiting for whatever barb he threw at me.

"So, what are you confused about?" He asked. There was no laughing or teasing, just honest curiosity.

"All of it." I said with a defeated sigh. "Sara and I have been working on this for hours and it still makes no sense to me."

"Sara wasn't the best at math either." Axel smiled. "We will take it step by step, okay?" I nodded and leaned forward as he began to explain the Pythagorean Theorem. Ten minutes later, he looked up at me. "Does that make sense?"

"I think so." I said slowly as I processed what he had explained to me.

"Why don't we do a few practice problems?" Axel suggested. I nodded and he wrote out a problem before handing me the paper and pencil. Taking a deep breath, I began working through the problem. When I was done, I looked up at him to see if I did it correctly. Our eyes met and his smile sent butterflies fluttering in my stomach.

"Good job, Trinity. Here, try this one." He grabbed the pencil from me and wrote out another problem. I took the pencil from his hand and went to work. This one was tougher and took me a little more time to work through. When I looked back at him, he was grinning at me. The pride in his eyes sent warmth to my toes.

"How's it going, Trin?" Sara asked as she skipped over to us.

"Seems like she's got it." Axel answered as he stood up.

"Yay! Axel was the only reason I graduated. Math is seriously the worst. Let's celebrate!" Sara clapped. "And the best way to celebrate is with loud music and good friends."

I looked across the kitchen to find that Matt and Liam had joined us. Sara turned up the music even louder and pulled me to the center of the room. Liam claimed the first dance. It was a fast song, and we were all laughing. At the end of the song, Liam took my hand and spun me. Matt grabbed my hand as they changed dance partners.

The next song was a little slower but still pretty fast. Sara was dancing with Axel and Noah watched them with a small pout on his face. When the song ended, Matt leaned down over my hand and laughing, I dipped into a curtsey. Axel walked over and asked if he could have the next dance. I agreed just before the song began.

'We'll Figure It Out' by Smithfield started and Axel took my right hand in his left. His right hand rested on my waist, and I tentatively put my left hand on his shoulder. Over the past few weeks, the tension between us seemed to be lessening by small degrees. It was rare that we weren't yelling or arguing with each other still. The fact that he helped me with my homework was completely out of the normal for us. We tended to ignore each other if at all possible. Despite our hostility towards one another, I couldn't help being attracted to him.

He began swaying us slowly to the music. I glanced over at Sara and Noah. He was holding her close as they danced. Matt and Liam stood in the corner smiling and drinking sodas.

Axel's jaw brushed against my cheek, and I closed my eyes. My heart was racing, and I was trying to calm it, to no avail. I wanted to lean my head on his shoulder and soak up the feeling of being in his arms. I gave myself a mental shake. What was I thinking? I couldn't give into the impulse. Axel and I were like oil and water. We didn't belong together.

Once the song ended, Axel slowly released me and stepped away. He cleared his throat and offered me a smile. This smile was a little forced and he started to act a little uncomfortable. Thankfully, Sara came up and put an arm around my shoulders and led me away before it could get too awkward. I was taking a sip of water when the music was shut off. Everyone turned to see what had happened.

Murphy stood there with a grim expression on his face. "Trinity, I need to speak with you."

"Okay." I said nervously and followed him out of the kitchen.

He led us to the office. Once inside, he closed the door and motioned to one of the seats in front of his desk. As I took my seat, Murphy walked around to the other side and sat in his chair. He sat there quietly as he stared out the window. Tension radiated from him, and I began to feel like something was terribly wrong.

"I found the information you wanted." He started to say. I sat forward, eager to know what he was able to find. "Seems like princesses can bestow blessings on their Enforcers. These blessings are more like conditions. They can be something like: If the Enforcer does anything that will threaten the princess the bond will be severed or if the princess gets married the bond will not be as strong or break." Murphy explained as he turned to look at me.

"How does a princess give a blessing?" I asked. This was just what I needed to be able to break the bonds with the guys. Over the last several weeks, I had thought long and hard about Enforcers and what their roles were, and how the position would affect them long term.

"There is a ritual that has to take place, but Trinity, Enforcers are in their own rights, blessings, given to the princess. The princess's magic picks the Enforcers for a reason. The bond is a powerful one that won't be easily broken. Are you sure you want to do this?" I started to nod my head yes. I have put a lot of thought into this decision.

He held up his hand in order to stall my answer. "I must also inform you of something else I found." Murphy looked worried and angry as he stared into my eyes. "We thought that once you turned eighteen that your aunts' guardianship would end because you would be an adult. That is not the case. Apparently, you are their ward until you are either married or twenty-one. You do not need their permission or approval for the marriage. But if the marriage is terminated for any reason before you are twenty-one, you will be their ward again."

I blinked at him in shock. *No!* This couldn't be happening. I was happy thinking I was finally free of them. I blinked back the tears that threatened to fall. I don't know why it surprised me anymore that my life was destined to be miserable. At least I had the power to free the guys from being trapped in this mess with me.

"What is the ritual?" I whispered.

"Trinity, if you do this, they won't be able to protect you as easily." Murphy tried to reason with me.

"The ritual, Murphy, what do I have to do?" I said again looking into his eyes.

He sighed in defeat. "The Enforcer will kneel before you and you must put your forehead to his. In your mind you must say a specific set of phrases before issuing your condition. If I was your Enforcer, it would sound something like: Enforcer Murphy, I, Princess Trinity, give you this blessing. And then you will say your condition. But Trinity please…"

"We should call the guys in." I cut him off. I needed to do this. Murphy squeezed his eyes closed before lifting his phone and typing something on it. He placed the phone back down on his desk and gave me a sad look. "I have to do this, Murphy, it's not fair to them to be stuck with me." I said just before the door opened.

Matt led the way as everyone filed into the room. Murphy got to his feet. "Boys, line up here and take a knee." Murphy said angrily. With confused looks on their faces they did as commanded. Sara looked worried as she sat on the edge of her seat. "No one is to move or say anything until this is done." My heart started hammering in my chest. I was nervous about breaking the bonds, or at least setting the conditions. On top of that, my fear of having to return to my aunts once again had my emotions all over the place. "Trinity, this is your last chance to…" Murphy looked pleadingly at me.

"No, Murphy." I cut him off again as I stood and walked over to him.

Tears were still burning my eyes and I tried to fight them. I took a shaky breath and stepped up to Matt who was at the end of the line. He watched me with concern but didn't say anything or move. I gently cupped Matt's face with my shaking hands and leaning down, I pressed my forehead to his. His hands touched my elbows softly, and I squeezed my eyes closed.

"Enforcer Matt, I, Princess Trinity, give you this blessing. When you fall in love, you will be released from your Enforcer Bond with me. Instead, your connection with your love will be just as strong as the Enforcer's Bond." I said in my mind.

I straightened up and a single tear fell. Matt was watching me with confusion but said nothing. I stepped to my left and repeated the process with Liam. My tears were coming quicker now. I stood in front of Axel. I wiped my cheeks and then gently cupped his face.

As our foreheads touched, I felt several tears fall. His hands reached up and held my forearms. I repeated the same blessing I did for the first two. When I finished saying the last word, his grip on me tightened and his breathing increased.

My eyes flew open in surprise as I straightened up. His eyes were squeezed shut as his grip on my arms stayed strong. His jaw was clenched, and he looked like he was in pain. He remained like that for several minutes before his grip slackened. Murphy pulled me back as Axel fell forward, catching himself with his hands. He stayed on his hands and knees, taking deep slow breaths. What had happened to him?

Murphy guided me to stand in front of Noah. I looked at him and my anxiety increased. If any of them had already met the conditions, I thought for sure it would have been Noah and not Axel. Will Noah end up in the same state?

I glanced back at Axel; he was still on all fours. Noah grabbed my hands, and I looked back at him. He placed my hands on his cheeks and gave me a nod. I touched my forehead to his and gave him the same blessing.

Pain exploded through my chest when I finished. Noah cried out in pain as well. I stumbled back a few steps before I fell to my knees and doubled over. Hands grabbed me and laid me on my side.

I curled into a ball and whimpered. A smaller hand touched my cheek, and I knew it was Sara. After several long minutes, the pain finally went away. I rolled to my back, breathing hard.

I opened my eyes to see Murphy, Sara, and Matt hovering over me. A laugh escaped me, and I put my arm over my eyes. I knew it! Noah was totally in love with Sara. I heard Noah groan off to my left and I looked over in his direction. He turned his head and our eyes met.

"Dang Trin, what did you do to me?" He panted out.

I started laughing harder. "If it makes you feel any better, that was much more uncomfortable than I thought it would be."

"That was 'uncomfortable'? What did your aunts do to you to desensitize you so much that you consider that merely uncomfortable?" Noah asked with disbelief all over his face.

I sat up and looked at him. "That, Freckles, is not up for discussion at the moment. How are you feeling?" I asked curiously.

He let out a short laugh. "Like a fire iron was taken to my back. It was twice as bad as when I got the Enforcer's Mark and I felt like someone was ripping something from my chest. How about you?"

"Same, minus the fire iron part." I shrugged.

Murphy muttered something under his breath, and everyone turned to him. When he saw me watching him, he sent me a glare. "You did it, Trinity. At least for one or two of them."

"Did what?" Noah asked as he got to his feet.

"She broke the Enforcer's Bond!" Murphy yelled. All eyes turned to me, and I dropped my gaze to my lap. "I bet that burning on your back was the mark being erased."

I heard people moving around. "What did you do, Trinity?" Matt growled out. "We are your Enforcers. We are here to protect you. Why did you break the bonds?"

I got to my feet and glared at him. "I didn't break the bond. I transferred it, and since only Noah reacted that way, I am assuming he met the conditions for it to move." I snapped at him.

"You transferred it? What condition?" Axel asked as he stepped closer to me.

"Yes, I transferred it, and I am not allowed to say what the condition is. What I can tell you is that when the condition of the blessing has been met, your connection to me will break." I gestured to Noah.

"Why?" Liam asked with a pained expression.

"Because you deserve better." I threw my arms out to my sides in frustration.

"This is our job, Trinity." Axel growled. "We have been chosen to protect you and you are throwing that away."

"You don't understand."

"You're right, I don't understand how you could do something so stupid!" Axel cut me off.

"Stupid?" I yelled. "I guess you would know from experience what stupid looks like."

"Will you two just stop?" Sara moved to stand in between me and Axel. "This is serious, Trinity. This decision affects a lot of people."

"I know that more than anyone. Now if you will excuse me, I am going to go play with Duncan." I pushed past Murphy and Matt and left the office.

As I settled down in the straw of the stall, Duncan came running over. He immediately climbed on my lap and settled down. I ran my hand over his soft back. The door to the barn opened and I held my breath. Axel's face appeared over the stall wall. My gut reaction was to yell at him, but something held me back.

"May I come in?" he asked softly.

I looked back at Duncan before giving a small nod. I didn't look over as the stall door creaked open and then clicked closed. Axel sat down next to me. He didn't say anything, and we sat quietly for a while.

Duncan eventually climbed off my legs and started biting my shoelaces. I pulled my knees up to my chest as I gently pushed Duncan away, but he was relentless. Axel tossed a toy and Duncan immediately pounced on it, tail wagging. When he settled back against the wall, his shoulder brushed mine and I took a shuddering breath.

"What's bothering you, Trinity?" Axel asked quietly.

I laughed humorlessly as tears fell from my eyes again. I leaned my head back against the wall and closed my eyes, not caring to wipe the tears away. What was bothering me? What *wasn't* bothering me? I was still a ward of my aunts, the man that killed my parents was most likely still looking for me, and I was responsible for trapping four good men into a life of danger and servitude.

A finger gently wiped the tears off my cheek. I looked over at him as he watched me with a concerned look. "Everything is going to be okay." he said softly.

I shook my head. "You don't understand, Axel. For me, nothing is going to be okay." I whispered.

"Help me understand then." He grabbed my hand and gave it a squeeze.

"Murphy just found out that I am still a ward of my aunts until I turn twenty-one. Which means they are still looking for me. Oh, and not only are they looking for me, but I also have the man that killed my parents looking for me too." Hot tears rolled down my cheeks as I explained a portion of the list of things that were causing my life to spin out of control. "I can't go back to them. The darkness, the chains, the needles, I can't. I just can't." I wrapped my arms around my legs trying to provide some comfort to myself.

Axel put an arm around my shoulders and pulled me to him so that I rested against his chest. His other hand cradled my head as he rested his head on mine. My silent tears turned to sobs, and I buried my face against him. Axel's arms tightened around me when I started to cry harder. He held me until I had no tears left and I felt completely emotionally drained. Axel started rubbing his fingers up and down my arm. The rhythmic movement relaxed me enough that I started to doze.

"There you are, Axel. I was wondering where you were. Have you seen Trinity?" Sara's voice called. "How is she doing?" Her voice was softer this time.

"Not good. She is completely terrified. Has she told you much about her past?" Axel spoke softly.

"Yeah, some. Why? What's got her so scared? We are here to protect her." Sara whispered.

"Apparently she is still a ward of her aunts." Axel's voice sounded frustrated.

"But she's eighteen. As an adult, her aunts can't do anything." Sara gasped. Her shock was evident in her voice.

I groaned as I sat up and leaned back. Axel's arm was still around my back, but I didn't care. "My guess is they petitioned the state to add a clause to the guardianship agreement. They sent me to a mental hospital for the first year after my parents' death. I had terrible nightmares and they claimed I was mentally unstable. I overheard them talking with someone about how they only had until I was twenty-one." I yawned and Axel pulled me gently to him.

"It doesn't make sense." Sara opened the stall door and walked in. She sat on my other side with a frown.

"Can we puzzle this out later? I feel completely drained." I yawned again.

Sara and Axel got to their feet before Axel reached down and helped me up. He kept a steadying hand on my lower back as we made our way back to the house. We used the back stairway on our way to the room. I felt like a zombie and just wanted to go back to bed. As soon as I saw it, I moved over to the bed and fell face first onto it.

"Trinity, you are covered in dirt, you're going to make the bed filthy." Sara protested as she tried to get me to get up.

"I don't care. I can wash the sheets tomorrow. As for right now, that pillow and I have a date that I don't plan on missing." I mumbled as I swatted her hand away.

"Axel, do something." Sara whined.

"Come on, Trin." Axel said as he scooped me up into his arms. Next thing I knew my head was on the pillow and a blanket was draped over me. "Let's let her rest, Sara." Axel said, but Sara started to protest again. "It's fine. She was tired enough to fall asleep in a barn, don't you think she should get some rest? The bed can get changed tomorrow." He said as the door clicked closed. I silently thanked Axel for coming to my rescue as I fell asleep.

*   *   *

"Trinity, sweetheart. I need you to go to the meadow and stay there until daddy or I come and get you. And no matter what, stay hidden okay?" My mom cupped my face in her trembling hands, forcing me to look her in the eye. "Promise me you will stay out of sight." My mother pleaded.

I was confused as to why Mom was sending me away. We were planning a big surprise to tell Dad that mom was pregnant. "Okay, momma." I whispered. Something was happening that had my mother trembling with fear.

"I love you, Trinity. Now go." She kissed my cheek and pushed me towards the back of the house as a knock came on the front door.

I ran for the back door and slipped through. I closed it quickly, leaving a small crack. Something had momma scared and I couldn't leave her there alone. I jumped as the front door flew open and crashed against the wall. I peered through the crack and saw a tall man with short blonde hair and a beard. He stalked towards mom with a triumphant smile on his face.

"It's been a long time, my princess." He stopped his advance only a few feet from her and looked up and down her body. "Just as beautiful as ever." He said and a shiver ran down my spine. His voice was higher pitched than most men I had heard, and it instantly put me on edge.

"Not nearly long enough." Mom snapped. I had never heard her sound so angry.

The man clucked his tongue as he looked disappointed. "That's not very nice, Clara. And I only came to offer my heartfelt congratulations." He took another step towards her, but Mom stepped back. "Imagine my surprise when I found out that you were alive and well, not to mention married." The man's tone changed from somewhat friendly to dangerous in an instant. "And rumor has it you also have a daughter."

"What do you want, Jason?" My mother asked with a tremor in her voice.

"For the longest time I wanted you, but a little birdie told me that you and your husband were blessed by your magic. Tell me Clara, is your daughter a magic user too?" I covered my mouth with my hand as the man grabbed Mom's neck.

"You will never have her." My mother wheezed out as she clawed at the man's hand.

"Being born from a blessed pair, Clara. Your daughter must be quite powerful." He smiled down at Mom before throwing her against the wall.

I felt the overwhelming need to hide. I turned and ran as fast as I could to the meadow. My foot landed in a gopher hole, and I fell to the ground. My ankle throbbed as I lay there trying to catch my breath. I felt I was well hidden in the tall grass and wildflowers. I was so scared, and I felt guilty for not being able to do anything to protect Mom. Hopefully, daddy will come back soon. He would be able to save momma.

"Find the girl!" I heard the man's high-pitched voice yell from across the meadow.

Chapter 12

I bolted upward in bed. I was breathing heavily as I looked around to get my bearings. I was in Axel's room, not in a meadow. I let out a heavy breath as I fell back on my pillow. I wiped the tears off my cheeks. Great, the nightmares were back.

I sighed as I looked at the clock, 3:00am. I groaned as I rolled over. I knew from experience that after having one of my nightmares, I was not able to go back to sleep. Needing to find something to do, I walked over to the closet. I spent the next hour and a half rearranging the whole thing.

My hands were still shaking when I finished. I pulled on a hoodie over my pajama shirt and headed for the door. Maybe a glass of milk or juice would help settle me. I walked down the darkened hall to the stairs. I hesitated for a moment before descending them and heading for the kitchen.

As I pushed open the kitchen door, I jumped and gave a startled squeak. Axel was standing in front of the open fridge taking a drink out of the milk carton. He choked at my sudden sound. Milk went everywhere as he whirled around to face me.

My heart was still racing from the scare by the time he was able to stop coughing. He wiped his mouth and chin with the bottom of his shirt. "What are you doing up?" he asked, still a bit surprised.

"I couldn't sleep, I came to get something to drink." I explained in a small voice. I still stood frozen in the doorway.

He reached for a towel to start cleaning up the floor but glanced up at my words. "Is everything okay?" He paused his cleaning to study me closer. The only light came from the open fridge, so there wasn't much he could probably see.

I gave a small shrug as I finally got my feet moving. I grabbed another towel out of the drawer and began cleaning up the counters. "Do you always drink out of the carton?" I asked without looking at him. I heard him start mopping up the floor again.

"Only when no one is around to see it." He muttered.

I laughed softly as I rinsed the rag in the sink and continued cleaning. "You do realize that we all are eating your spit when we eat cereal in the morning?" I asked him.

He stood up from the floor and moved to the sink to rinse out his rag. "I don't backwash." He sounded offended.

I stopped wiping the counter and turned to face him with a raised brow. "Everyone backwashes when they drink, Axel. It's nothing to get offended about." I stepped around him and turned on the light above the stove before moving over to the fridge. I closed the door before moving to the pantry.

I looked around the shelves trying to find something to munch on but could not find anything that sounded good. "Now that we have discussed my bad drinking habit, what has you up at this hour?" Axel stood behind me. I turned around to face him.

He was leaning against the pantry door frame as he watched me. I dropped my eyes to the floor and didn't answer. Axel grabbed my hand, and I looked back up at his face. His joking smile was gone, replaced by a look of concern.

"Does it have to do with anything you said earlier?" His voice had softened. Suddenly my toes were the most interesting thing in the world. He gently pulled me a step closer.

I shrugged and he tugged me another step towards him. "Axel, I really don't want to talk about it." I whispered. I was standing so close to him that I could feel his breath on my forehead.

"Okay. We don't have to if you don't want to." He whispered. I blinked back the tears that threatened to fall. How did he do that? The moment he showed me any sort of support I wanted to spill everything to him, and I was a blasted watering pot. His arms came around me and I leaned against his chest.

My arms found their way around Axel's waist, and I bit my trembling lip trying to keep the tears from falling. I sniffled and one of Axel's hands moved up my back to rest on my cheek. I lifted my eyes to his. Concern, uncertainty, and something else swirled in their depths.

He leaned down and rested his forehead against mine. I closed my eyes, not knowing what else to do. My heart was racing, and my stomach was doing flips. What was happening to me? I took a deep breath and let it out slowly.

Several minutes passed before Axel lifted his head. Our noses touched as he did. I opened my eyes and met his deep blue ones. Our faces were only a few inches apart. "I think I should go to bed." I breathed out. I stepped back slightly as Axel blinked a few times. I rose up on my toes and placed a light kiss on his cheek. "Thank you again, Axel. I don't know how you did it but I'm much calmer now." I said as I moved past him.

I didn't look back as I left the kitchen. Why did I do that? I had never kissed anyone before, well, besides my parents. What was happening to me? I couldn't let myself get attached to him. He was just my Enforcer. No, that wasn't correct. When I gave my blessing, he had reacted to it like Noah had, just to a lesser degree. Was he even my Enforcer anymore? I went back to the room and laid in bed. My eyes were closed as I tried to puzzle out what had happened in the barn and the kitchen.

I must have dozed because the next thing I knew, my door burst open. I bolted upright in surprise to find Sara skipping into the room. "Rise and shine sleepy head." She sang out as she closed the door behind her. "You need to get up, showered, and dressed because your test begins in two hours."

"I'm up." I said as I jumped out of the bed and headed to the closet. I opened my drawers but couldn't find any clean shirts. I shook my head at myself. I had forgotten to do my laundry yesterday and most of my clothes were down in the laundry room.

"While you shower, I'm going to get you some real food for breakfast. None of that sugar crap the guys are always eating." Sara called before I heard the bedroom door close.

Giving up, I grabbed clean underwear and a pair of shorts before turning around and grabbing one of Axel's T-shirts. Hopefully, he wouldn't mind. I planned on staying in the room all day while I took my GED test anyway, so no one would see me wearing it. I entered the bathroom and started the shower. The warm water felt good and relaxed me. I stood in the water for a while until a knock came on the bathroom door.

"Trinity, you have been in there for over an hour. Your food is cold, and your test starts in thirty minutes. Come on!" Sara's voice sounded irritated.

"Okay, okay. I'm getting out. Just leave the food and I'll eat it while I take my test." I called back as I turned the water off. "And don't forget that your job is to make sure none of the guys come up here and bother me."

"Don't worry, Trin. I'm already on it. I told them you had cramps." She laughed and I rolled my eyes as I smiled. "They quit asking about you immediately. Oh, and Trinity?"

"Yeah?" I said as I ran my brush through my hair.

"Good luck." Sara called. A moment later I heard a door close and when I walked out of the bathroom, I was alone.

I took a bite of the breakfast burrito as I turned on Sara's laptop. I settled back on the bed with my back against the headboard. I placed my notebook next to me and put the laptop on my lap. I logged in and waited.

I had five minutes until the test would start. I closed my eyes and took a deep breath to calm my nerves. I was still a little on edge from my nightmare. A soft knock came at the door. "Come in!" I called thinking Sara forgot something.

Axel stepped into the room and paused when he saw me sitting in the bed. "Are you feeling okay?" he asked with a furrowed brow.

"Yup. Did you need something?" I asked as I fought the blush I knew was trying to warm my cheeks. I remembered the feeling of his arms around me and me kissing his cheek.

"Just came to get a shower and some clean clothes." He said as he stayed close to the door, studying me. "You look comfortable."

I looked down remembering I was wearing his shirt, and I felt my cheeks grow hot. "I forgot to do laundry yesterday." I stammered out.

"I will have to remember to return the favor next time I run out of clean clothes. Except I don't think your clothes will look as good on me as mine do on you." Axel cleared his throat and moved to the closet. "What happened here?" He said in amusement a moment later.

"Oh, I...um...before I went downstairs last night, I may have tried to work my anxious energy out." I said as I got to my feet and walked to the closet.

Axel stood in the center of it and looked over at me with a smile. "Hmm. Well, could you help direct me to my clothes, please?"

My blush deepened as I moved to the back of the closet. "I put your shirts here, pants there. Your jackets and sweatshirts are over there. And your workout clothes and equipment over here." I pointed out the locations before turning back to look at him. He still had a smile on his face as he watched me. "What?" I asked as I wrapped my arms around myself.

He shook his head, but his grin grew. "I didn't realize you cleaned when you were unsettled." He moved over to where I was and began gathering his clothes. No teasing remarks. No wicked witch comments. What had changed between us? It was weird not arguing with him.

My computer beeped and I jumped. My test was starting. I slipped around him as I ran from the room and hopped back on the bed. I was all keyed up again thanks to Axel's unexpected appearance and odd behavior. He came out of the closet and headed for the bathroom. "What are you doing?" I asked.

"Taking my shower. It's my scheduled time, remember?" He shrugged as he closed the bathroom door. I stared at the closed door with my mouth open. Was he serious? I was still in here.

"You can't just take a shower while I am in here!" I called after him.

I shook my head when I heard the water turn on. Oh well. I had a test to take, and I couldn't change where I was taking it now. It had already started, and it was timed. I ignored the sound of the running water as I concentrated on the first part of the test. Thirty minutes passed and the water shut off. I glanced up briefly from the essay I was writing when the bathroom door opened.

Axel came out looking much more refreshed. His hair was still damp and his face freshly shaven. He leaned against the door frame as he watched me. My heart stuttered and I had a hard time concentrating on what I was writing. Why was he just standing there? Why wouldn't he leave? He was far too distracting standing there looking like he just stepped out of a modeling catalog. How did he get cuter in the last few days?

"What are you working on?" he finally asked.

I looked back up at him quickly and gave him a smirk. "None of your business." Maybe if we were at odds again, he wouldn't be so stinking attractive. My cheeks once again heated as I thought about last night and the way he held me in the barn. His brow quirked up.

"Hmm. He must be some guy for you to be blushing like that." Axel muttered as he started to walk towards the door. He was tense and looked like he wanted to hit something.

"What is that supposed to mean?" I asked, giving him my full attention.

Axel stopped with his hand on the doorknob and looked back at me. "Your face is nearly crimson, Trinity. You're hyper focused on your computer. It's not rocket science to know that you are messaging a boy."

"What is your obsession with me and boys?" I snapped.

"Girls your age are always going on about boys." Axel turned so he fully faced me. "Believe me. I have lived with Sara long enough to know how girls think."

I was fuming. "Oh, do tell." I balled my hands into fists. "What is it that I am currently thinking? You have always been spot on when it comes to knowing what's going on in my head. Is this going to be another Duncan kind of thing, or have you moved on to a different pasture?"

"You can't let that one go, can you?" Axel's eyes narrowed as he crossed his arms over his chest.

"You know me so well, Axel. It's a wonder why I even have a brain in my head when you know exactly what I'm thinking all the time."

"So, I am right about you messaging a boy?" He growled out, his face was turning red.

"Why even ask me when you are so smart?" I was practically shaking with anger. He had no idea what was going through my head and if he did, he would be yelling about that instead. How can the man be so infuriating yet so cute at the same time?

"Enjoy your date." he said stiffly before storming from the room, closing the door hard enough to shake the pictures on the walls. I blinked in surprise as I stared at the closed door. I was prepared for a longer fight. They usually lasted longer than this one did.

A door slammed somewhere downstairs, and I shook my head. What had just happened? I looked back at my computer and gasped. I only had nine minutes left to finish my essay and submit it. I got back to work. I could try to figure out Axel later.

I let out a sigh of relief as I pressed the submit button with two minutes to spare. I got up and stretched. I had a ten-minute break until part two started.

The rest of the day was relatively uneventful. I finally finished my last section and sat back. I closed down the computer and set it off to the side. It was done; all that was left to do was wait. According to the website, I would know if I passed in about a week or two.

I was exhausted. I had done nothing but sit on the bed all day, how did I feel this tired. It was only 3:00pm, Sara said she would be back around 5:00pm to check on me. Maybe I could get a nap in. I laid down and closed my eyes. It didn't take long, and I felt myself drifting off to sleep.

* * *

The grass swayed in the breeze around me as I laid face down in the dirt. I heard men's voices calling for me, but I was too afraid to move. My tears were cutting tracks down my dirty face as I trembled in fear. Suddenly, the grass was grabbing me as if it were hands. I screamed out in terror as I was being held down and grabbed all over. Sharp talonlike nails scratched along my skin as the 'hands' attempted to pull me towards the trees. I screamed for help and the pain increased.

Suddenly my father was scooping me up and running for the side of the house. I held tight to his neck as I sobbed in relief. Dad opened a secret door by the wood pile that led down to our safe room. He held me close for another minute before setting me down and looking me over. The momentary look of relief on his face was quickly replaced with fear.

"Are you hurt, Trinity?" he asked anxiously. I shook my head no, even though my ankle throbbed and my back stung. "Where is your mother?" He held me out at arm's length as he watched me.

"The m-man. Momma...in the house. H-he hurt her." I cried out.

Father pulled me back to him and kissed my forehead. "Trinity, I need you to be my brave girl and wait here for me. I am going to get your mother and be right back, okay?" I nodded and he stepped away from me. Just before he closed the door to seal me in, he looked down at me. "I love you, baby girl." I was plunged into darkness as the door closed.

I sat down against a wall and waited. I was shaking from fear as I strained to hear anything. My anxiety rose higher and higher as the minutes passed with still no sign of Mom or Dad. *Daddy can save momma.* I kept telling myself.

A few minutes later, screaming broke the silence. That was momma. The high-pitched man's voice boomed over the screaming. "She will be mine one way or another!" A loud cracking sounded just before the ceiling above me collapsed.

I became aware of my surroundings sometime later. My head hurt and I felt heavy. I panicked when I realized there was a large beam lying on top of me, trapping me there. I cried and screamed for help until I lost my voice. But still, no one came.

Chapter 13

"Trinity, wake up!" A hand shook me, and I bolted upright. Sara's anxious face was looking at me. I blinked at her and then glanced around. I was still in Axel's room. I raised a shaking hand to my forehead and was surprised to find I was sweating. "Are you okay, Trinity? What happened?" Sara asked.

"Just a dream." I let out a heavy sigh. "It was just a dream." I closed my eyes and tried to breathe normally.

"You were screaming like someone was murdering you. I heard you from my room." Sara's voice trembled.

"I'm sorry, Sara. I didn't mean to..." I started to apologize but she cut me off.

"Of course you didn't mean to. When I got in here you were tossing and turning and drenched in sweat, screaming in a way that could have woken the dead. I can't even imagine what the guys would have done if they were here." Sara babbled on. "I have been trying to wake you for at least twenty minutes."

"The guys are gone?" I asked. They had never left Sara and me home alone before.

"Axel left this morning and hasn't come back yet. He looked mad about something, and he hasn't been answering any of our calls. Matt and Murphy had to go to the diner to check on repairs. Noah went to get dinner and Liam is out on patrol." Sara continued to watch me with concern in her eyes.

Now that the initial fear of my nightmare was wearing off, I felt gross from all the sweat. "I think I am going to jump in a quick shower. After I'm all cleaned up, would you like to watch a movie? I am officially done with my GED testing, and I could use a break." I suggested with a forced smile.

"Yeah, that sounds great. I'll wait for you here and we can go down together." Sara gave me a smile.

I nodded and gathered some clean clothes. I had to grab another one of Axel's shirts since I still hadn't done my laundry. It was a comfort knowing that Sara was in the other room. My nightmare was still pretty fresh, and my shaking hands fumbled with the shampoo bottle a few times. I went as quickly as possible so I wouldn't keep Sara waiting.

As I was dressing, I felt a chill all the way to my bones. That man's voice kept coming back to my mind and it would send a shiver down my back. One of Axel's sweatshirts was thrown on the floor. He must have left it there earlier. I picked it up and slipped it over my head. It smelled strongly of his aftershave, and I took a deep breath. The smell calmed me slightly and I stepped out into the bedroom.

Sara smiled tentatively at me as we walked down the hallway. She was still watching me carefully, but I ignored her. "We should watch a comedy tonight." I suggested, as I tried to lighten the mood.

"That sounds like a great idea. Do you have anything in mind?" she asked, looping her arm through mine. I shook my head with a smile. My movie knowledge was still very limited. "How about 'How To Lose A Guy in 10 Days' or 'Hitch'?" We entered the lounge and sat on the couch together.

"Either one is good. I picked last time so you get to pick this time." I shrugged.

Sara grabbed the remote off the arm of the couch and navigated to Hitch. We were almost halfway through when Noah showed up with Chinese food. We ate quietly as we finished watching the movie. Sara still seemed unwilling to leave my side and Noah seemed to sense that something was off.

"You guys up for another one?" I asked. Even though I was exhausted, I wasn't ready to try to sleep again. I was worried that I would have another nightmare.

Living with my aunts, I had learned to sleep light. I would have all these same dreams. Relive every moment of that terrible day over and over again, but I never slept deeply enough for them to trap me in them. Not since the mental hospital. There, they just drugged me enough that I was like a zombie. Once back at my aunts, they never gave me the medication. They said it made me useless. The second night I was back with them, I had a nightmare. I was beaten into unconsciousness. I had been afraid to go to sleep after that, so I trained myself to wake at the slightest sound.

"Sure, Trin. What would you like to watch?" Noah asked. He was hesitant as he tried to understand what was going on.

"Ever After?" That had been one of Mom's favorites and one of the only movies I could name off the top of my head. "You don't have to stay, Noah, if you don't want to." I added. "I know guys typically don't like to watch those kinds of movies."

"No, I'll stay." Noah said quickly. There seemed to be an unspoken conversation happening between Sara and him. I ignored their worried looks and settled back as the movie started.

The movie ended and I still didn't want to go to bed, but I was having a hard time keeping my eyes open. I asked about another movie but yawned as I did. Matt stood up and walked over to me. When had he gotten there? He crouched down in front of me.

"Trinity, you have been falling asleep for most of the movie. I think it is time we all head to bed." He said gently.

I sat up straighter and pushed him over as my fear of falling asleep came out in a surge of anger. He fell backward with wide eyes. "I'm sorry *dad*, I didn't realize I had a bedtime." I snapped at him before storming off.

"Trinity, that's not what I meant." Matt called after me, but I didn't stop.

I marched up to Axel's room and slammed the door. I glared at the bed as if it was the reason for my nightmares. I walked into the closet and settled down in the back corner behind Axel's button-down shirts. I didn't want to even see the bed.

After a couple of hours, my head started to droop. I kept shaking it to keep awake but when my head bumped into the wall again, I stood up quickly. I began to do jumping jacks. There was no way I was going to allow myself to fall asleep right now. I didn't want to be trapped in my nightmares for the third day in a row. I had been doing so good for weeks. Then Murphy mentioned that I was still my aunts' ward, and the nightmares came back with a vengeance.

After I got tired of jumping jacks, I started to do sit-ups until I couldn't anymore. I looked at the clock. It was 6:00am. I jumped into the shower again;

this time I had the water as cold as possible. I was a shivering mess by the time I was done. Getting dressed in another one of Axel's shirts, I shook my head.

If I kept going like this, Axel wasn't going to have any clean shirts either. A smile spread across my face. I could go do laundry. I left the room bundled in Axel's navy-blue hoodie and headed for the laundry room.

Two hours later I was folding laundry on my bed when a knock sounded at the door. I walked over and opened it. Axel stood there with a grim look on his face. His eyes were directed downward as he avoided making eye contact with me. Was he mad at me?

"Is it alright if I come in?" He asked.

"Sure." I stepped back and walked over to the bed. I picked up another shirt and folded it.

"I see you did laundry." Axel said from behind me.

"Yeah. It became a necessity." I smiled slightly and covered my mouth as I yawned.

"You seemed to be managing just fine yesterday." He commented. His voice sounded like it was coming from the closet.

I grabbed a stack of my shirts and headed to the closet to put them away in the drawer. "That was before I ended up going through three of your shirts and one of your hoodies." I didn't look over at him, but I could tell he had stopped what he was doing and was watching me.

"How did you go through three shirts and a hoodie in less than twenty-four hours?" he asked, perplexed.

I ignored his question. "I figured if you were going to have any clothes to wear, I needed to wash my stuff." I turned around to grab another pile to put away but paused when I saw Axel's concerned look. "What?"

"You look pale." Axel took a step closer.

"I'm fine. It must be the lighting in here." I said as I brushed past him. "I'll let you get ready for the day and finish putting my clothes away later." I was almost to the door when Axel grabbed my arm and spun me around.

"It's not just the lighting, Trinity." he said as he tucked my hair behind my ear. "And there are dark circles under your eyes." His brow furrowed as he studied my face. His hand moved to my forehead as if checking for a fever.

"Cut it out. I'm not sick, Axel." I pushed his hand away in irritation. "Now, I am going to say this in the nicest way possible." I smirked as I patted his chest. "Go take a shower because you stink." A smile tugged at his lips as I turned around and left.

I found Sara and Noah playing pool in the game room. When I walked in, they both looked up and smiled. We played several rounds as we laughed and joked. I yawned frequently and they had to repeat themselves a few times because I had missed their questions or comments the first time they had said them. I didn't miss the looks Noah and Sara shot my way.

Sara was definitely worried. "I need to go get lunch ready. Trinity, would you like to help?" She asked with a smile.

"Sure. Anything special you were planning to make?" I followed Sara as she left the game room, leaving Noah to put everything away.

"No, not really. I just wanted company." Sara shrugged.

We entered the kitchen and Sara immediately went over to the radio and turned it on. I crossed my arms over my chest and gave her a stern look.

"You mean you wanted to keep an eye on me." I stated. The guilty look on her face said it all. "I am fine, Sara. I have been dealing with these nightmares for ten years. I promise I'm not going to shatter if something touches me."

"I'm sorry, Trin. I know you aren't going to shatter. But you freaked me out." Sara turned to me with tears shining in her eyes. "Your screams, Trinity. I have never heard anything like them." I walked over to her and put a hand on her shoulder.

"I know." I gave her a sad smile. "I know how terrifying it is. But I promise, I am fine. Just treat me like you normally would."

"Okay." Sara sniffed and wiped her cheeks. "What should we make for the guys?" We decided on sub sandwiches and chips. I suggested we make chocolate chip cookies and Sara wholeheartedly agreed.

We got to work with Sara building the subs while I mixed the cookie dough. After we placed a batch of cookies in the oven, I helped Sara load a large platter with the subs. Sara insisted that I stay in the kitchen to watch the cookies while she set the table and rounded up the guys. Sara left and I was alone.

I felt weird just standing there, so I turned the music up and sat on the counter as I waited for the oven timer to ding. My eyes closed as I listened to the music.

We were listening to the radio as we smiled and planned the big reveal for Dad. We were laughing when Mom glanced out the window. The smile fell from her lips, and she went pale. Fear filled her eyes, and her worry caused me to instantly become terrified. I had never seen Mom so scared in my whole life. Not even when Dad almost cut off his leg while chopping wood.

I was screaming in pain and Dad was suddenly there. The smell of smoke caused me to cough as Dad took me down to the safe house. He promised to be right back with momma and then he was gone. As I sat and waited, I could hear momma's scream. A loud boom and then a heavy weight. The smell of smoke got stronger as the house above me burned.

Hands shook me as someone yelled my name. I was shaken harder, and my eyes flew open. I jumped when I saw Sara's tear-streaked face in front of me. She gripped my arms tightly as she shook me again. Movement behind her caught my attention.

Noah was throwing open windows and turning on the vent while Matt was turning the oven off and pulling the chard cookies out. The room was filled with smoke. I pulled away from Sara's vice-like grip as my awareness came crashing back to me.

"I'm so, so sorry. I don't know what happened. Here, let me help." I rushed over and started to help clean up the mess. I found a small fan and set it on the counter, pointing it out the window. My hands were shaking from my nightmare and the adrenaline of almost setting the kitchen on fire.

Once the smoke was mostly cleared, three pairs of eyes turned to me with a mixture of emotions. Matt was the first one to speak. "What happened, Trinity?"

"I don't know. I was waiting for the timer to go off and sat down to listen to the radio. Next thing I knew, you all were here. I really am sorry." I looked between them. I could tell by the look on Sara's face she knew there was more to what happened.

"In the eight months I have known you, I have never once seen you burn anything. Or even fall asleep while on the job. What's going on?" Matt crossed his arms over his chest. He glared at me, daring me to lie to him.

"I have been studying a lot lately and putting in some long hours. I must just be tired, Matt. I'm sorry." I admitted. It wasn't an outright lie. I did spend the last several days studying really late to get ready for my test. I just didn't say that my nightmares have been keeping me up when I tried to sleep the last two days.

"Since you are so tired, Trin, why don't we let the boys finish up here and we can go watch a movie." Sara said, grabbing my arm and dragging me from the room. Once we were far enough from the kitchen, she lowered her voice to a whisper. "It was another nightmare, wasn't it?"

We got to the lounge, and I plopped down on the couch. "Yeah." I said softly.

"You were breathing hard and starting to sweat again. I tried to wake you, but you weren't really responsive." Sara came and sat down next to me. "When was the last time you slept, Trin?" she asked, keeping her voice down.

I laughed softly. "Less than ten minutes ago." Sara glared at me with her lips in a tight line. "I'm fine, Sara. I promise. Like I said earlier, I have been dealing with these for ten years. It's nothing to worry about, okay?"

"You better be telling me the truth or so help me I am going to slip sleeping pills in your food so you can actually sleep." She grabbed the remote and turned on a random movie. "Have you seen yourself in the mirror, you look like a ghost with those dark circles under your eyes, and you are so pale. Not to mention the fact you are now shaking." she muttered.

Not long after the movie started, Matt, Noah, and Liam came into the room and handed us plates of food. They all eyed me with suspicion as they took their seats. I smiled at them and took a bite.

I wasn't very hungry but to not cause any more issues, I forced myself to eat. Noah collected our plates and when he returned, he was whispering to Murphy. They both looked over at me and out of the corner of my eye, I saw Murphy's lips pull into a thin line.

The day went on in a lazy manner. The guys kept glancing at me frequently and I was beginning to get irritated. It was Matt's turn to fix dinner, so he left most of the way through the movie we were currently watching.

To be honest, I had no idea what movies we watched. I jumped when Sara's hand came down on my leg. I looked over at her and she gave me a look that said I missed something. I looked around and saw that Matt had returned and everyone was getting up. Dinner must be ready. I stood up and stretched before following everyone to the dining room.

I took a seat next to Sara and smiled when I saw spaghetti in the center of the table. I hadn't had spaghetti since my mom's. We dished up and started eating. Conversation carried on normally, but everyone occasionally watched me.

I tried to ignore them, but it was hard. I focused on my happy memories of eating my mom's spaghetti and laughing with my dad as he made slurping sounds as he ate. Mom had turned Dad's noodles into shredded zucchini because he was goofing off at the table again. Dad did it just to irritate her. She hated it when he slurped his food because I would imitate him. She said she was trying to raise a lady and he wasn't helping.

"Trinity?" I looked up to see Murphy watching me with amusement.

"Yes?" I glanced around and everyone was watching me, including Axel. When did he come in?

"Will you please return my spaghetti to normal?" Murphy's eyes sparkled with laughter.

"Huh?" I looked at his plate. His spaghetti noodles were shredded zucchini. "I'm so sorry, Murphy. I didn't…I wasn't…" I felt my magic swirl in me, and the zucchini turned back to spaghetti. "I'm sorry." I said again as I looked down at my now empty plate. I didn't even remember eating.

"Is that something your mother taught you to do?" Murphy asked. I could tell he was trying to lighten the tension around the table.

"Mom would change Dad's spaghetti because he always ate it in a goofy way, and I would always follow his example. She would scold him for teaching me such bad manners while she was trying to teach me to be a lady. I haven't had spaghetti since…" I swallowed hard. "I was just remembering. Thank you, Matt. It was delicious." I said quietly.

Dinner continued around me after an awkward moment of silence. Sara gave my leg a comforting pat before taking another bite. Liam and Noah helped clear the table. I offered to do the dishes, but they insisted on doing it. I swallowed hard when Murphy headed up to bed followed by several of the others. Panic started to well up in my chest at the thought of going to sleep. I could just stay up all night again. I already had one nightmare today and I wasn't keen on having another one.

Chapter 14

Morning finally came. That had to be the longest night in history. I spent the night trying to read but that only made me start to fall asleep, so I scrubbed the entire bathroom from top to bottom. When that was completed, I again started to do different exercises to keep myself from falling asleep.

It was getting to the point that if I stopped moving, I felt like I was going to pass out. At 5:30am, I jumped in another freezing shower. With teeth chattering, I got dressed in a pair of sweats and one of my hoodies.

I walked downstairs to the kitchen to make some toast. I wasn't really hungry, but it was something to do. While I was munching on my toast, I glanced around the kitchen. This room could use a good cleaning too.

I pulled out the cleaning supplies and began scrubbing everything from the walls to the floor, the oven to the microwave. I was cleaning the window frame when a throat cleared behind me. I glanced over my shoulder and saw Noah standing there.

"What are you doing?" he asked as he leaned against the doorframe.

"Cleaning the windows." I replied and refocused on my task.

"I see that. Why?" Curiosity filled his voice.

"Well, I'm done now so you don't have to concern yourself." I said as I returned the cleaners under the sink and washed my hands.

"Okay." He said slowly. "Since you seem like you want to be busy, would you like to help me set out breakfast?" He moved towards the pantry.

I followed him silently. He passed me two boxes of Fruit Loops before grabbing a basket of fruit. We didn't talk as we placed our items on the table and returned to the kitchen. Noah handed me the spoons as he grabbed plates and bowls. As we walked into the dining room everyone was taking seats. I set the spoons down and grabbed a banana.

Noah sat next to me. He leaned over and whispered. "I'm not an idiot, I know something is wrong and I don't need the Enforcer's Bond to tell me that. During the last few days, the guys have said they can feel your anxiety and know that something is off with you."

I shook my head and stood. I threw my banana peel in the trash before heading out to check on Duncan. I played with him for an hour before heading back inside. I avoided everyone as much as I could. I was tired of all the looks they kept giving me. After lunch, I snuck into the library and pulled out a book on magic users. I sat in the window seat and began to read.

I kept having to shake myself to stay awake. It was getting harder to keep myself from falling asleep. Just a little longer and maybe I would sleep so deeply that the nightmares wouldn't get me. I laughed at myself. They always found me.

A loud thump caused me to jump. My book was on the floor. I slapped my cheeks a few times and picked up the book. The door to the library opened and Sara walked in. When she saw me sitting by the window, she smiled.

"Hey, we are getting ready to watch a movie, wanna join us?" She asked. I gave her a smile. This was exactly what I needed. A movie should be able to keep me awake.

"Sounds great. What movie are we watching?" I asked as I put the book down and walked over to her.

We left the library and headed for the lounge. "I don't know. I let the guys choose and since Murphy won't be back until late, my guess is a scary movie." She shrugged her shoulders and shot me a grin.

Great. I hated scary movies, but if I were too scared, maybe I could stay awake. We got to the lounge and the boys were already sitting. There was one open seat on the couch. I sat down without even looking to see who was next to me. Sara flipped the lights off before making her way over to Noah. She sat in the recliner with him, and he pressed a kiss to her temple.

"Noah, remember to be a gentleman with my sister." Axel warned from beside me.

"I'm always a gentleman, Axel." Noah retorted and Sara giggled.

I smiled as someone started the movie. Sara guessed right; it was a horror movie. The first jump scare happened, and I barely reacted. The room was warm and with the lights out, my eyes began to droop.

My head nodded and I jerked up. Not even a scary movie was keeping me awake. I got to my feet and began to pace. I needed to stay awake. What could I do to get me through another night? I ran my hand through my hair as I thought. The lights clicked on, and I jumped.

"Now she reacts." Liam muttered.

"Leave her alone, Liam." Sara snapped at him. "Some people don't do well with scary movies."

I looked over at them with my brow furrowed. "What are you guys talking about?"

Matt stood by the light switches. "If the movie is too much for you, we can change it."

I whirled around and looked at the TV in surprise. That's right, we were watching a movie. I quickly moved back to my seat and sat down, rubbing my palms on my jeans. "I'm sorry, I forgot." I muttered, tucking my legs up under me as I ran a hand down my face.

"You forgot we were watching a movie?" Axel asked, concern lacing his voice. He turned my face to look at him so he could study me. "Matt?" Matt moved over to us. "Look at her eyes. Am I seeing what I think I'm seeing?" Axel turned my face to look more at Matt.

"You mean how glassy and unfocused they are?" Axel nodded. "Trinity, when was the last time you slept?" Matt asked.

"Last night." I lied as I tried to pull away from Axel's hold. His hand moved behind my neck to keep me from moving away without hurting me.

"Without the nightmares?" Sara added. I squeezed my eyes closed and shook my head. "Trinity, you can't keep going like this." Sara moved to my side.

Axel released me and I looked down at my hands. "What day is it?" I asked.

"Sunday." Liam answered like I should have known.

"Wednesday night was the last night I got any sleep." I whispered. "So, three, no four days? I don't know. You do the math."

"Trinity." Sara pulled me to her. She nearly pulled me off the couch, but Axel's arm came around my waist, keeping me in place.

"Why haven't you slept, Trin?" Liam asked as he moved over to the group gathering around me.

"I don't want to see it anymore." I said as I shook my head. I was so tired.

"See what?" Noah asked in confusion.

"The day my parents died." I whispered. Everyone went quiet. I finally looked up and my gaze locked with Axel's. No one seemed to know what to say. I blinked and looked back down.

"How about we compromise, you go to sleep..." Axel began to say, and I started to shake my head. "Let me finish. You go to sleep and if you start having a nightmare, we will wake you up. You need sleep, Trinity."

I looked over at Sara, who was watching me hopefully. I glanced at Liam, Noah, and Matt; all wore matching expressions of concern. I turned back to Axel. He lifted a brow in question. "We can all feel your restlessness and exhaustion, Trin." Matt put a hand on my knee.

"Fine." I sighed in defeat. "But I'm warning you, if I have another nightmare, you won't taste another Fruit Loop for a month." All four men laughed.

They moved to their seats again and started the movie. I leaned my head back on the couch. Matt tossed a blanket over, and Axel caught it. He spread it out over me. I closed my eyes and took a deep breath. After a few minutes, I felt my head slipping but I didn't stop it this time.

"That was quick." I heard Matt mutter.

"Shh." Sara chastised him. "She probably isn't fully asleep yet." That was the last thing my brain registered.

The blonde man's high-pitched voice reached me. I was in the dark and shaking. I just wanted to be up on my towel and out of the basement. The chains were biting into my wrists as I tried to get away from him. He lowered his scarred face to my neck. I felt his hot breath on my skin, and I let out a whimper as fear continued to build within me. I hated and feared this man.

"Trinity, wake up." Someone shook me. I jerked awake. The TV was paused again. I groaned as I laid my head back down and I buried my face into something hard. My heart was racing, and I shivered as I remembered the man from the basement. "Trin, respond to me so I know you are fully awake." Axel's voice came again.

I lifted my head and looked around. I was once again laying on Axel's chest. "I'm sorry." I muttered sleepily as I tried to sit up more, but he kept me there. He even shifted a little, so he was more reclined, and I was laying more against him.

"It's okay, Trin. You were just having another nightmare. Go back to sleep." Sara said softly.

"But…" I felt so heavy, and my eyes began to droop again.

"You're fine, Trinity. Just sleep." Axel whispered close to my ear as the movie started again. He placed his hand on my head as my body relaxed.

"That was quick. She was only out for like five minutes." Noah commented.

"I guess that explains why she hasn't really slept in four days." Liam said.

Axel's hand ran slowly through my hair. "I'm scared." My voice was barely audible. I hadn't even meant to say anything. Axel's arm around my waist tightened and I knew he heard me. His hand in my hair stopped moving and he softly stroked my cheek with his thumb. I listened to the steady beat of his heart. I tried to fight falling asleep but the rhythmic rise and fall of his chest lulled me back to sleep.

* * *

Voices roused me from a deep sleep. I groaned and curled more into my pillow. I was still so tired. At my movement, the voices stopped. I relaxed again with a sigh. A soft hand tucked hair behind my ear and I whimpered in protest.

"Leave her alone, Sara." The voice was deep and vibrated through my pillow.

"Axel, her hair was in her face. That would have driven me crazy." Sara's voice registered slowly in my sleepy mind.

"She has been sleeping like that for hours without having an issue. It's not worth waking her up." Matt's voice sounded irritated.

I tried again to open my eyes. I felt like they were packed full of sand. I needed to talk to Murphy. I remembered the high-pitched man being in my aunts' house. He knew where I was.

I rubbed my eyes and I stretched. I tried to roll onto my back but couldn't. I forced my eyes open and blinked against the brightness of the sun coming through the window.

A hand cupped my cheek, and I blinked a few more times to clear my sleepy vision. Axel was looking down at me. It took me a moment to remember I had fallen asleep on the couch with Axel during the movie last night.

"Hey Trin, how are you feeling?" Axel spoke gently.

"Mmm. Tired." I muttered. Axel smiled down at me, and I heard Matt laugh. "I need to get up." I yawned.

"Why don't you go back to sleep if you're still tired?" Axel asked.

"Because if I don't get up, I am going to pee on you." I answered.

Axel tensed. "Fair enough." he said as he tightened his arms around me. As he got up, he lifted me with him. He set me on my feet, and I wobbled slightly. Keeping an arm around my waist, he studied me. "At least you don't look as pale."

I found my balance and stepped away from him. "Thanks." I said sarcastically as I turned around and walked out of the lounge.

I headed upstairs to my room. I grabbed some clean clothes and headed for the bathroom. After I took a shower, I got dressed and headed out of the bathroom. Sara was sitting on the bed, and I moved to sit next to her.

"Feel better?" She asked with a smile.

"A warm shower did wonders. How long was I asleep?" I yawned.

"You've been out nearly sixteen hours." Sara replied.

"Did I...have many nightmares?" I didn't remember much, so I hoped I didn't keep everyone up.

"Only one right after you crashed. Seriously, within like five minutes your breathing increased, and you became restless. Matt paused the movie, and it took Axel a couple tries to wake you. You fell back asleep quickly and whenever you started getting restless, Axel would whisper in your ear, and you would settle down. It was kinda cute. I have never seen him be so soft with anyone before." Sara bumped my shoulder as she smiled at me.

"Don't get your hopes up, Sara. I'm not looking for a relationship. My life is in enough chaos as it is." I looked over at her. "Plus, it was probably just the Enforcer's Bond making him want to protect me from my nightmares." I fought the blush that wanted to stain my cheeks. I couldn't deny that I really liked waking up with Axel close by. He made me feel safe and I had not felt so rested in a long time. I gave myself a mental shake.

"I thought both Noah's and Axel's bonds broke. They both reacted after the blessing thing." Sara pointed out.

She was right, Axel had reacted after the blessing. He must be in love with someone then. Guilt filled me. Here I was crushing on a guy whose heart was already involved with someone else. I needed to put distance between me and him.

"Hmm. I don't know. Maybe." I said with a shrug. I needed to move out of this room. I saw too much of him since we shared the space. "Hey, I have an idea!" I jumped up and smiled at her excitedly. "You mentioned being roommates at college if we ended up going to the same place." Sara nodded slowly as she tried to see where I was going with this. "Why don't we room together now? That way Axel can have his room back and I don't have to worry about the guys coming in on me." I suggested excitedly.

A smile grew on her face, and she hopped off the bed. "I know where we can get an extra bed!" She hugged me before pulling me from the room.

For the next two hours we arranged her room to accommodate the extra bed and dresser. Next, we took a few laundry baskets and loaded all my clothes into them before moving them down into my new room.

With both of us working, it only took two trips: one for my clothes and one for all my toiletries. We took apart the bed in the room across from Sara's and moved it into her room. We were laying on our beds laughing and eating cookies when yelling came from down the hall.

Sara furrowed her brow and went to the door. When she cracked it open, all was quiet. "Stay here. I'll go check it out." She slipped out into the hallway and closed the door. Sara returned several minutes later with a confused look on her face. "Everyone is gone."

"That's weird. I wonder if something happened at the diner?" I shrugged.

"Maybe." She still looked worried. "I think we should go to the bunker until they get back, just in case." I felt the color drain from my face. Bunker?

"It's okay, Trin. It's actually really cool. That is where the gym is, and you can't even tell it is a bunker." Sara smiled encouragingly at me as she took my hand.

I was shaking as she led me down the hallway near the back staircase to a second set of stairs that led downward. She opened a heavy steel door and the lights immediately clicked on. Sara was right, the room was a massive gym. There were punching bags, weight machines, and a boxing ring. As she closed the door, she pressed a button, and I heard a heavy metal bolt slide into place.

"Isn't this awesome? Murphy even installed a security area over here." She led me to a door. She opened it and there were several monitors that showed areas around the house and grounds. "The bathroom is over here, and the bunk room is through that door." She pointed to the other two doors across the mats.

My earlier panic about being in the bunker had quickly faded. This place was nothing like the one I had been trapped in. "What should we do until they get back?" I asked, looking around.

"We can crank up the music and workout or we can stare at the monitors until we see them?" Sara shrugged.

"Put the music on." I laughed and she did as I requested.

"Here. We are about the same size." She tossed me some yoga pants, sports bra, and a light blue tank top. Sara was a little smaller than I was, and the stretchy material of her workout clothes hugged tightly to my body. She led me to the weight machines. Sara was much stronger than she looked. After a while, we moved to the punching bags, and she helped me learn a few basic techniques. When she found out that I had no knowledge of any self-defense moves, we relocated from the punching bags to the ring.

We spent the next several hours going over moves. I was having a lot of fun and was picking it up quickly. We had moved onto light sparring to practice what Sara had taught me. We were standing facing each other in the ring, Sara lunged toward me, and I dove out of the way, rolling to my feet. But before I could turn around to face her, Sara was on my back. She placed me in a choke hold.

Something I learned early on about Sara was that she was ticklish. Instead of defending like she had taught me, I reached around and began tickling her. She screamed as she let go and fell to the ground, tripping me on her way down. We lay there laughing and breathing hard.

The music cut off and we both sat up. Murphy, Liam, Noah, Matt, and Axel were all standing there watching us. "Where did you guys go?" Sara found her voice first as she got to her feet. She reached down and helped me up. We walked over to the edge of the ring and stepped out.

"What do you mean? We went out looking for you two." Noah crossed his arms over his chest, clearly frustrated.

"What are you talking about? You guys took off and left us here, so we came to the bunker." She shot back.

"We checked the whole house, Sara. You two were gone and all of Trinity's stuff is missing." Axel stepped toward his sister, anger flowing off of him. I started laughing. They must have gone looking and missed us as we were moving my stuff. Axel glared at me. "You find this funny?"

"A little." I replied. "You have to admit, it is a little funny." Sara looked over at me and smiled. "Can I talk to you for a second, Sara?" I grabbed her arm and dragged her over to the security room.

I gestured for her to sit down at the computer and whispered my suspicions. She rewound the tape. The screen was small and only she and I were able to see it. I watched over her shoulder as she played the footage from hours ago.

Sara sped up the time a little. We watched as Sara and I took the last load of clothes down to her room. Not long after we went downstairs, Axel and Matt entered his room, only to come running out seconds later. All the men went into a flurry as they searched the house.

When they looked in Sara's room, we were dismantling the bed across the hall. When they were rechecking Axel's room, we were in Sara's. They even went outside to the barn. We were in Sara's room when they ran back inside only long enough to grab the keys to the vehicles before taking off.

Sara and I started laughing. They kept barely missing us. Our laughter continued and someone growled in frustration behind us. I was pushed to the side and Sara let out a startled gasp as she was pulled from the room. Axel appeared next to me and before I knew it, he threw me over his shoulder and walked out to the main room.

"Put me down Axel!" I yelled as I hit his back. "You are acting like a complete caveman. Let me go!"

Sara was yelling at Noah to put her down and he finally obliged by dumping her onto the training mats. Axel dropped me right beside her. Sara and I looked at each other and started laughing again. The guys surrounded us, cutting off all escape routes.

"Will you ladies please explain what the heck has happened over the last five hours?" Murphy finally asked.

"Trinity and I have decided to room together. It makes more sense for us girls to share a room instead of having to have a schedule to know when the guys can use Axel's room and when Trinity can have complete privacy. I don't know why we didn't think of it before. All this time wasted!" Sara laughed. "We were moving her stuff around and apparently kept missing the search party." Sara explained with a smile. "We heard yelling and by the time I got to the front to see what was going on, you all were gone. Not knowing what was going on, we came down here to be on the safe side."

Murphy smiled at us. "I am so glad you girls were smart enough to come here to wait for us. But next time can you inform us of your plans before you go into ghost mode?"

"We weren't hiding anything. It's not our fault that the search and rescue team missed us. I honestly don't know how they did. It's not like we are the quietest people in the world." Sara laughed again.

"Do you have any idea how worried we were?" Noah snapped at her. "Matt and Axel came running down the stairs saying Trinity's stuff was gone and then we couldn't find either of you. For all we knew, you two were kidnapped." I had never seen Noah so worked up. He was red in the face and his hands were on his hips as he glared at Sara. If he was a cartoon character, steam would have been coming out of his ears.

Sara's eyes were wide in surprise. She slowly got to her feet and moved over to him. "Noah, I'm sorry." she said softly. When she got within an arm's reach, Noah wrapped his arms around her and pulled her quickly to him. Sara wrapped her arms around his neck as he kissed her.

I glanced over at Axel to see his reaction. His brow was lifted in surprise, but he didn't say anything. Noah finally broke the kiss and rested his forehead against Sara's. "I don't know what I would do if anything happened to you." He whispered.

"Just tell her how you really feel." Liam coughed out with a grin on his face.

"Thanks, Liam." Noah said sarcastically as he glared at his brother.

Sara giggled and turned Noah's head to look back at her. "I love you, too." She placed a quick kiss on his lips.

I smiled as I watched the two of them for a minute longer. I glanced at my feet. I was missing a shoe. Where and when did I lose my shoe? I began to look around from where I sat and caught Matt's eye.

He gave me a big smile and pointed to the security room. I glanced over there and sure enough, my shoe was sitting in the doorway. I got to my feet and went to retrieve it. A movement on one of the cameras caught my attention.

Two women and three men were walking up the driveway. I stepped farther into the room to get a better look and my blood froze. Aunt Lucy and Aunt Grace were back.

Chapter 15

"A-A-Axel." I stammered out, not much louder than a whisper. I watched as a tall man knocked on the door. "Axel." I tried again. My voice came out somewhat strangled as my anxiety and fear spread through me.

"What's wrong?" he asked from directly behind me. I pointed to the screen with a shaky hand, and I felt him step closer. "Matt! Murphy! We have company!" He called out, causing me to jump. He wrapped an arm around my middle and pulled me back against him to allow room enough that Murphy could see the monitor. I grabbed ahold of his forearm as my eyes remained glued to the screen.

"Everyone upstairs! Now!" Murphy barked. "Axel, you stay here with Trinity."

Axel pulled me after him as everyone quickly left the bunker. Once the door was closed, he pressed the lock button. He still had a tight hold on my hand as he moved back to the security room. Fear had my limbs fumbling and he was practically dragging me around. Axel took a seat on a computer chair before he finally let go of me.

I was trembling as I watched my aunts speaking with Murphy on the front porch. One of the men looked strangely familiar. My legs felt like jelly, but I moved closer to the monitor to get a better look. The man had blonde hair. He was looking down at the ground, making it hard to get a good look. I felt Axel's eyes on me, but I kept my focus on the screen. Who was the man?

He was the only one with his body angled away from Murphy. He glanced up quickly before turning his gaze back down. It couldn't be him, could it? I sat down in a daze and Axel's arms came around me. I jumped back to my feet when I realized I had sat in his lap. I turned to look at him and he had a spark of amusement in his eyes. I cleared my throat.

"Could you rewind to the moment that guy looks up at the camera and pause it?" I asked, stepping aside to allow Axel more room.

"Sure. Do you want me to enlarge it too?" He began to press buttons and in no time at all I was staring at the man that haunted my dreams. The close-up showed the blonde man with burn scars that covered the side of his face. He was one of the men from my aunts' basement. He had been a regular.

"Can you close the enlarged photo?" I asked in a soft voice. Axel did so, and the man at a distance with his face somewhat pixelated, looked just like the man that hurt mother. I stumbled from the room and tripped over my shoe that I had dropped. I started having trouble breathing. I couldn't seem to get a breath.

Axel cupped my face and turned it to look at him. "Breathe, Trinity. Slow, deep breaths." He tried coaching, but I couldn't get my body to function. He picked me up and carried me over to a couch in the corner. He sat down with me straddling his lap. "Come on Trinity. Work with me." He wiped the tears off my cheeks as he cupped my face with both hands. I didn't even realize I was crying.

"Axel." I gasped as I grabbed his wrists. "H-he was there." I tried to explain but I was having a hard time forming words. Axel removed one of his hands from my face and wrapped it around my waist. I needed him to understand who the man was. "A-Axel." I tried again.

His hold on me tightened as he stroked my cheek. I shook my head before burying my face in his neck as I wrapped my arms around him. "Shh. It's okay. I have you." His voice was soft and soothing. I shook my head as I trembled. His hand started to rub my back in slow circles. "You're safe, Trinity."

"P-please A-Axel." I begged. "Jason." Axel tensed slightly but continued to hold me for several minutes. "Jason." I cried again. Axel needed to know the man was Jason and Murphy needed to know that it was Jason who killed my parents.

He finally pulled back slightly to look into my eyes. I'm sure my terror was still evident all over my face. He pressed his forehead to mine. "We need to slow your breathing, Trin, or you're going to pass out." I closed my eyes and took a deep breath. Axel was right, I needed to get control over myself. I was no longer a helpless eight-year-old little girl. I took in another shuddering breath. "That's it, Sweetheart. Just breathe." I put my hand on the side of his jaw as Axel whispered softly. After several minutes, my breathing was less chaotic, and my panic attack began to fade.

I was still terrified, and my body was still trembling. "Jason..." I whispered. But Axel cut me off.

"Shh. Let yourself recover a bit, Trinity. Then we can talk about Jason." I nodded before I moved my head to his shoulder. "Trinity, move your leg over here for me. I think you will be more comfortable." He lifted me slightly and I moved my leg to the side, so I was sitting in his lap instead of straddling it. I closed my eyes and continued to concentrate on my breathing, matching my breaths with Axel's. I was starting to relax against him even though I still gripped his shirt with a tight fist. I thought I felt him kiss my head. I dismissed the thought. He was in love with someone else.

"You two look cozy." Matt's laughing voice called from across the gym. I jumped and Axel stiffened but he didn't let me go.

"Trinity recognized one of the men with her aunts and had another panic attack." Axel explained. His voice was all business. All the softness in his tone from a few minutes ago was gone. His hold on me was still protective and gentle though.

Murphy's angry voice joined the conversation. "Who do they think they are? They won't get away with this." I jumped as the metal door slammed closed.

Sara ran over to the couch, and she sat down next to Axel. "It's going to be okay, Trinity. None of us are going to allow them to do this." Tears and fury were in her eyes.

"What are you all talking about? What are they trying to do?" Axel asked, his voice a mixture of frustration and concern. His hold on me tightened slightly.

"They have a marriage contract with the ugly blonde guy. He came with her aunts to collect his bride-to-be." Liam growled out.

I jumped to my feet; all my recently acquired calm was gone. I ran a shaking hand through my hair as I began to walk around the room. "They cannot make you marry him, Trinity. You are an adult and even as your legal guardians, they can't force a marriage on you." Murphy tried to stop my anxious pacing, but I brushed him off.

"As my legal guardians, they can force me to be at the church. And if he is the same man I think he is, he will give me no choice but to say yes." I said with a small lift of my shoulder. Silent tears were starting to roll down my cheeks. The man I was now contracted to marry was dangerous and I knew that somehow, he would find a way to blackmail me into accepting him.

The room was quiet for a few minutes until Sara stood up. "He can't marry you if you are already married. He only has a marriage contract. The agreement is only between him and your aunts. Your signature wasn't on it. And to get an actual license, both the bride and groom must show a form of identification." Sara grabbed my arm to stop my pacing and looked me in the eye. "What if you marry someone else before they get back here on Friday?"

"Why Friday?" Axel asked, confused.

"They said they would be back by Friday to take Trinity because they know she is here, and they have evidence to prove it. Either she is waiting for them on the front porch or there will be a police raid." Matt answered.

"Sara is right, Trinity. If you are married, your aunts lose their guardianship over you and that man will no longer be able to force your hand." Murphy said. "Now, we just need to figure out who?"

"I think it should be one of you three." Noah said. "As her Enforcers, it would allow you to stay close."

"Axel, you are the strongest fighter, I think you should be the one." Matt said. I looked at everyone in disbelief. They were discussing this as if they were picking out what kind of ice cream they should buy.

"I agree with Matt." Liam gave a small nod to signify his agreement.

They all looked over at Axel who was still sitting on the couch. He was watching me. "I can do that." He finally said.

"Are you all insane?" I cried out. Everyone's attention turned to me. "You have no idea who you are up against! You have no idea the danger I have put you all in! This plan of yours isn't going to work, not by a long shot!"

Axel slowly got to his feet and walked over to me. He placed his hands on my shoulders and looked into my eyes. "Everything will be okay, Trinity. We will be able to protect you. That man and your aunts won't be able to get to you."

I let out a humorless laugh as more tears fell. I took a step away from Axel and glanced at everyone before turning my attention back to him. "And that is where you are wrong, Axel. My mother being married to her Enforcer didn't stop them from being killed. I can still hear their screams." I wrapped my arms around myself. "He is after me and he will stop at nothing to get to me." There was no emotion in my voice now. I was putting up my walls again. The same walls that got me through the mental hospital and living with my aunts. It was safer to not allow anyone to see my emotions, but the walls were shaking, and I knew they would crumble any second. "I'm going to take a shower." I said as I walked towards the bathroom that Sara had shown me on her tour.

I locked the door and turned on the hot water. Stepping into the spray, I let out a sob. Jason Monroe was working with my aunts all this time. He looked different than he had ten years ago. Instead of a thick beard, his face was disfigured with burns all along his left side. But his voice was the same high-pitched tone. Someone scratching their nails over a chalkboard was a beautifully composed symphony compared to his voice.

How had I not seen it before? To be fair, I was in a panic every time he came to the basement. My fear of the dark and people touching me made it hard for my brain to register much else in the moment.

Maybe Sara was right. Maybe the only way to get away from him and my aunts was to get married. It's not like I was totally opposed to the idea of marriage. I just hadn't thought too much about it. I was broken. And no man should ever have to settle for a woman who was broken with nightmares and the fear of touch.

No, I wouldn't force anyone to marry me. Especially Axel. I couldn't do that to him. He was in love with someone. If he married me to protect me from my past demons, he would be giving up the chance to live a happy life with the woman he loved.

My heart ached at the very thought. A pang of jealousy struck me, and I froze. Why did the thought of Axel in love with another woman hurt so much? I covered my mouth and shook my head.

Oh, no. No. No. No. How could I have allowed this to happen? He was in love with someone else and I knew that. Yet I still somehow fell for him. Even more reason to not agree to this mercy marriage. It would break my heart to watch him sacrifice his own happiness to protect me, knowing he could never feel the same way I did. It would also paint a target on his back if he married me. No, I could not put him in any more danger.

My shoulder burned as I dried off. I sucked in a quick breath and squeezed my eyes closed until the pain passed. What was that? I tried to look at it, but I couldn't crane my neck enough to see it and there was no mirror in the room. Giving up, I got dressed into the borrowed workout clothes, since my clothes were out in the main part of the bunker. As I walked out, I kept my eyes on the floor. I sat on the ground with my back against the couch next to Sara and Noah.

I glanced up to see Murphy, Matt, Liam, and Axel as they discussed plans on the other side of the room in hushed tones. Liam had a laptop in front of him and Matt would occasionally point at the screen. Axel glanced in my direction, and I quickly looked away from him.

"They sent in yours and Axel's I.D.'s. Murphy's contact should be dropping the marriage license off soon. And they are setting up a preacher or someone to come perform the ceremony for Wednesday." Noah said quietly.

I pulled my knees to my chest and laid my head on top of them. A hand started running through my hair, gently untangling the wet strands. After a few minutes, Sara stopped and patted my head softly. "Hey, you seem exhausted. Why don't we go lay down in the bunk room for a little while?"

I nodded mutely, and she guided me into a room lined with bunk beds. I took the closest bunk and laid down, facing the wall. She began to run her fingers through my hair again. I closed my eyes, but sleep didn't come. I felt so numb. I didn't know what to do in order to protect everyone. I needed to think of a plan because a wedding wasn't the answer.

Jason wasn't going to give up so easily, even if I got married. He would just end up killing the poor man once we were discovered. Murphy and the guys wouldn't give up easily on this either. They believed this was the best course of action to keep me safe from my aunts. They were probably right on that score. My aunts would be removed from my life if I got married, but I wasn't prepared to pay the price that small amount of freedom would cost.

That is why I gave the blessing I did. I didn't want to be the one to rob them of their future happiness. If Noah was still my Enforcer, he and Sara wouldn't be able to start a life together.

"How is she?" Axel spoke softly from the doorway.

"I don't like this, Axel. She is completely withdrawn. Even being sleep deprived, having a panic attack or sick with fever, she still had some spark in her. Now there is just…nothing." Sara's worried voice whispered.

I heard him move closer, but I held still. The mattress sank with the weight of someone sitting. "Trinity?" Sara's hand stopped running through my hair and Axel touched my cheek. I didn't allow myself to react. I hated how much I liked his touch. "Trinity?" He tried again. I scooted farther away from him as I curled more into a ball. "I know you are awake, Trin." He whispered close to my ear. I remained silent and he let out a sigh. He rested his forehead against the back of my head. "Everything is going to be okay; I promise." His hand travelled down my arm until he laced his fingers through mine. His arm was draped over me, and he held me for several minutes.

"Axel, phone call." Matt called from the other room.

"You will see, everything will work out for the best, Trin." Axel's whisper was just loud enough for only me to hear. He moved his mouth next to my ear and his breath tickled slightly. "We'll figure this out." He gave my hand a squeeze before he stood.

"I'll stay with her." Sara said softly as Axel left the room.

I lay there thinking. Friday was coming quickly, and the raid was going to happen whether I willingly went with them or not. I would once again be helpless and forced to watch those I cared about be destroyed. If I went willingly with Jason, my life would be endless torture before he eventually killed me for my magic. If I married Axel, he would take me away. We would be safe for a time and then, like my parents, Jason would find and kill us.

Death and destruction. Those were the two main things that made up my life. But I had a choice: I could enjoy what little time I had with the people I cared about before everything went up in flames, or I could take the fight to the source and keep everyone safe from my fate.

I made up my mind, I was going to take the fight to Jason before he could hurt my family. I rolled over to find Sara sitting on the opposite bunk looking at her hands. When she saw me roll over, she quickly moved to my side.

"Hey, there you are. I've been worried you slipped into a shock induced coma or something." She said with a small smile.

"Sara, I need to go home." I whispered to her. Her brow furrowed in confusion. "It's the only way. Jason is dangerous. He won't like the fact that the guys are keeping me from him." I needed her to understand. I had no money, and I needed her help in order to buy a bus ticket.

"Axel, Matt, and Murphy are setting up additional cameras right now. Why don't we talk to them tomorrow about this? They will know what to do." Sara patted my hand, and my heart sank. There was no way they would allow me to do what I was planning on doing.

"Okay." I said with as real of a smile as I could muster. Sara looked relieved and I felt a little guilty. I had no intention of talking with the guys. If everything goes smoothly, I should be on a bus tomorrow. Sara moved over to the other bed and laid down.

I was pretending to be asleep when I heard someone enter the room, and I held my breath. "Sara, scoot over, Love." Noah whispered. I heard the bed squeak as he settled onto it. I cracked my eyes open and hid a smile. Sara was cuddled up to Noah's chest. He pressed a kiss to her forehead before letting out a sigh.

I waited until they were both asleep before quietly climbing off my bunk. I tucked an extra blanket under the one I was laying on before I put my shoes on. Once I cloaked myself, I snuck from the room. Liam was passed out on the couch and snoring loudly. Murphy and Matt were leaving, and Axel pressed the lock button once they were gone. I needed money for my plan to work. I watched as Axel walked to the security room.

Axel usually had his wallet in his pocket. I just needed to figure out a way to get it. I followed him silently, not sure what to do. I watched as Axel sat in the computer chair watching the monitors. I uncloaked and took a small step into the room.

"Axel?" I said softly. He whirled around, almost falling off the chair.

"Trinity." He got to his feet and cleared his throat. "How are you feeling?"

I gave a small shrug and took another step forward. How was I going to get the wallet? "I don't know if this is a good idea." I looked away from him and stared at the monitors.

Axel moved closer to me and hooked his finger under my chin. I looked up at him. He was studying me closely. "What's bothering you, Trin?" he asked, keeping his voice low.

"Come on, Axel. Getting married isn't going to solve this problem. At best it will only delay it." I stepped around him before leaning against the table. Axel had moved to stand directly in front of me and I stopped talking.

"Are you done?" He asked. I blinked up at him and my stomach flip flopped. He put one hand on my hip and the other cupped the back of my neck. "We will figure it out, Trinity. The important thing is that we keep you safe." I squeezed my eyes closed. Oh, how I wanted to figure things out with him, but I couldn't be selfish.

"Who's to say we are even compatible? We hardly even get along and I don't even know if I'm capable of having a relationship." I looked back at him.

"Is that what you're worried about?" His mouth pulled up on one side. "Compatibility?"

My breath caught in my lungs as he lowered his head towards me. He paused just short of his lips touching mine. He waited, giving me time to pull away. I couldn't move. On some level, I knew I should push him away but at the same time I wanted to know what it would feel like to kiss him. Especially since I was going to confront Jason. I would never get the chance to know what a kiss would feel like.

His lips pressed lightly to mine and my pulse picked up. The kiss started out soft and hesitant but became insistent. My hands found their way around his neck. I was starting to get lost in the sensation of his lips on mine when I remembered why I came in here. The wallet. My hand slipped down his chest and Axel moved his hand from my waist to my face as he deepened the kiss. He pulled away slightly and rubbed the tip of his nose against mine. His wallet was safely in my pocket, but I wanted something good to remember when I faced Jason.

Raising up on my toes, I kissed him again. Axel didn't seem to mind as he pulled me against him. We were both out of breath when I finally ended the kiss. Axel smiled down at me, and I blushed. I cleared my throat and looked everywhere but his face. I needed to get out of here before I changed my mind about leaving. Kissing Axel had been unexpected but would definitely be a highlight of my life when it flashed before my eyes in a few days.

Suddenly, tears burned my eyes, and I took a deep breath to calm my rising emotions. I hadn't imagined saying good-bye would be this hard. Axel's hands were back on my waist as we stood quietly until our breathing returned to normal.

"I think we can say we are pretty compatible." Axel smirked. "But if you need more convincing..."

I was tempted to kiss that smirk right off his handsome face, but I bit my lip and moved away from him. "Good night, Axel." I said softly.

I could still feel the heat in my cheeks as I left the security office. Overwhelming guilt slammed into me. Guilt for stealing his wallet. Guilt for kissing him. He was in love with someone else and only kissed me because he planned on marrying me, all in the name of protecting me.

I glanced around and made sure Liam was still asleep and Axel hadn't followed me. I cloaked myself again and moved to the laptop. I quickly looked up the bus schedule. I purchased five tickets to five different locations that would leave within a few minutes of each other. I left Axel's wallet next to the computer with a note that said, 'I'm sorry' and slipped out the bunker door.

I made my way up to Murphy's office. Sara mentioned that Murphey kept cash in the desk for emergencies. I kept cloaked and moved things as little as possible so that Axel wouldn't catch the movements on the cameras. Opening a drawer in the desk just a crack, I spotted a credit card and a roll of fifty-dollar bills. I slipped them out and ran to Sara's room.

I changed out of the yoga pants and put on a pair of jeans. Then I pulled on the combat style boots that Sara bought for me. One of Axel's sweatshirts was on the floor, and I quickly put it on. I walked over to the window and slid it open. Axel would no doubt be watching the doors. I climbed out and jogged across the grass. I could hear Duncan barking as I ran past the shed and tears began to fall. Someone was bound to notice me missing soon so I couldn't take the time to say good-bye to him.

I headed in the direction of town. In a car it would have taken only fifteen minutes, but it took me an hour. I avoided all the roads and hid whenever a vehicle approached even though I was cloaked. As I got closer to the bus station, I uncloaked in a group of trees. All I needed was for someone to see me poof in out of nowhere.

I walked up to the counter and purchased a ticket for Bellsview. The clerk handed me my ticket with a smile. "Thank you." I returned his smile as best I could. I was so nervous that one of the guys was going to show up any second. "You don't by chance happen to have a paper, pen, and envelope, do you?" I asked and he handed me the items. I thanked him again before walking away.

I still had thirty minutes until the bus would leave, so I found a quiet corner and sat down. I wrote a letter and sealed it. I put my aunts' address on it and returned it to the clerk.

"Hey, I have a huge favor to ask. Would you be willing to deliver this letter for me? I don't have the heart to tell them in person that I changed my mind about which school I will be attending." The clerk agreed with a sympathetic smile and tucked it into his shirt pocket.

"Parents can be so hard to talk to sometimes." He said as he accepted the pen back.

"Tell me about it. My dad wants me to do one thing while I know I need to do another." I glanced around as more and more people began arriving. There was a total of seven buses leaving in the next fifteen minutes. "Thanks again." I waved as I moved back to the side of the crowd.

I really hoped he would deliver it. My nervousness was increasing as the time slowly ticked by. The buses of the five tickets I purchased earlier were starting to board. If Murphy and the others discovered I was missing, they would most likely be showing up soon. I should have purchased tickets for later in the day so I wouldn't have to worry about the possibility of being seen.

I saw my bus and quickly boarded, finding a seat near the back and in the center. I didn't want them spotting me through the windows when they got here. A commotion outside drew my attention. I glanced out the window and spotted Liam and Matt as they were shoving past people trying to get to a bus that was pulling away. Axel was climbing onto another one just before the doors closed behind him, and it started to leave. Noah and Murphy were talking to the clerk who pointed at the bus two spots behind the one I was on.

I held my breath trying to calm my racing heart. The bus doors closed and began to move. I let out a sigh of relief. I closed my eyes and sent up a prayer of thanks that I got away. Someone sat in the chair next to me, but I didn't look up. I knew it wasn't any of the guys because I saw all of them as we pulled away.

Chapter 16

"They are going to kill you when they find you, you know that right?" I jumped and looked over at Sara. She had a very stern look on her face.

"Sara, I can explain." I whispered.

"Please do, because I have never in my life seen five grown men so panicked. Matt and Liam kept saying they could feel your anxiety and Axel was so angry. He found his wallet next to the computer and cursed up a storm. I swear a sailor would have been shocked, and then he threw the computer across the room when they saw the bus schedule. The whole ride here, he kept muttering about a dirty trick and he'll get you back for it." she said, keeping her voice low as she glared at me. "What were you thinking?"

"I couldn't let him throw away his life, Sara. You said it yourself; the Enforcer's Bond broke that day in the study. My life has been nothing but one tragedy after another and I will not add you guys to that list." I stated.

"You are trying to protect us?" Sara asked slowly. She studied me for a long moment before speaking again. "What was the blessing you gave? I mean I know you said you couldn't talk about it but..."

"I can tell you." I cut her off. "I just didn't want it to influence anything with the guys."

I glanced around to make sure no one was close enough to overhear us. There were only six other people on the bus and there were at least four rows between us and the nearest person. I leaned my head back on the seat and turned to look at Sara.

"I released them from their Enforcer's Bond with me when they fall in love." Sara's mouth fell open in shock. "I did not want them to miss out on having a family because they were bound to me. Noah obviously really likes you. I wasn't surprised that my bond with him broke immediately." I smiled at her.

A blush rose on her cheeks. "Thank you for releasing Noah." She smiled shyly at me before her face turned serious again. "But wait, Axel's bond broke too."

"That's exactly why I have to do this. He is in love with someone but willing to give that up to protect me. It's not fair to him." I turned and looked out the window. "And you're welcome."

Sara grabbed my hand and gave it a squeeze. "Where are we going anyway?" She asked.

"First stop will be in two hours. Then we get to purchase camping gear." I turned back to her. "I hope you like hiking."

"As a matter-of-fact, I do." She smiled at me. The sunlight glinted off something on Sara's hand. She followed my line of sight, and her smile grew. She moved her hand so I could see better. "Noah asked me last night, before your aunts showed up." A beautiful diamond ring sat on her finger.

I sat up straighter and grabbed her hand as I looked at the ring. "Holy crap! Congratulations!" I threw my arms around her and hugged her tight. "Why the heck did you follow me then? Noah is going to be so mad when he finds out you are with me." I pulled back.

"Leave him to me. And you better know what you are doing because you are my maid-of-honor." She beamed at me, and my heart dropped to my stomach. "So other than a camping trip, what is the plan?"

"We will spend a day and a half hiking up to my parents' house. I told you I needed to go home." I said and Sara raised a brow. She wanted more details. "I sent a letter to my aunts letting them know and to tell Jason I would be there." I looked down at my hands.

Sara waited to hear what I was going to say next, but that was it. I didn't have a plan beyond getting there. I knew my life had an expiration date on it, but I had made up my mind to end it on my own terms. Come what may, I was going to protect my new family at all costs.

"That's it?" She sounded horrified. I shrugged as I fought the tears that stung my eyes. "But, Trin..."

"Jason is planning to kill me anyway. Whether I married Axel, and it wasn't for a few years, or I ended up marrying Jason. The fact is still there, I am not surviving this. At least going back home, it will happen on my terms."

Sara wrapped her arms around me, and I could feel her shaking as she cried silently.

We remained quiet for the rest of the way. Eventually we reached the top of the mountain and pulled into a small town. We left the bus and headed for the Walmart across the street. I used most of the cash to purchase backpacks, food, camping gear and some extra clothes. We also purchased a shotgun and a handgun with a couple boxes of ammo.

We were packing our bags when Sara's phone began to ring. We both paused what we were doing and looked at each other. Sara fished her phone from her pocket and my heart began to race painfully in my chest when I saw Axel's name on the screen. I gave her a nod and she answered it.

"Hey Axel, what's up?" she said cheerfully. Axel yelled into the phone and Sara pulled it a little from her ear. "Take a chill pill, I went out with the girls." she said calmly. She listened for a minute but seemed at a loss as to what to say.

I took the phone from her. "Axel?" I said softly.

"Trinity? Thank heavens. Where are you guys?" The relief was evident in his voice, and I closed my eyes as I fought the tears that threatened to fall.

"Are all the guys there? Can you put it on speaker?" I asked. There was some noise and then everyone started to speak all at once. A small sad smile curved my lips. "Axel?" They all went quiet as I started to speak. "I am sorry for stealing your wallet. I truly am. I had no other choice. Liam, you are such a good man and I appreciate your friendship. Murphy, you were a father figure for me when I needed one the most, and Matt, you are the closest thing I have ever had to a brother. I love you guys. Noah, you hurt my best friend and I will come back and make your life miserable." I sniffled as the tears broke free. Sara touched my shoulder in a gesture of comfort.

"Trinity, why does it sound like you are saying a final good-bye?" Liam asked, tension filling his voice. In the background I heard a muffled voice demand someone to trace the call.

"Trinity, come back home and we can figure out what our next steps should be." Axel's pleading voice caused my tears to come faster.

"Promise me you won't take this out on Sara. She saw me get on the bus and followed me." I whispered.

"Trinity, stay where you are. We will be there in a few." Axel sounded near to a panic attack.

"I can't, Axel, and I think you know that I won't be here when you arrive." Sara finished packing her bag and moved to mine to help me while I was on the phone.

"How are we supposed to protect you if you don't let us?" Matt's voice broke and a sob escaped from my lips.

"No one can save me, Matt." I sniffed. "It will never end. The only thing that will change if I go back is the number of people who will die because of me."

"That's what families do, Trinity. We fight and protect each other." Noah said desperately. "Come back home."

"That's what I am doing, Noah. I am fighting and protecting my family. And I won't sit back and watch the people I love get killed again. I can't do it. I love you all." I took a deep breath. "Oh, and Axel?" My voice sounded stronger. I knew this was the right course of action.

"I'm here, Trin." I closed my eyes at the sound of his voice. A muffled voice in the background said they found our location.

"Hurry up, Trinity, we need to buy our bus tickets." Sara said with tears in her eyes.

"Don't get on that bus. Please, Trinity. Just wait for us to get there." Axel begged.

"I stole one of your hoodies again, I'll have Sara give it back to you when she returns home." I said as I hung up the line.

*   *   *

Axel

Finally, Sara's phone was ringing. Noah and I had been alternating calling her for the past hour, but it kept going straight to voicemail. "Hey Axel, what's up?" Was she serious?

"Where the heck are you, Sara?" I yelled into the phone and Noah came running over.

"Take a chill pill, I went out with the girls." she said calmly. I was ready to wring her neck. We were worried sick about Trinity disappearing, then Sara had run off somewhere. We had called around to her friends and all of them said they hadn't seen or heard from Sara all day.

"You are a terrible liar. Do you think we are stupid? When you weren't in the jeep and we couldn't get ahold of you, we called your friends. Now where are you?" I growled out. I was so angry with her.

"Axel?" Trinity's soft voice came over the line.

Relief flooded my body and I dropped to my knees on the pavement outside the fast-food joint we were using the Wi-Fi of. Matt was trying to see if there were any other buses that left around the time the other five buses did. "Trinity? Thank heavens. Where are you guys?"

"Are all the guys there? Can you put it on speaker?" She asked. I gestured for everyone to gather around as I pressed the speaker button. Liam, Matt, Murphy, and Noah all started talking over each other. "Axel?" They stopped and listened when Trinity spoke up. She sounded close to tears and our relief quickly turned to unease.

She continued speaking as my mind replayed our kiss. Had she only kissed me in order to steal the wallet or had it meant something to her? For me, that kiss changed my world. I was attracted to Trinity. I had been since I first saw her at the diner. Kissing her had made me realize that my feelings were deeper than just thinking she was cute. I wanted to get to know her more. I wanted to see what would happen between us. I wanted there to be an 'us'. I had been disappointed when she told me goodnight instead of letting me kiss her again.

Trinity sniffled and her voice was thick with emotion. "Trinity, why does it sound like you are saying a final good-bye?" Liam asked. His body was tense, and he looked pale. I leaned over and whispered to Matt to start a trace on Sara's phone. Something was wrong. I was sure Matt and Liam could feel it just like I could. Deep sadness, anxiety, fear. It was driving me insane and the feelings only intensified hearing Trinity's voice.

"Trinity, come back home and we can figure out what our next steps should be." I pleaded. If she didn't want to get married, we could figure something else out. I just needed her safe and with me.

She ignored me as she begged us not to be angry with Sara. I was near a panic attack. My gut was telling me that something bad was about to happen. I needed her to stay put so I could get to her, but I knew the likelihood of that happening was almost nonexistent.

"How are we supposed to protect you if you don't let us?" Matt said as he fought the tears in his eyes.

"No one can save me, Matt." She sniffled. "It will never end. The only thing that will change if I go back is the number of people who will die because of me." She couldn't honestly believe that she was the cause of her parents' death, could she?

"That's what families do, Trinity. We fight and protect each other." Noah said desperately. "Come back home."

"That's what I am doing, Noah. I am fighting and protecting my family. And I won't sit back and watch the people I love get killed again. I can't do it. I love you all." Trinity said. Her voice was stronger, and I knew she was dead set on going through with whatever she was planning. "Oh, and Axel?"

"I'm here, Trin." I picked up the phone, desperate to be nearer to her. Matt called from the jeep where he was checking the tracking on Sara's cell phone. He had their location.

"Hurry up, Trinity, we need to buy our bus tickets." Sara's voice called and my stomach knotted.

"Don't get on that bus. Please, Trinity. Just wait for us to get there." I begged as I squeezed my eyes closed. *Please, Baby. Don't get on that bus.*

"I stole one of your hoodies again, I'll have Sara give it back to you when she returns home." She hung up and I slammed my phone down onto the ground, shattering it.

Murphy touched my shoulder, and I looked up at him. "Let's go get them." He said and I got to my feet.

The car ride was tense and quiet for the first hour. "What do you think she is planning?" Noah asked.

"Your guess is as good as mine." I said stiffly as I glared out the window.

"Did she say anything to you during her panic attack that might help us understand her mind set?" Murphy asked as he moved into the right lane.

"Not really. She just said she recognized the blonde guy. She said he was there, then just kept saying my name. She seemed to be begging for something. Then she asked for Jason." I continued looking out the window.

Whoever this Jason guy was, I wanted to punch him in the face. I wasn't usually a jealous man, but I didn't want any other man near Trinity. If I was to be honest with myself, I haven't liked the idea of Trinity being around other guys for a while. Not since she allowed me to hold her in the shower when her aunts first came looking for her.

Murphy slammed on the brakes. Horns honked at us as he swerved onto the shoulder. My head slammed into the window by the abrupt movement, and I let out a curse. Before the dust settled, the jeep was thrown into park. Murphy threw the door open and walked to the front of the jeep and began to pace. I exited the jeep and slowly approached Murphy. His fiery gaze snapped at me.

"What were her exact words, Axel?" Murphy demanded through clenched teeth.

I furrowed my brow as I thought about holding her and her desperate pleas. "She said 'he was there. Axel, please.' And then she said 'Jason'. She was terrified and I figured she wanted her boyfriend." I tried not to show how much it bothered me.

Murphy slammed his fist down on the hood and I jumped. "Back in the jeep!" He yelled as he ran for the driver's door. I was barely in the car before he peeled out. There was more honking, but Murphy only increased his speed as he wove through traffic dangerously. "Jason was the man rumored to have killed the royal family when Princess Clara disappeared. If he was there, Trinity was probably talking about the day her parents were killed."

Silence once again filled the vehicle. Tension radiated from all five of us. Jason wasn't her boyfriend but the man that took everything from her. She had tried to tell me, but my jealousy blinded me. How could I have been so stupid? I punched the passenger seat in front of me. Noah reached over and patted my shoulder.

"We'll get her back, Axel. She is tougher than she thinks she is." I nodded and buried my head into my hands as I grabbed my hair.

We reached the coordinates an hour later and climbed out of the jeep. We fanned out around the Walmart parking lot. They could have gone anywhere. Across the street I noticed the bus station and took off at a run. I reached the counter with Noah right on my heels.

"Can I help you, sirs?" The male clerk asked, a little alarmed at our sudden arrival.

"I sure hope so." I said breathlessly. "We are looking for two women. One has brown eyes and dark brown hair that is to her shoulders while the other has blue eyes with light brown hair. Have they come through here?" I asked desperately.

"You guys must be the men they were talking about." The clerk smiled at us sympathetically.

"What do you mean?" Noah asked.

"The blue-eyed girl was trying to convince the dark-haired girl to change her mind on something, saying the guys weren't going to like it. Both had been crying. I could tell because their eyes were all red. Anyway, when Brown Eyes saw me watching them, she gave me a sad smile. The kind that literally makes your heart break. She said she was going to visit her parents' graves, and their guys didn't want her to because of the hard memories that came with it. Then they bought tickets." The clerk rambled on.

"Tickets? To where?" Noah asked quickly.

The clerk laughed as he turned to his computer. He printed two sheets of paper and handed them to us. I assumed he printed off tickets, but when I looked down, I let out a groan. It was a list of bus routes. Noah showed me his and it was the same thing. Just a list of bus routes. Except Noah's had completely different locations than mine.

"What's this?" I asked, confused.

"That is a list of all the tickets they purchased. I put it all on one document for you after they left. I figured you would show up eventually and would need it." The clerk gave us a sympathetic smile.

"Which one did they get on?" I asked as Matt, Liam, and Murphy walked over. I handed the paper over to Matt and his mouth pulled into a thin line.

"How did they get enough money to purchase all these?" Liam asked in disbelief.

"Sorry, man. I tried to keep an eye on them, but in the crowd, I lost sight of them." He apologized. "And the name on the card was Murphy Edwards."

"Do you have security cameras?" Matt asked. The clerk nodded hesitantly. "Can we take a look at them?" The young man looked ready to protest.

I stepped back up to the window. "Please. I need to find her." I kept my voice quiet so the others couldn't hear me. I could see the clerk's resolve was cracking. "Whatever you want, I will give you. You want money, name your price. You want me to beg, I will. Please, she is my everything." I ignored Matt when he stepped up to my side. I looked the clerk in the eye and his shoulders finally slumped.

"Okay, it's in the back." The clerk stood up and let us into the ticket office.

He showed us to the back room. It wasn't very big but there were three monitors along a crowded desk. Matt sat down and began rewinding the footage. He slowed down whenever a bus pulled into the depot. It didn't take long before we spotted the girls getting off a bus. They talked for a little while before heading across the street. An hour later they had come back to the station with backpacks. Sara gave Trinity a long hug before they approached the ticket counter.

"Is that a shotgun?" Noah asked as he pointed to Sara's pack.

I leaned forward to get a better look. "Yeah, that's a shotgun." The uneasy feeling in my gut intensified. Why would they need a gun? I almost didn't want to know the reasons.

They handed over a card before accepting their numerous tickets. They slowly walked around the entire station, occasionally stopping and pointing at the various cameras.

"Those little devils." I muttered under my breath. "They are marking cameras." Once they were out of sight of the ticket counter, Trinity threw something away before they continued their slow walk around the mostly empty waiting area.

"They are trying to figure out a way to leave without us spotting which way they went." Matt let out a laugh. "Smart girls."

Murphy smacked Matt on the back of the head. "Smart enough to throw their trail, but not smart enough to avoid walking into a snake pit." Murphy said.

We continued watching as a large crowd began to form around the station. The girls quickly disappeared into the mass of people.

"There!" Noah pointed to the screen. Just barely visible in the top right corner were two pairs of legs walking out of town.

"Not on a bus, then. Did her parents live close by?" Liam asked.

"I never learned where they were living. They came to visit me when Trinity was only a month old. All I know is they lived in a pretty isolated location. Clara made a remark about it taking four hours to get to a store." Murphy said thoughtfully.

"It's getting dark, we should drive the direction the girls went and hope to find them along the way. The time stamp says they left two hours ago." Noah commented as he headed for the door. We followed him out with a quick thank you to the clerk.

I stared out the window hoping to catch a glimpse of either my navy-blue hoodie or Sara's light blue jacket as we drove. We were driving for an hour when I had a feeling we were going the wrong way. I sat up and tapped Murphy's shoulder as I looked around.

"This doesn't feel right." I commented. "Pull over at the next exit."

We pulled over and everyone looked at me to explain. I got out of the jeep and looked around. My eyes kept returning to the way we had come.

"What is it, Axel?" Murphy asked.

I looked back at the jeep and all four guys were leaning against the side of the car watching me. "I don't know. It feels like we are going the wrong way." I ran my hand over my face in frustration.

"Matt, Liam, do you feel the same?" Murphy asked curiously.

"Fear, anxiety, desperation. The same as earlier when we first realized she was missing. I feel like she is in danger, and I need to get to her." Liam said.

"Same for me too. She is in danger, and we need to find her." Matt said.

I began pacing again. I was restless and the fact that Liam and Matt confirmed my feelings of Trinity being in danger just made me more anxious to find her. I ran my hand through my hair and let out a groan. Murphy put a hand on my shoulder to get me to stop.

"What happened the day Trinity blessed you all?" Murphy asked.

"What does that have to do with what is happening right now, Murphy?" I yelled. Why was he talking about the blessing when we still needed to find Trinity and Sara?

"Matt and Liam didn't respond when she was done. Noah and Trinity were both in extreme pain when she did his, and his Enforcer's Mark is gone. Something happened to you, but not to her. So, I will repeat the question. What happened, Axel?" Murphy growled out.

I threw my hands in the air. "Pain, burning. Just like the night of her birthday. That's it. Now let's head back to the station and see if we missed something." I started walking toward the car when Murphy started laughing.

I stopped and slowly turned to face him. He looked over at me with a large smile on his face. Had he lost his flipping mind? We needed to find the girls. "That explains so much. I don't know why I didn't see it before."

"See what, Murphy?" Matt asked as he stood up straight. He looked between me and Murphy with a confused expression that, I'm sure, matched my own.

"Axel and Trinity." Murphy started walking toward us. We looked at him with dumbfounded expressions on our faces. "It would be easier to show you. Remove your shirt, Axel." Murphy stepped up to me and waited. The quicker we got this over with, the faster we could get back on the road. I yanked my shirt off in frustration and turned my back to Murphy. He pointed to a spot on my shoulder blade.

"What the heck? When did you get that?" Noah asked.

"Get what? It's the Guard's Shield and the Enforcer's Mark just like Matt's and Liam's." I said turning around to face everyone.

Matt shook his head. "Your mark is different. It has a second wolf's head at the top left of the shield." He stepped behind me and took a picture before handing me his phone. "The wolf on the top is even slightly different from the Enforcer's Mark."

Chapter 17

Trinity

Sara pulled me into a hug. She took her phone back and turned it off before sticking it into her backpack. We shouldered our packs and headed to the bus station. Using Murphy's credit card, we purchased two tickets for every bus on the schedule for the next two days. We took note of all the security cameras. There were too many of them, so we decided to start heading down the road and when we were no longer in town, we veered into the trees.

Without a trail to follow, walking was a bit more difficult. We remained quiet as we hiked. It was getting dark, and I could tell that Sara was getting tired. We decided to set up camp in a small clearing. It didn't take long to put up the two-man tent we purchased and pull out our beef jerky.

"Do you think they made it to the town yet?" Sara quietly asked as we lay in our sleeping bags.

"Oh, I'm sure they have. They probably went way over the speed limit, too." I whispered back. "I think you should go back, Sara. Noah is probably losing his mind." I propped myself up on my elbows as I looked over at her.

"There is no way I am leaving my best friend to face this alone." She rolled her eyes at my attempt to get her to go back. "Can I ask you something?"

"Go for it." I said laying back down and looked up at the roof of the tent.

"You love him, don't you?" she asked cautiously.

"Who?" I tried to play it off, but my heart started beating faster. The feeling of Axel's arms around me and the sense of safety I always felt with him had my emotions rising to the surface.

"Axel, who else?" I could feel her watching me.

Warm tears leaked from the corners of my eyes. I gave a small nod. "Yeah." Sara scooted closer to me and touched my arm until I looked at her. She had tears in her eyes. "Okay, stop, no more tears. He loves someone else, remember? His bond broke before I realized how I felt about him. And it doesn't matter because I'm meeting up with Jason soon."

Sara didn't say anything else, and we fell asleep. My nightmares returned and Sara ended up waking me several times. In the morning, we broke camp and began hiking again. Neither of us got any sleep and I could see how exhausted Sara was. I hooked my arm through hers and without her noticing, I healed her tired and sore muscles. She seemed to be doing better after that, but my exhaustion got worse.

My only thought was putting one foot in front of the other and getting to the clearing. By this afternoon I would see my childhood home for the first time since I was rescued from the basement. As we drew closer, my hands began to shake, and my anxiety grew.

"Trinity, what is your plan once we get there?" Sara asked softly.

I stopped walking and faced her. "You will be up in my tree house while I go down to the house. You will stay up there no matter what and when the danger is gone, you can head home."

"I don't like the sound of this plan." Sara's face was pale as she studied me.

"And I told you before that I was going down on my own terms. You will stay in the tree house where it is safe. I am going to confront Jason. Maybe he will just take my magic and be done with it." Murphy had said taking someone's magic would kill them, but Sara didn't need to know that. Not that I would let him. There was no way I was letting him get more powerful than he already was.

It was just past noon when we came to a stream with a huge tree that sat on the edge of it. There was a rope swing attached to a large branch that hung out over the water. The stream in early spring was much deeper than it is now. I remember Dad setting up the rope and we played there for hours.

Sara caught sight of it and grabbed my hand. We were within a mile of home now. I knew exactly where we were. I changed our direction and followed the stream for ten minutes before crossing. Sara kept hold of my hand the whole time. Once on the other side, we walked away from the water.

We neared a clearing, and I slowed my pace. I looked up at the trees, scanning each one until I found it. Nestled about twenty feet up was a tree house. I pointed up to it and we quickly climbed the ladder. Surprisingly, everything was in good shape. We got to the top and crawled through the door. Spider webs were everywhere but the wood looked sturdy. I found a stick and used it to pull the spiderwebs down. I peeked out the window and I could see the charred remains of my childhood home.

"Okay, you stay here. Remember to stay quiet and unseen. When the danger is over, you can head back the way we came." I turned to see tears flowing down Sara's face.

"I don't want to lose you." She whispered.

"We talked about this, Sara." I scooted toward her and pulled her in for a hug. "I love you." I squeezed her tight. "Oh, I almost forgot." I pulled Axel's navy-blue hoodie off and handed it to her. "I told him you would be taking it back." Before I could change my mind, I climbed back down the ladder.

I closed my eyes and felt my magic swirl through me. I sealed the tree house so that only I could remove the barrier. Whether in person or by my death. Sara was going to be so mad at me for locking her up there.

Steeling myself, I made my way back to the stream and skirted the meadow. If Jason was already there, I didn't want him to see me anywhere near the treehouse. I finally made it far enough away from Sara and walked out into the meadow.

Memories flooded me. Picnics, laughing, playing tag, singing, and dancing. I slowly walked toward the pile of burned wood that used to be my house. I felt tears sting my eyes and my hands started to shake. I cautiously stepped into the rubble and began sifting through it. I was hoping to find some sort of memento that would remind me of the good times, not that it would matter much considering I didn't expect to live long.

Hours passed, and I was still alone in the meadow. I was near the front of the house when I tripped over a beam. I looked back and saw the corner of my parents' trunk under several boards. Hope grew within me, and I spent a good thirty minutes unearthing the trunk. The once thick leather was burned in many places exposing metal plating underneath. With shaking hands, I lifted the lid.

The hinges creaked as ash and dirt slid off the top. The contents of the trunk were completely untouched. I slowly started going through it. When I got to our photo album, I started crying. I sat down in the ashes, not caring that I was completely covered in black soot, and reverently opened the cover.

My parents' smiling faces stared up at me as my mother showed off her ring to the camera. I turned the page and there they were holding an infant with Murphy standing next to dad. I closed the album and hugged it to my chest as I sobbed. I missed them so much.

After a while, I wiped my face and returned the book to the chest. I spied my mother's journal and picked it up. A folded piece of paper slipped out from between the pages, and I picked it up. I unfolded it and gasped. At the top of the page, in my mother's handwriting, was written: Trinity's Powers. Listed under the title were: advanced healing, cloaking, transfiguration, repair, and shielding/protective barriers. Each item was accompanied by what age I was when the power manifested.

I had all these even without having my full powers? I reread the list before slipping it back into the pages of Mom's journal before replacing the book in the chest. I closed the trunk's lid and pulled some of the debris back over it. I didn't want Jason to find my treasures and destroy them too.

I found a comfortable place to sit and rested my back against a charred wooden beam. I knew I could heal, cloak, and transfigure things, but I had no idea that I could create protective barriers and repair things. I glanced over in the direction of the tree house.

I had placed a protective barrier around Sara without thinking about it. I looked down at my hands curiously. How did the barrier thing work? Could I use it to protect myself from Jason or was it like my healing powers that only worked on others? My hands were covered in a thick layer of black. Even my arms and clothes were covered in ash.

I sat there for hours as the sun began to sink below the horizon. Well, it looked like Jason wasn't coming today. Hopefully, Murphy and the boys hadn't found our trail yet. I really didn't want them to show up. If they did and Jason was here, he could use them to make me do anything. I would do everything in my power to protect them and I'm sure Jason knew that.

What was I going to do when Jason actually showed up? I needed to make a decision. My time was running short. I shifted and the handgun in the back waistband of my pants dug into my back. I repositioned again to get comfortable and let out a heavy breath. It was fully dark now.

Hours passed and it was getting late, and I started to doze off. Falling back into old habits, I fell into a light sleep. Every little sound made me jump. It was a long and tense night. Every sound made me think Jason had arrived.

My nerves were in tatters by the time the sun was finally lighting the sky. I got up and stretched before walking around the meadow to exercise my legs, keeping close to the house.

Two hours after sunrise with still no sign of Jason, I was beginning to think the clerk didn't deliver my letter. My letter said I would be at my childhood home in two days from the date I listed.

I scanned my surroundings and caught sight of the treehouse. How was Sara doing? She had all of our food and water with her, so she was fine in that regard. I looked back at the house and debated if I should pull out the trunk again while I waited.

The sound of a stick breaking behind me caused me to tense. "I'm curious, was it the good memories or the bad ones that came first when you got here?" My earlier resolve to show no fear was quickly crumbling with the sound of that familiar voice.

I slowly turned around to face the newcomer. "Good morning, Aunt Grace." I said as my hands began to shake slightly. I tried not to whimper in fear when I fully turned around and saw, not only Aunt Grace, but also Aunt Lucy, Jason, and a boy around nine or ten years old, standing there.

"We can dispense with that awful name. I am no more your aunt than that house behind you is habitable." Grace sneered at me.

"What?" I breathed out. That couldn't be true. For ten years I had lived with them. What did she mean she wasn't actually my aunt?

"My dear girl, you are so gullible." Jason laughed, his high-pitched voice making the laugh sound like a hyena. "Lucy and Grace are *my* sisters. When you went missing, thanks to your father, my sisters searched for you. I was in the hospital for burn injuries. Your mother apparently had fire magic as well as healing. We overheard that a girl had been found among the rubble. We falsified the necessary documents, and your new 'aunts' took custody of you." Jason had a sick smile on his disfigured face.

"Why?" I asked, barely able to breathe. All this time, all the abuse I suffered was from Jason's sisters. He had known where I was the whole time. My parents sacrificed their lives to keep me from him, but their sacrifice had been in vain.

"Because I need you." Jason shrugged his shoulders as he took a step towards me. I took a matching step back. "Your mother would have been enough, but she went and bonded herself to another man. That bond stopped me from collecting her magic. But it also brought you and you are so much better. A royal offspring with magic or children born from a bonded couple, each on their own, are very powerful. But a child born from a bonded pair with royal blood is even more so. The only question is, do I just harness your magic, or do I have you produce a child for me first? With me being a magic user as well, our child would no doubt be a force to be reckoned with." Jason looked me up and down, and I felt sick to my stomach.

"You're too late for that one." I said, taking another step back. There was no way I would ever bear him a child. I was determined to end my own life if it came down to it.

"What do you mean, girl?" Lucy took a threatening step towards me, but Jason grabbed her arm. His smile had changed to a glare, and he was looking at me with fire in his eyes.

"What do you think I mean?" I asked, realizing they misunderstood my meaning. I meant I would never allow him to touch me. If he had come to me and offered me his hand in exchange for escaping my aunts, I might have accepted his offer but not now. Not now that I have lived with Murphy and had tasted what a real life was like.

"She is with child." Lucy sneered.

I quickly looked between everyone as I frantically searched my mind for anything that might help get me out of this. I remembered reading in

Murphy's book about magic users, that those who were pregnant had a bond with the child that protected them. If the child came to any harm, the mother's magic would pull from the mother to protect the baby. Maybe I could delay getting killed or worse if they thought I was already pregnant.

"You better pray that isn't the case. Because if you are, I will beat it out of you." Jason threatened.

"You don't know much about pregnant magic users, do you?" I crossed my arms over my chest. I tried to appear confident, even though I was terrified. Where was Axel when I needed him? I was always calmer when he was near me. No. It was good he wasn't here. "The child is protected by the mother's magic. Whatever harm you do to the child, the mother pays the price. The magic will even pull the mother's last breath from her in order to try to save the child's life. So, if you want me alive, I suggest you refrain from doing anything stupid." I glared at him.

I could see the wheels turning in his head as he tried to figure out what to do. I wasn't lying. I never said I was actually pregnant. They were the ones who jumped to such a conclusion, and I just explained the bond between mother and child.

"Then I guess we'll just take your magic." Jason took a step forward but froze with wide eyes as I pulled the gun from my waistband and pointed it at my head. "What are you doing?" he asked nervously.

"If I am going to die, I will do it on my own terms." I said evenly. My hands were no longer shaking as a stillness came over me. I was not going to let him get what he wanted.

"Put the gun down before you hurt someone." Jason said softly as he took another small step forward. I clicked the safety off, and his face paled, but he stopped moving.

"You stupid girl, do you think we don't know about your friend in that tree?" Grace yelled angrily. "Stop playing these games or we will hurt her."

My pulse sped up as Jason's face took on a dark expression. Something dangerous flickered in his eyes before he turned to look at the treehouse. The tree erupted into flames.

"Sara!" I screamed as I sprinted towards the flames. I needed to save her. A hand grabbed me by the arm and spun me around. A cloth came over my nose and mouth as pain exploded in my left shoulder. I screamed before everything went black.

Chapter 18

Axel

I looked around the abandoned parking lot of the bus station. Night had fallen and we were still no closer to finding Sara and Trinity. After Murphy's revelation about the second wolf's head on my shoulder, we climbed back into the Jeep and headed back to the bus station.

Murphy had quickly explained that the second mark was the magic picking me for Trinity. The guys had teased me for a few minutes before the situation with the girls missing pressed heavier on us. Matt sat next to me and kept glancing over. I could tell he wanted to talk, but not in front of the others.

When we got back to the bus station, we checked the trashcan that we had seen Trinity toss something into and found all of the bus tickets. On the back of one was a hastily written note. Trinity told us to take care of each other and Duncan. She expressed how glad she was to have experienced what life could be like away from her aunts. She once again apologized for leaving without saying good-bye before saying she loved us all. Matt had stormed off and was gone for close to half an hour before returning.

It was getting late, and Murphy suggested we get hotel rooms and pick up the search at first light. We found a rundown motel with three vacant rooms. Matt volunteered to bunk with me, and we made our way silently to the room. As soon as the door closed, Matt began his questions.

"Did you know that you were bonded to Trinity?" he asked excitedly.

I sat down on the end of one of the beds. "No." I sighed.

"Does she know?" He asked.

"I don't know." I felt emotionally drained and didn't want to be doing this right now. I just wanted Trinity back. "Matt, no offense but I'm tired and not in the mood for questions. So, go to bed." I snapped.

Matt turned off the lights and climbed into his bed. He didn't say another word and soon his snores filled the room. I felt bad for snapping at him. He was my best friend and a brother. Murphy had trained us together and we were inseparable. I was going to need to apologize in the morning. After tossing and turning for hours, I finally fell into a restless sleep.

I woke before the sun had fully risen. We spent the morning showing pictures and asking the workers around Walmart if they had seen Sara. I told them that my sister had run off with a friend and we were worried about her. Not many people recognized her. We all grew more and more irritable as the day wore on with no leads.

It was close to midday when we talked with a guy in the outdoor section that said her picture looked familiar. He thought he had helped Sara and another girl get a tent and other camping gear. I wished I had a picture of Trinity that I could show him. He said he saw them at the hunting area looking at the gun display case. We thanked him and talked with the person there.

The man recognized Sara immediately. He said he almost refused to sell them the shotgun and handgun because of how upset the other girl had seemed. He was worried because at first, she seemed really depressed. The man got a big grin on his face when he said she started flirting with him and she had given him her phone number. He leaned on the counter and commented how he couldn't wait to give her a call.

Matt asked if he could call her now so that we could figure out where Sara went. My phone rang and I answered it. Matt, Noah, and Liam laughed when we realized that Trinity had given the poor guy my phone number. The man seemed irritated and less forth coming with information after that.

With no one else to talk to, we left the store and headed back to the bus station. Where had they gone? I was standing in the parking lot looking into the trees near where we saw the girls on the security camera when Noah came running up. He shoved his phone in my hand, a panicked look on his face.

"Hello." I said as I raised the phone to my ear.

"Axel." Sara was crying on the other end of the line. My heart took flight with anxiety, and the relief from hearing her voice nearly made me drop to my knees.

It finally registered in my brain that Sara was crying, and I was immediately on high alert. "Sara, what's going on?" I asked as fear started to settle in.

"She is planning on a suicide mission." She sobbed and I felt the blood drain from my face. "She said she was going to die anyway, and she would rather go out on her own terms. She took the gun."

"Where are you?" I asked as my hands began to shake.

"We walked along the road heading east for about half a mile before we turned into the forest. I'm not sure how far we walked but we went south in a straight line." She sniffled. "We camped last night and got here less than thirty minutes ago."

"Is there any way for you to stop her?" I asked desperately as I began to jog down the road. "Liam, grab my rifle!" I called over my shoulder.

"She must have done something because I can't get out of the treehouse. She was going to meet with the guy that killed her parents." Another sob came from Sara. "I can see her. She is going through what is left of a burned down building." Several sniffles later, Sara spoke again. "I'm scared for her, Axel. Please, hurry."

"We are already heading into the forest. Hang tight, sis." I said before tossing the phone back to Noah. "Sara said they went this way. Trinity has a handgun and isn't anticipating living through whatever it is she is planning."

Matt cursed as he pulled even with me, matching my stride. I wished I could increase our pace, but a sprained ankle would only slow us down. "Hey, Matt?" I glanced over at him as we jumped over a fallen tree.

"Yeah?" he asked, glancing over at me.

"Sorry for last night. I just...I just. I'm just worried." I finally said.

"Hey man, I get it. If the woman I loved disappeared in the wake of a crazy murderer threatening her, I would be going out of my mind too." Matt sent me a half smile. I tripped, barely managing to keep upright as I came to a stop. I stared at him blankly as I tried to process his words. "So, when did it happen?" The others caught up and looked between us, confused as to why we had stopped. "Are you saying I'm wrong?" Matt crossed his arms over his chest with a lift of his eyebrow when I continued to remain silent.

"Wrong about what?" Liam asked.

"Axel being in love with Trinity." Matt said.

"My money is when you helped her with her math and then we had our makeshift dance party." Liam commented.

"I'm betting it was when they fell asleep watching the movie after Trin woke up from healing him." Noah laughed.

Murphy walked past us. "Let's keep going. And it was most likely the night of her birthday."

Noah took off again and I silently followed. We remained quiet for the next several hours as we jogged south. We stopped in a small clearing to take a quick break. I was breathing hard, and my shirt was drenched in sweat. We had no water or food with us so all we could do was lie in the shade to cool off and catch our breath.

I closed my eyes and covered them with my arm. I thought back on all my interactions with Trinity. Her dancing and singing in the diner's kitchen. Her bleeding and panicked as she ran and locked herself in the bathroom. Her dressed in my clothes and angry. Her burning with fever and sitting with her in the bathtub praying it would help. Arguing with her just to see her cute little nose scrunch up in frustration. Helping her understand her math problems. Slow dancing with her in the kitchen. Getting angry over her messaging that boy while dressed in my shirt. Comforting her in the barn and holding her while she slept. Kissing her last night. I cursed under my breath as I sat up.

"There it is!" Matt laughed. "I'm surprised it took you so long."

"Shut up." I snapped as I got to my feet and walked over to a different patch of shade. I glared at the ground as I waited for everyone to be ready to head out again. A piece of paper caught my eye, and I bent down to pick it up. It was a balled-up receipt. I smoothed it out and started reading down the items. "The girls were here." I breathed out as I scanned the area.

"What do you mean?" Murphy asked as he walked over to me.

I passed him the receipt as the rest of the guys gathered around. "They got everything. Enough food, water, extra clothes, a tent, ammo, even a portable charger for a cell phone." I pointed out. "Sara said it took them half the day to get to the clearing from here."

"Let's go." Noah led the way. I knew he was as desperate to get to Sara as I was to get to Trinity.

An hour later the sun set, and we were forced to slow to a walk. The slower pace allowed my mind to wander, and I didn't like it. How much further? Were Sara and Trinity safe? What would I do if we were too late? I loved her and that knowledge only fueled my need to get to her.

Matt seemed to sense my swirling emotions and moved closer to me. He patted my shoulder but said nothing. We walked through the night, and we were all exhausted and thirsty. The sun was just beginning to rise when we stopped to rest again. I couldn't seem to settle. Anxious energy had me shifting restlessly as I waited for the signal to move out. Matt and Liam seemed equally unsettled.

"Axel, when I grabbed your rifle, I also grabbed the earpieces." Liam said. "I think we should spread out and continue more cautiously. Something doesn't feel right." He handed us each an earpiece so we could still communicate with each other while keeping our hands free.

Liam passed my rifle over to me. I checked to make sure it was loaded and ready to go before slinging it over my shoulder. He also handed me my vest with all my extra ammo. Murphy had drilled me for years on shooting. Even though I hated having to use guns, I had become quite a proficient sniper by the age of eighteen.

We spread out and began to slowly move forward. We had been traveling like this for nearly two hours when I heard voices. I crouched down and waited.

"Eyes on Trinity. She is talking with four unknowns. Two female, two male. One of the males appears to be a child." Matt's voice came softly.

"Approach just enough to hear their conversation but not be seen. Hold those positions." Murphy said.

I inched my way forward until I could see her. She was wearing her workout shirt from the other day and a pair of jeans, but I could hardly see the color of her shirt through all the ash that covered her from head to foot. A high-pitched male voice cut through the quiet morning air, and it made the hairs on the back of my neck stand on end.

"Because I need you." The man said as he took a step towards Trinity, and she took a step back. "Your mother would have been enough, but she went and bonded herself to another man. That bond stopped me from collecting her magic. But it also brought you and you are so much better. A royal offspring with magic or children born from a bonded couple, each on their own, are very powerful. But a child born from a bonded pair with royal blood is even more so. The only question is, do I just harness your magic, or do I have you produce a child for me first? With me being a magic user as well, our child would no doubt be a force to be reckoned with."

"You're too late for that one." Trinity said as she took another step back. *What?*

"Trinity is pregnant?" Noah asked in disbelief.

"Axel." Murphy growled.

"It's not mine." I whispered as my heart stalled for several seconds.

"What do you mean, girl?" A woman took a threatening step towards Trinity, but the high-pitched man grabbed her arm.

"What do you think I mean?" Trinity asked. My heart squeezed painfully in my chest. Trinity was pregnant with another man's child. I felt like a steel ball dropped in my stomach.

"You better pray that isn't the case. Because if you are, I will beat it out of you." The man threatened. It took everything in me not to rush out and beat the man senseless.

"You don't know much about pregnant magic users, do you?" Trinity crossed her arms over her chest. I swallowed hard as I listened to her tell the man that if he tried to hurt her unborn child, her magic would protect it by hurting her. I fought the urge to call out to her, to rush to her. I needed to hold her and make sure she was okay.

"Then I guess we'll just take your magic." The man started for Trinity but froze. She had reached behind her and pulled a gun from her waistband before putting it to her head. "What are you doing?" The man asked nervously.

"If I am going to die, I will do it on my terms." Trinity said evenly. She was dangerously calm, and I started to raise my rifle to my shoulder. *Please Baby, no. Don't make me do it.* If I had to, I was going to shoot her arm to stop her from pulling the trigger. I could deal with her healing from a bullet wound but I couldn't lose her.

"Put the gun down before you hurt someone." The man said softly as he took another small step. Her hand shifted slightly and I felt like I couldn't breathe. *Don't do it, Trin. I need you and I don't want to hurt you.* I silently begged her to put the gun down.

One of the women yelled angrily, and the blonde man turned to look south. A tree erupted into flames. Trinity screamed in horror as her gun hand lowered. She took off running towards the flames ignoring the four people in the meadow with her.

I looked through the scope as I aimed at the man's right shoulder as he chased after Trinity. I let out my breath as the man grabbed her arm, and I pulled the trigger. He spun them both around to face me at that exact moment. Time seemed to slow down. He held her against his chest while pressing something over Trinity's mouth.

"No!" I yelled as her body went limp. Did I hit her? I watched as Trinity's limp body slumped against the man before the four unknown people and Trinity disappeared. I ran from my hiding place and sprinted to where I had last seen them. I examined the ground and found blood. I slowly laid the rifle down as I dropped to my knees. A hand came down on my shoulder. "I shot her." I said in an emotionless voice.

"We don't know that, but Trinity was worried about Sara in that tree. Let's save your sister and then we can figure out where they took Trinity." There was an urgency in Matt's voice. It snapped me out of my shocked state.

I got to my feet and ran to where I saw Noah and Liam. The tree was an inferno. Most of the flames were near the top while the bottom part of the trunk was a blackened mess. I looked up and saw a treehouse among the flames nearly twenty feet up.

How were we going to get to Sara? Noah had tears in his eyes as he ran his hands through his hair. Liam was trying to calm him down. We could push the tree over and hope the fall didn't hurt Sara too much or wait for the fire to die down.

Making a decision, I grabbed Matt's arm as I moved away from the tree at a jog. "Our only option is knocking the tree down." I explained.

"How do you plan on doing that?" Matt asked skeptically.

"Running into it and praying." I said as I sprinted towards the tree. Matt and Murphy were the only ones that knew I was a magic user. I could change the density of my body. I had been training with it in private since Matt had been laid up. I wasn't perfect at it, but I could at least hit the tree much harder than if I wasn't using it. I felt my magic flowing through my veins as I ran. I slammed all my weight into the hot trunk like a battering ram. Pain shot through my shoulder as I collided with it. I heard a crack. I moved to the side not sure if the crack came from the tree or from a bone.

A second later, Matt slammed into the tree just like I had. Another crack and the tree began to tip. I used my good shoulder and pushed, putting everything I had into it. Matt was right beside me and a minute later the tree gave way. "Timber!" I yelled, jumping back.

The tree hit the ground with a loud boom. I stumbled for the treehouse. I always felt weaker after using my magic. Noah and Liam beat me to it. Noah yanked the door open and dove inside. He came out carrying Sara before anyone else reached the treehouse. Her arms were wrapped tightly around his neck, and she was sobbing. We moved away from the burning tree and closer to the burned down house. Hopefully, the fire didn't spread.

"Axel, let's take a look at your arm." Murphy said as he grabbed my shoulder. I hissed in pain but let him continue to examine my arm. "I think you dislocated your shoulder." Murphy gave a quick yank and I heard and felt a pop as pain once again exploded through my shoulder.

"What happened to the fire?" Matt asked in confusion. We looked back at the tree and sure enough, the flames were completely gone. All that was left was a blackened trunk and a completely untouched treehouse. "Am I the only one seeing this? I mean the treehouse was on fire a few moments ago, right?"

"I think it was Trinity. I think she did some sort of protection on it." Sara sniffled.

I turned and walked over to her. "Are you okay, Sara?" I pulled her away from Noah and gave her a hug. I held her tight, relieved that she was unharmed. I looked across the meadow and saw a boy at the tree line. I blinked and he was gone. I kissed the top of Sara's head before stepping back and nudging her back to Noah. He immediately put his arms around her and kissed her forehead.

"I'm fine, but they took Trinity." Sara began to panic.

"I know, we saw." Murphy said dryly.

"You're Trinity's friend, right?" Liam asked and Sara shot him a glare. "Did she mention anything about being pregnant?"

"What? No. Trinity is not pregnant." Sara answered clearly shocked by the question.

"You're sure?" I asked hopefully.

"At least she never said anything to me about it. She is a private person, so I guess it's possible. She has been a total mess emotionally lately. But no, she would have told me, right? I mean I would hope she would tell me something like that. Why would you even ask that question?" Sara asked, agitated.

"We heard her tell the man she was." Matt said angrily. "How the heck did she get pregnant and who is the father?"

"Oh." Was all Sara said as hurt filled her eyes.

"Did you hear where they were going to go?" Murphy asked to change the subject.

"I couldn't really hear anything from the tree house. Only a gunshot as I saw her body jerk." Sara answered and my heart stopped.

I walked several steps away from the group. My breathing had become uneven, and I felt like I couldn't catch my breath. Trinity was most likely pregnant. That thought sent a stabbing pain through me. That pain was nothing compared to the thought of shooting her.

Tears gathered in my eyes and my legs gave out. Sara had mentioned seeing Trinity jerk with the sound of the shot and the blood on the ground...Oh man, what have I done?

"Axel, are you okay?" Sara's quiet voice asked from behind me.

I shook my head as I lowered it into my hands. "I shot her!" I cried out in despair. "I killed her!"

Chapter 19

Trinity

My shoulder was on fire, and I couldn't seem to open my eyes. My brain felt foggy, and I had a headache. I let out a groan as the pain in my shoulder got worse. I heard someone scoff in disgust as they moved a little closer.

"The girl lives." That sounded like Lucy.

"Not for much longer if she continues to bleed like that." Grace said. "Dump her in the cell and see what that witch can do for her. We have to figure out what to do with Jason."

Someone picked me up and I cried out in pain. The person carrying me attempted to move more carefully, but it didn't help much. I kept my eyes squeezed closed as I fought the urge to vomit. The jingle of keys proceeded a heavy door opening and closing. Then I was lain on a cold hard surface.

"What happened to her?" A woman's voice sounded horrified. I must really be losing it because I thought I heard…no that couldn't be possible.

"I guess she was shot. Her heart stopped and I did CPR to bring her back. The mistresses want you to do what you can to save her." A man said before a door slammed.

I felt myself slipping closer to unconsciousness. "Oh, my dear child, what have they done to you?" The woman whispered. "Adam, get me some clean rags. We are going to have to clean her up after we stop the bleeding."

When I regained consciousness, I felt much better. My headache was gone and the pain in my shoulder was non-existent. I opened my eyes and looked around. I was laying on a wooden table in some sort of cell turned living quarters. There were three bedrolls against the far wall and some sort of couch made out of a wooden crate. A thick door was on the opposite wall from the bedrolls. No windows were visible, and the room's light came from two lamps set in two opposite corners.

I jumped when the door banged open and a young boy was thrown into the room, landing in a heap on the floor. The door slammed closed. "Was that really necessary?" He yelled at the closed door.

The boy stood up and turned around with a scowl on his face. His eyes went wide when he saw me watching him. I slowly sat up while keeping an eye on him. It was the same boy from the meadow.

"Hey, you're awake." He stated. "Are you thirsty? Mom said you would be thirsty when you woke up." I nodded my head slowly as I eased myself off the table. The boy returned with a bottle of water. "Here. But keep in mind we only get so many of these for the week and with you here, I'm not sure if they will increase the number of supplies or not." The boy offered the water to me with a small smile. "My name's Trenton. But everyone calls me Trent. What's your name?" he asked as he sat on a stool.

"Trinity." I responded after taking a sip. "You were at the meadow." I said, my voice feeling a bit odd from disuse.

"I'm sorry about that. Jason doesn't really give me a choice on where I can be." The boy looked embarrassed. Trent was talkative and cheerful. His eyes were a beautiful shade of blue with golden brown hair. "I'm a magic user like my parents, except I can only do one thing like my dad. Jason uses my magic to get around. Are you okay? There was a gunshot, and the bullet went through your shoulder and hit Jason." He looked around and lowered his voice like he was afraid of being overheard. "The bullet barely missed your heart, but not Jason's and he died. The mistresses are so mad. I heard them talking about taking your baby for revenge." The boy's face paled as he covered his mouth, his eyes going wide. "I'm sorry, I shouldn't have said that. Dad's always telling me to watch my mouth."

"It's fine, Trent. So, Jason is really gone?" I was shocked. I hadn't expected Jason to be dead. I didn't know exactly how I felt about the news. Overjoyed, unsatisfied that I didn't get to see it, relieved he was gone? The boy gave an affirming nod. "Who are you and your parents? How did you end up here?" I asked as I sat on the couch-like box. I was curious about this kid and how he ended up here.

"Mom and Dad are great people. They told me Jason brought them here a long time ago to make someone do something. I was born here, and when I was old enough, Jason put me to work. Mom and Dad clean the place and stuff. They said I used to have a sister, but Jason took her from them. Dad says Mom's never been the same." Trent smiled sadly at me.

"I'm so sorry. Jason took my parents from me and now my second family." A tear slid down my cheek. Had Sara survived the fire? I had trapped her in the treehouse to keep her safe, but with the fire...I really hoped she was okay. I would be devastated if she died in that stupid treehouse because of me.

"Don't tell anyone, but after bringing everyone back here, I snuck out. The girl in the treehouse was fine, a bit shaken up but fine. The tree was on fire and two of the guys knocked it down. It was crazy to see them run full speed into it. I don't know how the first guy managed to split the wood when he hit. He has to be insanely strong. I did try to teleport in there to get her out, but there was some sort of shield around it. Was that you?" Trenton stood and moved over to sit by me. "The treehouse was completely untouched by the fire and when the tree fell, the girl was like floating inside of it until it was on the ground."

"You went back to save her?" I asked in surprise.

A blush rose to his cheeks. "Jason has forced me to do a lot of things I'm not proud of. He has my parents and if I step out of line, I watch them get punished. The same thing goes for them, but they watch me. That girl did nothing. They were going to kill an innocent for you being pregnant and I didn't like the idea of leaving her there to die. But I'm no hero." Trent shrugged as if it was no big deal.

I was so overwhelmingly grateful that I threw my arms around him and hugged him tight. "Thank you."

I jumped back from Trent when the door banged open again. Lucy and Grace waltzed in. I got to my feet to face them. "Look at that, you actually survived. Your little stunt killed our brother." Grace raised her hand and slapped my face so hard that I stumbled into the wall. "Greg, bring her." She demanded; her voice was full of hatred.

A large man stepped in and grabbed my arm. As I was dragged from the room, I looked back at Trent who watched helplessly. I was taken to a small room not far from Trent's. Greg put my wrists in chains forcing me to stand there with my hands pulled straight over my head. The chains bit into my skin as I stood on my tip toes.

This was the same way Lucy and Grace had chained me for years. I was spun around so that I was facing the wall. Panic began to overwhelm me, and I squeezed my eyes shut. Axel's handsome face appeared as he had coached me through several of my panic attacks. And I felt slightly calmer.

"It has been over a week since you got our brother killed and since Jason is no longer with us, we will collect your magic and finally be done with you." Lucy coldly informed me. My shirt was cut from my body and a sharp object was dragged down my back. I screamed out in pain. "Doesn't this bring back fond memories?" Lucy's voice had taken on a demonic sound. There was another long slow drag down my back and I screamed again. "You have a lot of magic, little one. We were able to extract some here and there through the years. We had to be careful not to leave too many scars though. We should have just finished taking your magic that day in the field."

"But Adam had to be noble and use his own magic to shield you from us. The stupid man, he made himself too weak to protect his precious princess by saving you." Grace added. Another slow drag. Another scream.

I remembered them doing this to me every few months. I had thought they were dragging needles across my skin. Had they really been extracting some of my magic? If so, Murphy was correct when he said that it would be a long painful process to take someone's magic.

I wasn't sure how long I had been screaming with Lucy and Grace getting more and more frustrated about something. Eventually they yelled at Greg to take me back to the cell. My body was shaking as I was dropped on the floor just before a door slammed closed. Warm hands touched me, and I screamed as the touch sent bolts of pain shooting across my back. I heard sobbing as the pain slowly began to fade.

A blanket was draped over me, and I was gently picked up and laid on a bedroll. I lay there trembling as a man tried to comfort the crying woman. After a few minutes, I rolled to a sitting position as I kept the blanket around me. Grace and Lucy had destroyed my shirt, and I was now only in my jeans. I looked around the room. Trent was sitting on the couch with tears in his eyes as he watched me, and a man was holding a woman over by the table.

I died. That is the only way I could explain what I saw in front of me. Tears began to blur my vision as I watched the couple closely. If I was dead, would Trent be there? My heart was beating wildly. I couldn't quite make out the words, but I could hear the deep soothing tones of the man's voice and it brought back so many memories.

I closed my eyes as I pictured my dad whispering to my mother late at night as they cuddled on the couch. His comforting words whenever I got scared. I began to sob. This couldn't be real; I was either dead or dreaming.

A hand touched my blanket covered shoulder, and I looked up into brown eyes that were the same as mine and my mother's. "Clara Sloan?" I asked through my tears. The woman looked surprised before she glanced quickly at the man behind her. She turned her gaze back to me. "Momma?" I whispered.

There was a pause before the woman broke down sobbing again. She tentatively reached out to me as if afraid to touch me. "Trinity?" Her voice was barely louder than a whisper. I nodded my head as tears continued to flow from my eyes. In the next second, I was pulled into my mother's arms and a second pair of arms wrapped around the both of us. We stayed like that for a long time.

"I thought you were dead." I finally managed to say.

"No, baby girl." My father grabbed my face in his hands as he wiped my cheeks. Tears continued to fall from his eyes. "Jason knocked us out and brought us here. Our mark made it impossible for them to collect mine or your mother's magic. Then when Trenton was born, they used him to get around."

I looked over at Trenton who was watching us with wide eyes. "Trinity is my sister?" He breathed out in amazement. "My sister is a freaking rockstar!" He launched himself into the midst of us and gave me a hug. "She was able to put a shield thing around her friend that I couldn't even get past like I can with yours, Dad. And she threatened to blow her brains out if Jason touched her."

"What?" My parents said in horrified unison. I ducked my head, embarrassed.

Over the next several hours, I told them a watered-down version of everything that had happened, from the moment Mom had told me to run, to the moment I was thrown back into this cell. I mentioned briefly Murphy, Sara, the guys, and even Duncan. I didn't mention that Murphy was Mom's guard, and they didn't seem to make the connection. Trent was really excited about Duncan.

"Oh, and Liam, Noah, Matt, and Axel were all chosen as my Enforcers." I finished.

"Four Enforcers? I have never heard of such a thing." My father's brow furrowed. "What is your symbol?"

"A wolf's head." I answered.

"Like the wolf's head on your shoulder?" Trent asked excitedly.

"What?" I asked, confused.

"You have a wolf's head tattoo on your left shoulder blade. I think it's pretty awesome." Trent said with a huge grin.

"I don't have a tattoo." I said as my brows furrowed.

My mother reached over and pulled down the collar of the shirt she gave me and gasped. "Adam, it's..." My mother whispered.

"I see it." My father said in disbelief. "Right where a Blessing Mark usually is." I looked between the two of them in confusion.

"Trinity, sweetheart, if your princess mark is a wolf's head and you have a similar mark on your shoulder, it means that your magic has found the person it deems worthy of you. It's a Blessing Bond." My mother explained and my mouth fell open. "And that bond seals your magic, no one can strip it from you."

I just stared at them in shock. Who was I bonded to? It couldn't be any of the guys, could it? Definitely not Noah or Axel. Both of them were in love with someone else and I didn't think my magic would be that cruel to bind me to someone whose heart belonged to another. Matt and Liam were like brothers to me, and it was weird to even think about them like that. I ran a hand through my hair as I tried to think of anyone my magic would have chosen but I came up empty. It was getting late, and Mom and Dad insisted we all go to sleep, saying we could pick this up in the morning.

Weeks passed with Mom and Dad leaving for their assigned tasks. Trent was occasionally pulled away to do stuff, while I was taken back to the room and chained up. My days were spent either being tortured or locked in the cell by myself. A few times they left me hanging there for hours after one of our sessions. Being trapped in this limbo, depression settled in as time crawled by.

*　　　　　*　　　　　*

Axel

I was glaring down at a map of the area around the meadow from where Trinity had disappeared. Matt was standing next to me with slumped shoulders. "We have combed the surrounding four miles with no trace of anyone but us, Axel. I think we need to start broadening our search to the towns and cities within a fifty or hundred-mile radius." Matt put both hands on the edge of the table.

I let out a defeated sigh as I hung my head. Were we ever going to find her? At least we knew she was still alive because our Enforcer Bonds were still intact. The problem with that was the constant feeling that Trinity was in danger. It was making Liam, Matt, and me irritable.

"It's been six weeks, why haven't we found any sign of her yet?" I asked in frustration.

"Hey man, we'll find her. It may take a little more time than any of us would like but we will get her back." Matt put a hand on my shoulder in a gesture of comfort.

"She doesn't have time, Matt. If she really is pregnant, then both her and the baby only have a few months left." I looked over at him. Even though I hated the fact that Trinity was pregnant with another man's baby, I couldn't deny the fact that I still loved her and my need to protect her extended to her child as well.

"We will save them both. And then you can kick the other guy's butt for touching your woman." Matt gave me a half smile.

"If Trinity wants that guy, then when we finally bring her back, she can have him. I am not going to stand in the way of her happiness." I said as I headed for the door of the office.

"Love sucks." Matt muttered. He didn't know half of it. We walked down the hall together as we headed out back.

Duncan came running up with his tail wagging. "Hey boy." I bent down and scratched his head. "You ready to go for a ride?" I hooked his leash to his collar before walking around to the front of the house.

I opened the back door of my new truck and Duncan jumped in. I was just about to climb into the driver's seat when Noah and Sara came out the front door. "You're really going then?" Sara asked with tears in her eyes. She had taken Trinity's disappearance as hard as I had. She was even refusing to set a wedding date until Trinity was back home.

"I have to, Sara. I need to find her." I stepped over to her and pulled her into a hug. "Matt and I will check out the towns and cities around the area to see if we can find any trace of her. We should be back in a few months." I placed a kiss on her cheek. "And be nice to Noah. He loves you and he's been having a hard time watching you struggle." I whispered in her ear.

She glanced over at Noah before giving me a nod. "I know. I just...miss her." Tears began to gather in her eyes and Noah moved to her side. She leaned into him, and I walked back to my truck.

"Take care of each other and we will keep in touch." I climbed behind the wheel and started the engine. I took a deep breath as I put the truck in gear and drove down the driveway. I didn't care how long it took; I was going to find Trinity.

* * *

Trinity

"Trinity sweetheart, it has been three months, you need to start eating more. I know this is hard, but please, you have to keep up your strength." My mother pleaded with me.

Dad and Trent were summoned to do whatever they were assigned to do, leaving Mom and me in our cell alone. "Why did the Monroe's attack the royal family? Why are they doing this?" I finally asked the question that had been bothering me for weeks. I took a bite of my sandwich as I waited for her to answer.

Mom let out a heavy sigh as she sat next to me. "This world is full of two kinds of people: magic users and humans. The humans don't know about us magic users and we want to keep it that way. Centuries ago, a highly respected family of magic users was appointed as rulers over all those who had magic. The magic community had voted and the magic approved of their choice.

"The royal family's job was to keep the peace between the two worlds. Which meant setting rules to keep magic users hidden from the world and discipline those who broke those rules or hurt humans. Because of the royal family's goodness and sacrifices to keep their people safe, the magic blessed the family with daughters who had more than one gift." Mom grabbed my hand and gave it a squeeze.

"The Monroes thought magic users were superior to humans and felt like we needed to come out of hiding. They wanted to show the humans that magic users were better. When Jason started to pursue me, my magic chose your father as my Enforcer to help protect me. My father learned of Jason's intentions toward me and sent him away. A few weeks later, the attack happened."

"He killed everyone but you. How did you get away?" I asked as I laid my head on her shoulder.

"Your father somehow sensed the danger and got me out, but he had received an injury to his back. Once we were safe, I had him take his shirt off so that I could heal him. Once I was done, I noticed his Guard's Mark was different from when my father confirmed the Enforcer's Mark. There was a second rose.

"I asked him about it, and he gave me a look that sent my heart fluttering. Trinity, your father had always been a flirt. He was my guard, so he would escort me around. When we walked down the hallways, and no one was around, he would brush his fingers against mine a few times before trying to grab my hand. He even tried to kiss me a few times." Mother got a small smile on her face at the memory.

"Your mother was a flat-out tease." Dad's voice filled the room as the door closed behind him. "She would let our fingers brush but whenever I tried to grab her hand, she would fold her arms and give me a smile. She toyed with me for years before then too." Dad sent Mom an adoring look before sitting next to us. "I had been in love with her since I was twelve and she gave me a black eye."

Mom laughed and placed a kiss on his cheek. "Anyway, his mark was different, and he refused to tell me why. We traveled for several months before finding our meadow. Your father purchased the land and began building the house. We lived in a four-man tent during that time. The day the house was finished, he asked me to marry him. We got married the next day.

"A week later, we were playing in the creek when your father noticed the rose on my shoulder. You were born just over a year after we were married. We found out where Murphy lived and went to visit him. We needed to know you would be safe if anything happened to us."

"The day Jason came to the house, he tried to take your mother's magic. His sister Lucy's magic allows her to take magic from others. However, Lucy couldn't pull the magic from your mother. Apparently, my second mark and your mother's mark are symbols of the bond that our magic gave us. It sealed our magic to us. Jason found a book that talks about the Sealing Bond. Children born within the Sealing Bond have stronger magic. Jason kept us alive to see if your mother would have another daughter. Trent was born and exhibited teleporting abilities early on. They kept us around only to keep him in line." Dad took up the story.

"But why did he wait ten years to try to take my magic? Wouldn't it be easier to do it when I was a child?" I was so confused and angry that I had to live for ten years with Lucy and Grace and all their abuse.

"As a princess, your full magic wouldn't manifest itself until you were anywhere between eighteen to twenty-one years old." Mother explained. "Jason wanted the full strength of your powers."

"He also wanted me to produce a child for him. He said because I was the child of a bonded pair and had royal blood, my kids would have great strength." I watched as Mom's face paled and Dad's jaw clenched.

"It's a good thing that he is already dead." Dad said menacingly. The door opened and Lucy came back in. She gave us a mocking smirk as she pointed to me. I got to my feet and Greg reached for me. "Please, don't. Not again. You have to know by now that you can't get her magic." My father pleaded.

Lucy had tried over thirty times to extract my magic. Thirty minutes of complete torture before she would give up and I was thrown back to my parents. My mother would heal me, and it started all over again several days later.

"She has a Bonding Mark." Dad was on his feet with tears in his eyes.

"You stupid girl. Not only did you get yourself knocked up, but you are also bonded to someone!" Lucy yelled. Her face turned red with her anger as she directed Greg to drag me out, my parents' pleas for them to leave me alone followed us down the hall.

Instead of going to the small room where they tried to pull my magic, I was taken to a small closet. Greg shoved me inside and the door slammed closed. I was surrounded by pitch blackness. Terror seized me and I screamed. After I lost my voice, I lay on the ground sobbing. Axel's voice entered my mind, and I took a slow deep breath. I could almost see him. He was cupping my face as we sat on the couch that last night. His soft voice coaching me to just breathe. Hours passed before the door opened and Greg was standing there with Grace.

"I presume you remember how to use these?" She pointed at a broom and mop bucket with rags. I nodded and she smirked at me. "The whole ground floor needs to be swept and mopped. And if you try to leave, one of your family members will be treated to the V.I.P. room. Do you understand?" I nodded as I gathered up the supplies. "You will be of some use to us until that child is born, then your usefulness will end." She spat at me before Greg showed me where to start.

Two days straight of scrubbing the floors and windows. I was exhausted and my feet dragged trying to keep up with Greg as he took me back to my parents. My father caught me before I hit the ground as Greg shoved me into the room. He helped me to the bedroll, and I fell into a deep sleep.

I woke up slowly and my whole body ached. It had been a long time since I had scrubbed so much at one time. Dad was the only one there and he brought me some water and a roll as I sat up. I gave him a tired smile as I accepted the food and water.

"Trinity, are you really pregnant?" He asked and I choked on my roll.

"Dad." I coughed some more and finally managed to dislodge the bread by swallowing half my water bottle.

"I'm not mad, sweetheart. I just, as your father, I don't like the idea of you...before you are married. And who is the father? It better be the man you are bonded to." Dad was clearly trying not to show how upset he really was.

I put my arms around his middle, and he held me tight while laying his cheek on the top of my head. "I don't know who I'm bonded to remember? But it doesn't matter because I'm not pregnant. Jason assumed I was, and I never cleared up the misunderstanding. I figured if he continued to think I was, he wouldn't try anything until I could escape." I whispered.

Dad sighed in relief. "Thank heavens." He murmured before placing a kiss on my head. "I was terrified that Jason might have actually..." He cleared his throat. "He has taken advantage of several young ladies. Greg's daughter is about six months pregnant."

"I thought Greg was loyal to the Monroes." I said in surprise.

"No. They have his two daughters. He refused to do something, and Jason took his sixteen-year-old daughter, Tracy, for the night. Greg was devastated when he found out what had happened to her and that she was pregnant. The poor girl nearly died trying to end the pregnancy. She has asked your mother and me to take the baby when it is born." Dad gave me another kiss on the head before getting back to his feet. "Soon you and Trent will have a little brother or sister."

My mouth fell open. I couldn't believe they had agreed to take the baby. After everything Jason had done to them, to us. Why would they even consider caring for his child?

"Don't give me that look, Trinity. That child and its mother are innocent. We can't hold the baby responsible for the actions of the man that fathered it. Your mother and I have talked this over, and we feel we can give the child a loving home so that it can escape the evils that started its life."

I immediately felt guilty. Dad was right, the baby didn't deserve to be blamed for Jason and his sick actions. I apologized and went back to bed. That could have been me instead of Greg's daughter. A shiver ran down my spine and for the thousandth time I wished Axel were next to me.

Chapter 20

Lucy and Grace kept us separated as much as possible. There was always at least one of us in the cell at all times. We were only in the cell all together at night. Trent said it was because he couldn't teleport out of or into the cell and as long as one of us was locked up, the others wouldn't leave. It was smart, they knew our weakness and used it to their advantage.

When I was let out of the cell, I was cleaning and scrubbing everything. I hadn't seen Lucy or Grace for nearly two months, which was a good thing, otherwise they would have discovered that I wasn't actually pregnant. My anxiety started to grow more and more each day. I would soon be delivering, if I were pregnant. Time was running out and we needed to escape.

Mom and Dad wouldn't leave until Tracy's baby was born. The plan was for the five of us to escape and bring back reinforcements to free everyone else. But we still didn't know how we were going to get out.

Trent and Dad were gone. Mom and I were sitting on stools at the makeshift table whispering, waiting for them to come back. "What if I cloaked myself and waited for them to come punish you? They will pull you out of here and Trent can teleport us to safety." I suggested.

"It won't work. Trent would not know when we would be implementing it." Mom said, shaking her head.

The door crashed against the wall as Greg rushed in carrying a teenage girl. She was drenched in sweat and whimpering in pain. "I think the baby is coming." Greg said in a panic.

Mom and I rushed to the girl's side as Greg laid her on the bedrolls. I took a step back and stared. The girl looked to be a few years younger than me. "You did good to bring her here, Greg. Trinity and I will take care of her. You should probably get back before they notice you are gone." My mother said, giving him a reassuring smile. Greg hesitated for a moment before walking out the door and closing it. "How are you feeling, Tracy?" Mom turned her attention to the girl.

"Please, make it stop." The girl begged. Her brown hair was drenched with sweat and her grey eyes were full of fear.

For the next couple hours, we helped Tracy feel as comfortable as possible while the contractions became more painful. Trent and Dad still hadn't returned, but that was probably for the best right now.

I was holding Tracy's hand and brushing her damp hair back from her face. Tracy was in a tremendous amount of pain, and she began to scream with the contractions. There was a particularly bad contraction and Tracy fell back exhausted. A second later a baby's cry filled the room. I looked at Mom with wide eyes as hers filled with tears.

"You have a little girl. Would you like to hold her?" Mom said softly to Tracy. Tracy began to sob as she shook her head and turned away from the baby. My heart broke as I watched Tracy. She had been so traumatized by what Jason had done to her that she couldn't even look at her baby.

Mom nodded and handed the screaming baby to me and motioned for me to go to the other side of the room. Trent had been slowly stocking up on infant formula and a few extra blankets. I cradled the baby close as I moved to the couch, lifted the secret compartment, and pulled out a soft green blanket. I wrapped it securely around the baby. I pulled out a diaper and premade newborn formula bottle and shook it. I sat down, put the diaper on her and offered the baby the bottle. She immediately started sucking down her first meal.

Tracy continued to cry until she finally fell asleep. Mom put a blanket over her and moved to my side. "How is the baby doing?" I gave her a shrug while continuing to observe the little girl. "She seems to be doing well. What should we name her?" Mom asked and I looked up to see my mother smiling adoringly down at the bundle in my arms. "Your father and I were talking about something like Tahna or Taylor or Tatum."

"Not another T name, Mom. You already have a Trenton and a Trinity." I rolled my eyes as I smiled. The baby finished eating and was asleep. I gently started patting her back and rocking her.

"What would you suggest then?" My mother gave a soft laugh.

"Aurora or Dawn or even Chloe are better than adding another T name." I ran a finger lightly over the soft dark brown hair that covered the baby's head. She was such a beautiful baby with her several inches of long hair.

"Which do you like the best, Trinity?" I turned with a furrowed brow to look at Mom.

"This is your baby. Tracy asked you and Dad to take care of her. You guys have to decide." I said as I studied my mom's face. Her eyes looked fondly at me but there was also uncertainty there.

"Tracy did, at first, ask your father and me. But Tracy just asked if you would adopt the child. She said she knows you will be the best mother for the baby." I blinked in surprise. "Tracy's magic allows her to see small glimpses of the future. She said that you should be the one to raise the girl."

"But I'm only eighteen and I'm not even in a relationship. How can I raise a baby on my own?" I started to feel completely inadequate.

"You would be the baby's legal mother. You won't be alone though, I will be there every step of the way, Trinity. You won't have to raise the baby by yourself." Mom tried to soothe my worries.

"I don't know, Mom." I looked back at the baby and my heart hammered harder in my chest. Was I ready to be a mom? Could I provide for her and keep her safe?

"Just think about it, okay? In the meantime, you can think of a name." Mom kissed my cheek before moving back over to Tracy.

I sat there for a long time holding the little girl and thought about what my future would look like if I agreed to adopt the baby. Would the man I'm bonded to hate me for taking on the child of an evil man? He would just have to learn to accept that this little girl is not her biological father, and his crimes are not hers.

My eyes moved from the baby to the door as Trent, Dad, and Greg stepped into the cell. They all wore worried expressions.

"How is Tracy? Did she…" Greg's voice trailed off as he looked over at his daughter.

"Tracy is doing very well. I healed her after she delivered the baby, so she won't have all the trauma of childbirth to contend with. She is sleeping right now." Mom said quietly as she moved over to the men standing near the door.

Trent saw me and moved to my side. He looked at the baby for a minute before touching her hand softly. "The baby is kinda cute." He whispered and I laughed quietly.

"Trent took me to the courthouse, and I was able to get the adoption papers. All that needs to be done is for Tracy, me, and both of you to sign them and a name to be given." Greg whispered.

"Actually, Tracy has asked Trinity to adopt the baby." Mom looked over at me and the men followed her stare.

I swallowed hard and glanced over at Trent. "So, I'm going to be an uncle?" Trent said excitedly.

I smiled at him and put the baby into his arms. He sat stiffly as he tried not to hurt her. "Trent, meet your niece, Evelynn Dawn."

I got to my feet and moved over to Mom who had a big smile on her lips and tears in her eyes. She gave me a hug and kissed my cheek. Greg and I filled out the paperwork and signed at the bottom. Mom and Dad signed the witness lines, and it was done. I was now a mother. I just needed to take the papers to the courthouse to file them in the next two weeks. I looked over at Trent and Dad. Dad held Evelynn and Trent placed a kiss on her little head.

Before Greg helped Tracy back to her room, she signed the papers and moved over to me. She pulled me into a hug and thanked me. Once they left, we gathered around the newest member of our family. My heart swelled with love for the little girl I had just adopted, while the weight of her safety settled heavily on my shoulders.

The next few days flew by in a blur. Trenton had snuck out again to get several outfits and some diapers. Newborn clothes were too big for her tiny body. Mom guessed that Evelynn was only around five pounds. She said that Tracy hadn't been due for a few more weeks and that Evelynn surprised us all by coming so early.

Tracy had taken up my chores when I was summoned so that I could take care of Evelynn. Mom and Dad were really supportive as they taught me the different aspects of taking care of a newborn.

The nagging feeling of needing to get away was growing stronger with each day. Trent, Dad, and Mom were at the table while I sat on the couch with Evelynn. They had just come back for the evening. They were eating when the door opened slowly.

"So, it is true, you have a baby." Lucy's cold voice spoke, and we all jumped to our feet. Evelynn started crying and I tried to soothe her. "Judging by the purple, am I to assume that it is a girl?" We all remained quiet, but that didn't seem to bother her. "Perfect. She will be a powerful little royal. Now, hand the brat over."

"No." I said firmly as I hugged my baby to my chest. There was no way they were going to touch my child.

"That isn't an option." Lucy stepped further into the room with Grace following in her wake.

They stalked closer to me, and I made eye contact with Trent. I motioned to the open door with my eyes, and he nodded his understanding. He whispered to Mom and Dad, and they hesitantly followed Trent's slow movements towards the door. Just as they were slipping through, Lucy and Grace reached me. Grace grabbed for Evelynn, but she was shocked by an invisible force.

She cried out in pain as she fell to the ground. Lucy dropped to the floor next to Grace, trying to help her. I ran towards the door. Dad was standing just inside the opening. A cry of anger rang through the air, and I turned to see Lucy charging towards us. I wasn't going to make it out before Lucy reached me. I passed Evelynn to Dad.

"Go!" I yelled as I was hit from behind. The door slammed closed between us, locking me in the cell with Lucy and Grace. We fell to the ground in a heap. "You will never hurt that child." I said as I stood.

Grace had recovered and advanced on me as Lucy got to her feet. I dove out of the way of Grace's attack. I remembered some of the things Sara had taught me about self-defense all those months ago. The only problem was, there was nowhere for me to run. They kept coming at me and I kept defending.

Grace let out a scream of frustration as she tackled me, and we fell hard onto the couch. The box shattered under our combined weight. All the hidden items were thrown around as we wrestled on the ground.

I heard the click of a gun and turned towards it. Lucy held the handgun that I had purchased with Sara. She was aiming it at me. My heart stopped in fear, and I closed my eyes as she pulled the trigger.

A heavy weight fell on me at that moment and my eyes shot open. Grace lay across me with lifeless eyes. I screamed as I tried to wiggle out from under the dead body. What had happened? Lucy ran to her sister, crying.

"No! Why did you dive on her at that moment, Grace?" I continued to scoot away, and Lucy's head whipped in my direction. Hatred. Pure hatred burned in her eyes as her gaze locked on me. "This is your fault! First Jason and now Grace!" She screamed as she once again lifted the gun to aim at me.

Time seemed to slow down as Lucy took a step toward me as I pressed myself against the wall. This was it. Now that I had so much to live for, I was going to die in a cell by my own gun. No! I was going to fight to the very end. Evelynn needed me and I was going to do everything I could to get back to her.

Just as Lucy pulled the trigger, I felt the warmth of my magic flowing through me. Everything went still. I was too afraid to move, but after the length of a breath, Lucy dropped to her knees before falling face first onto the stone floor. I sat stunned, not able to take my eyes off Lucy's motionless form.

The door burst open, and I felt hands grab me. I pointed to the two bodies with a shaky hand and Dad let go of me before moving cautiously towards Lucy. He grabbed the gun before checking for a pulse. Next, he moved to Grace before looking back at me.

"What happened?" he asked in bewilderment.

"Lucy tried to shoot me and somehow Grace got in the way. Lucy got angry and tried to shoot me again. I think it ricocheted off something." I said still in shock.

Dad moved back to the door. "Greg, get everyone out. Lucy and Grace are dead. Evacuate the entire place!" He yelled before turning back to me. He grabbed my arms and pulled me to my feet. I was still shaking. "Come on, Trinity. Trent is waiting to take us to your mother and daughter." I followed wordlessly.

In the hallway, Trent ran to us and threw his arms around me. In a blink, we were suddenly standing in the meadow with a screaming Evelynn in

Mom's arms. Mom passed me Evelynn and I hugged the infant close to my chest. I placed a kiss on her head as I began to cry. Mom held me for a long time until my adrenaline levels came down and I was no longer shaking.

We decided to make camp there in the meadow until we knew where to go. I noticed that the tree that had the treehouse in it was lying across the ground. "Mom, can you hold Evelynn? I want to check something."

She took the baby, and I jogged over to the treehouse. I looked inside and laughed. Both Sara's and my backpacks were still there. I grabbed them and headed back over to Mom. I pulled out the tent and set it up. I spread out the two sleeping bags and handed Mom a few granola bars.

Dad and Trent got back with supplies for Evelynn, food, water, and another tent. Dad set up camp while Trent and Mom gathered wood for a fire, and I fed Evelynn.

Dad and Mom took the bigger tent while Trent and I took the smaller one with Evelynn. I found the extra battery pack that Sara had for her cellphone and plugged her phone in. Hopefully, in the morning I could place a call. The night was calm, and I fell into a peaceful sleep for the first time in a long time.

*   *   *

Axel

My phone rang and I was prepared to ignore it. Matt sent me a glare and I rolled my eyes. I picked it up and pressed the accept button before putting it to my ear. "Hey, Sara." I said with a glare sent in Matt's direction. He knew how frustrated I was with Sara's constant calling. He too was irritated with the daily calls. Trinity's level of anxiety was only growing each day which caused us to be more ill-tempered. Last time I told Sara I would reach out if anything changed. Why couldn't she just lay off for a few days.

"Axel, we have a problem." Sara's anxious voice came over the line.

I sat up in bed and set Duncan off to the side. "What's going on?" I asked and Matt picked up on my change in demeanor from irritated to tense.

"Murphy has gone missing. He was in the library when he got a phone call. He seemed off the rest of the day but refused to tell us what was bothering him. When we got up the next day, he was gone. He hasn't responded to any of our phone calls." Sara explained quickly.

"Calm down, Sara. He probably went on a business trip or had to deal with something at the diner." I rubbed the back of my neck. These hotel beds weren't very comfortable. After four months, I was ready for my own bed.

"No, Axel. Something is wrong. He would have told us if it was anything like that. We need you to come home. Please." She begged.

Matt ripped the phone from my hand. "We will head home in the morning." Sara's relief was evident as she thanked Matt before he finally hung up.

"I'm not ready to go back. I haven't found her yet." I glared at Matt.

"Axel, we need to figure out a different strategy. This isn't working. We have been gone for four months. You know that Murphy isn't one to just disappear for days without informing someone where he is going!" Matt yelled. "We are headed back in the morning. You can hate me all you want, but we are leaving."

I sat there stunned. Matt was right, Murphy wouldn't just disappear. We needed to head back and check on things. I gave Duncan a scratch behind his ears before laying back down. I was a mess. Everything fed into my anger, and I couldn't seem to think straight. Matt was growing tired of my moodiness, and I didn't blame him. But he was just as insufferable as I was. This Enforcer's Bond was driving us all to madness. I let out a sigh. It would take us five days to get back home anyway. Hopefully, I could put myself together by the time we got there.

* * *

Trinity

It started raining as the sun rose. Everyone was still sleeping, and I slowly got up, trying not to wake Trenton or Evelynn. I grabbed Sara's phone after tucking blankets around the baby. I ran across the meadow and climbed into the treehouse. I pressed the power button on the phone and waited. I let out a chuckle as the screen lit up.

I debated on who to call. My first thought was to call Axel, but I was so scared he would be angry with me for taking off in the first place. It had been six months, but still, I wasn't sure I was ready to forgive myself for what I did to him.

As I scanned Sara's contact list, Murphy's name came up. I pressed the call button and held my breath. "Hello?" Murphy's confused voice came over the line. Hearing his voice made me so home sick that I began to cry. "Who is this?" Murphy asked with a strange note in his voice.

"I need your help." I sniffled.

"Trinity?" He breathed out my name as I heard him start to cry. "Where are you? Thank goodness, we have been so worried."

"I know, Murphy. I'm so sorry." I cried. "I'm sorry."

"Shh. It's okay, honey. Just tell me where you are." His voice was filled with relief, worry, and excitement.

"I'm at the meadow, but I can't hike out." I answered while trying to stop the tears. "Sara knows the way."

"That's okay, we can get something up there." Murphy sounded like he was digging through drawers.

"Just you Murphy, please. I have four others with me, and I don't want to make a scene." I clutched the phone tightly. "And could you pick up an infant car seat?"

"Oh, Trinity." Murphy said softly. "We heard most of your conversation with Jason. We weren't sure, but you really were pregnant?"

"I will explain everything once you get here, okay? We aren't prepared to hike for two days with a newborn. You won't be able to call me again. The phone I found doesn't have much battery left." I explained.

"I'm on it. I will see you within a week." Murphy said and I thanked him.

The phone beeped saying it had five percent left. I tapped Axel's name and closed my eyes. I needed to hear his voice, even if it was yelling at me.

"Hello?" Axel's deep voice said, and my stomach tied into knots. "Listen Sara, I told you I would update you in a few days." He sounded irritated and I held my breath. I didn't know what to say. What could I say? "I promise to call you soon, okay?" His voice had softened. "I love you, talk to you soon." He hung up the phone and I started crying. After I got control over my emotions, I ran back to the tent.

We were trapped in our small shelters as the rain continued to fall over the next three days. I was worried that Murphy wasn't going to be able to make it up here with how wet the ground was getting. Any vehicle was bound to get stuck.

Trent didn't seem to be bothered by the rain. I laughed as he ran around and got muddy. Mom and Dad also watched him with large smiles on their faces. It was great to see the nine-year-old being so carefree. Mom and Dad spent most of the days holding each other and watching me and Trenton.

Chapter 21

It had been nearly a week since my phone call with Murphy and still no sign of him. The storm had finally passed, and Dad was out looking for dry wood to build a fire. We had discussed where we could go, but with no money and Trent's limitations on teleporting, we were stranded until we could hike out. He could only teleport somewhere if he had already physically been there and the meadow was the closest location to Murphy. I hadn't told anyone about the phone. I wanted to surprise Mom and Dad with their old friend.

Evelynn had been up all night again and I was taking a nap with her when I heard the sound of a helicopter. I sat up quickly and picked Evelynn up. I climbed out of the tent and looked up at the sky.

"Trent, get everyone to the treehouse!" Dad yelled from across the meadow. I blinked and suddenly I was in the treehouse with Mom and Trent. I could see Dad standing near a tree, watching the sky.

It didn't take long until I saw the helicopter starting to land near where the tents were. Dad tensed as he crouched down to hide behind the tree. My heart was hammering in my chest. Who was it? Was it Murphy?

We all remained still as the chopper blades began to slow down and two men exited the chopper with firearms raised. I was just about to put up a protective shield when I heard his familiar voice.

"Move slowly. Don't fire unless you have to." Murphy's voice carried through the meadow on the wind. I passed Evelynn over to Mom and I bolted from the treehouse. I heard Dad yell at me to stop but I didn't. Murphy turned in my direction just as I jumped into his arms. He pulled me tight against him. "Trinity." His voice was thick with emotion.

I pulled back and smiled at him with tears in my eyes. "Hey, don't get all emotional on me just yet."

Murphy smiled down at me. "And why not? You have been missing for six months. The last time we saw you, we heard you were pregnant, and Axel shot you. I'm just glad you are safe."

"Axel was the one who shot me?" I asked in disbelief.

"Well, he accidentally shot you. He was aiming for that Jason guy. Just as he pulled the trigger, you were pulled into the line of fire." Liam said as he moved up to us.

"Liam!" I jumped into his arms, and he returned my hug. "You are a sight for sore eyes." I said with a smile. "I missed you."

"It's good to see you too, Trin. Now, who is that coming toward us with a shotgun?" Liam lowered his voice.

I turned around to see my Dad stomping towards us with the shotgun in his hands. His lips were pulled into a thin line, and he looked angry. "Adam?" Murphy asked in shock.

"Murphy?" Dad stopped in his tracks as his eyes went wide.

I whistled and waved my arms, telling Trent to bring Mom and Evelynn over. In the blink of an eye, they were there, and I felt Liam jump a little at their sudden appearance. "Liam, Murphy, these are my parents, Clara and Adam Sloan, Trenton my brother, and Evelynn." I smiled up at Liam's shocked expression. "Mom, Dad, Trent, this is Murphy and Liam. Liam is one of my Enforcers." Mom handed Evelynn back to me before pulling Murphy into a hug as she sobbed.

"Who is Evelynn?" Liam asked quietly.

I turned to fully face Liam. He was studying the baby in my arms with a mixture of emotions on his face. "Technically she is my daughter." I said trying to hide a smile. I knew he thought I had been pregnant.

"Technically? Trinity, she either is or she isn't." Liam said with a serious expression on his face as he studied the baby.

"She is my daughter, but not by blood." His eyes snapped up to mine. "I know you thought I was pregnant, but I never was. Evelynn is the biological child of one of Jason's victims who couldn't take care of her. I was asked if I would, and I agreed. She is my adopted daughter." I explained and I saw the shock on his face turn to disbelief and then relief.

"Well, she is pretty cute." Liam said, softly touching her head. "Congrats, Trin."

I leaned against Liam's chest and gave him a one-armed hug. "I missed you guys." I whispered. He put both arms around me.

"Just promise me you will leave the heroics to us Enforcers. You have no idea how bad we have been without you." Liam said quietly. I nodded and he let out a sigh of relief.

I turned to see my father embracing Murphy. We spent several more minutes talking before Liam and Murphy helped Dad and Trent break down camp. Once everything was packed into the helicopter, Murphy handed me baby ear protection as we climbed aboard. Liam sat in the pilot's seat and Murphy in the co-pilot's chair.

An hour later, we were landing at an airstrip. True to his word, Murphy had a car seat waiting in a SUV for us, along with a diaper bag full of diapers, wipes, and blankets. We had been driving for a good hour when I finally leaned my head on Liam's shoulder and fell asleep.

Someone shook me. "Trinity, wake up. We're almost back at the house." Liam whispered. "And if I had to guess, Sara will be ecstatic to see you." I sat up straighter and looked out the window at Murphy's house as we drove up the driveway.

Evelynn was in her seat to my left and Liam on my right. As the SUV rolled to a stop, Liam quickly jumped out and pulled me out behind him. I barely found my footing when a scream came from the front door, followed by me being slammed into the side of the car. My head smacked the window as arms came around me. I laughed as Sara and I fell to the ground.

"For crying out loud, Sara, you're going to kill her." Liam lifted Sara off of me while Dad helped me to my feet. As soon as I found my balance, I launched myself back at her, causing us to fall back to the ground. "Really, Trinity?" Liam laughed.

After a few minutes of us hugging and crying, we were able to get to our feet. I was pulled into a hug by Noah. "You had us so worried, Trin. Where have you been?" Noah's voice was thick with emotion.

I opened my mouth to answer but a loud wail came from the back seat. I turned back to the SUV where Evelynn was just waking up. I hurried around to the other side to get her out. When I returned to the group on the porch, Sara's eyes were wide. I gave her a small smile.

Before I could say anything, Murphy spoke up. "I think this can all be discussed inside where Trinity and the Sloans can finally sit and rest." Murphy said quickly as he walked inside.

Murphy led the group to the library, and everyone sat. I handed Evelynn over to Mom, so I could make a quick bottle. By the time I got back, Sara was holding Evelynn with a look of amazement on her face. I passed her the bottle and winked. She smiled at me before leaning back against Noah and putting the bottle in the baby's mouth. Evelynn eagerly started to eat.

I turned back to the room and took a deep breath. "I guess I have some explaining to do." I said and Noah scoffed. Sara elbowed him in the ribs, and I bit back a smile. I told them of my desire to protect them and my fear that I would get them all killed, like my parents had been. I went on to explain my kidnapping and finding my family. I finished up with telling them about my confrontation with Lucy and Grace in the cell and the final outcome.

Noah let out a low whistle. "So, you weren't actually pregnant? Like this baby isn't actually yours?"

"She is my daughter, but I adopted her from one of Jason's victims. She is barely seventeen and couldn't handle raising the baby with the trauma she had been through. She asked if I could take the baby." I explained.

"Axel is going to be so relieved." Noah muttered under his breath to Sara, who elbowed him again.

Murphy stood and instructed Noah and Liam to go prepare a couple of the rooms for Mom, Dad, and Trent. Liam grudgingly left after threatening me that if I wasn't still here when he got back, he was going to chain me up in the bunker. Trent looked horrified, but I just laughed. I listened to Murphy and my parents discussing the last ten years.

An hour later, the boys returned. Murphy led my family out to show them around the house and to their rooms so they could get cleaned up and rest. Sara, Noah, Liam, and I were left in the library.

Sara passed Evelynn back to me before snuggling closer to Noah. "Now, that you got the lowdown on what I have been up to, how about you guys? What have you been doing?" I asked as I settled back into the couch with Evelynn laying on my chest.

"Looking for you." Liam said in disbelief. "Do you honestly think we would have just let it be after seeing you poof into thin air? Matt and Axel have been gone for four months, hitting all the towns and cities within fifty miles of that meadow to see if they could find any sign of you. Sara and Noah have been holding down the fort here while looking for leads online. I have been with Murphy, meeting with anyone and everyone who might have any sort of connection that might help us find you."

"What?" I said, shocked. "That would be like looking for a needle in a haystack."

"No kidding. There were literally no tracks to follow, so we were exhausting every possible option we could think of." Noah said in exasperation.

"There were no tracks because Trent teleported us out of there. I don't even know where we were, exactly." I explained. "I wasn't allowed outside and the only time I saw the sky was through the windows as I scrubbed the floor."

"I knew I recognized that kid. He was the one from the meadow." Liam sat up straighter. "And he is your brother?" I could see the anger in his eyes and my defense rose instantly.

"Don't you dare start judging him. If he didn't do what he was told, he was forced to watch his parents being tortured. Plus, he even tried to go back to save Sara, but couldn't get past my shield. He watched as you guys knocked the tree over and pull Sara out of the treehouse." I defended Trent and sent Liam a glare. He put his hands up in surrender. "I'm sorry, Liam. It's been a long six months." I apologized and sighed tiredly.

"Why don't we get you two settled in for the night?" Sara stood and put an arm around me as she walked with me to our room. All my stuff was still there. "I can hold Evelynn for you if you would like a shower." Sara offered.

"That would be amazing." I smiled at her as she took the baby from me. "Can I ask you for a favor?" I asked and felt my cheeks warm.

"Sure." She looked at me curiously.

"Do you think I could get one of Axel's hoodies?" My cheeks heated even more as I glanced down at my hands.

I just needed this small thing one last time. I told myself in the meadow that I was strong enough to face him and walk away when the time came to leave again. I was planning on finding a little house close to wherever my parents ended up for me and Evelynn. But returning to Murphy's house and seeing everyone but him had left me feeling like something was missing. I just needed something of his for a few hours to regain my balance.

Sara laughed softly. "You got it. I'll go get you one after you are done with your shower." I smiled my thanks as I headed for the bathroom.

I showered quickly and changed into clean pajamas. It felt so good to be clean and in my own clothes again. When I walked out of the bathroom, I took Evelynn from Sara and she left to get Axel's hoodie for me. While she was gone, I decided to bathe Evelynn too. She had yet to have a bath. I was just drying off a very upset little girl, when Sara returned. She put the hoodie on my bed and sat on hers as she watched me put Evelynn in a clean jumpsuit. I quickly pulled the hoodie on before picking the baby up and rocking her.

"How old is she?" Sara asked me.

I took a moment to think about it. "She is nine days old." I answered her.

"Wow. No wonder she is so small." Sara smiled over at me.

"Mom said she came several weeks early, making her even smaller than she should be." I kissed the top of Evelynn's head. "So, when are you and Noah going to make Evelynn a best friend?" I asked Sara with a big smile.

"Slow down, Trinity. We need to get married first." Sara laughed.

"You're not married yet? What the heck?" I yelled but softened my voice when Evelynn jumped. "It's been six months, I thought for sure you would have already tied the knot."

"And I told you that you were my maid-of-honor, and I wasn't about to have my wedding without one." She shot back.

"I'm so sorry, Sara. This is all my fault." I sat down and closed my eyes as I battled the guilt that washed over me. It appeared that everyone's lives were put on hold while I was away. It wasn't supposed to be that way. I was supposed to confront Jason so they could all live peacefully without me and the chaos that I attracted.

"Don't sweat it, Trin. None of us have been emotionally ready to celebrate. I don't think we even had music playing since you left." Sara said as she lay down on her bed. "Now go to sleep and we can start planning a wedding tomorrow while dancing in the kitchen. We need to introduce

Evelynn to the proper way of getting things done." I laughed and we turned out the lights.

It was early morning when Evelynn woke up for another feeding. I carried the screaming girl down the hall to the kitchen to make her a bottle. I made my way to the lounge and settled into one of the rocking chairs and gave Evelynn her bottle. I hummed a little as she ate.

When she was done, I raised her to my shoulder and burped her. It was nearly 5:30 in the morning and I didn't want to wake up Sara. I settled back in the recliner and started to doze. Evelynn had woken up at least six times during the night. She ate a little each time but mostly she seemed to just want to be held and bounced. I was exhausted. This routine had been going on for about a week now.

A loud commotion down the hall woke me and I got up. My heart was pounding, what was going on? My first thoughts were that Lucy and Grace were back, but I reminded myself that they were gone. I held Evelynn tight before slowly moving to the door. Sara and Mom came down the hall laughing when I stepped out of the lounge to see what the fuss was about.

"It seems we have two very excited grandpas." Mom said, smiling.

"What?" I laughed in confusion.

"They were at the store as soon as it opened, and I think they bought the whole place out." Mom explained as she reached for Evelynn.

"You and Dad have been in a dungeon cell for ten years. How does he have the money to purchase anything?" I asked as I watched Mom and Sara sit on the couches.

Mom's eyes sparkled as she laughed. "Trinity, baby. I am a princess, remember? We have plenty of money. You do too. Your father can get you the information for your account." My eyes went wide as I stared at her, causing her to laugh even more. "Go check it out. I don't think I have ever seen two men more excited about baby furniture. They are in the first room on the right at the top of the stairs."

Axel's room? Why would Murphy put Evelynn's stuff in Axel's room? When I walked into the entryway, delivery men were carrying boxes up the stairs and I followed behind them. My eyes went wide, and my hand covered my mouth as I took in the room. Dad and Murphy were trying to put together a baby crib and there was a rocking chair already in a corner.

"What's going on?" I asked in disbelief when I finally found my voice.

"You're up." Dad said with a smile. "Murph and I were talking, and we realized that you and Evelynn needed a few things. What do you think?" Murphy and Dad looked at me with proud smiles and I couldn't help but laugh.

"I think Evelynn isn't even two weeks old and she is already the most spoiled little girl I have ever known." I looked around again. Axel's things had all been moved to one side of the room. I can't believe Murphy was taking over Axel's space again. "You do realize that this isn't my room, right?" I asked with a raised brow.

Murphy looked around in surprise but raised his shoulder before turning back to the instructions in his hands. "Axel can move to one of the smaller rooms if he wants to."

I shook my head at him. "You can't just kick Axel out of his room, Murphy. It wouldn't be fair of me to waltz back in here after six months and take over his space."

"We can cross that bridge when we get there. Until then, enjoy having a space for you and Evelynn." Murphy sent me a quick smile. Dad winked at me before grabbing another screw.

I left the room with a smile on my face. I walked down the stairs and nearly ran into Noah and Liam. "Where is my favorite niece?" Liam asked.

I laughed. "Her grandmother has her at the moment because her grandpas are setting up a nursery."

"A nursery? Where?" Liam's brows drew together.

"Axel's room. I told Murphy he couldn't kick Axel out just because I'm back but...yeah he doesn't seem to think it will be an issue."

"I'm with Murphy on this, Trin. It's not going to be a problem." Noah was trying hard to not smile.

"It's not my room and I doubt Axel would want to share a room with a baby, especially when he was always irritated when having to share it with me."

They laughed as they jogged up the stairs to see what they could do to help. I stared after them for a long moment before shaking my head. I felt like I was missing something. I went back to the lounge and found Sara and my mom laughing as they talked. Sara told us about how she and Noah had finally set a date.

We talked about the wedding until it was lunch time. Sara ran upstairs and asked for a bassinet to be brought down to the kitchen so that we could make lunch while Evelynn napped. Noah brought it down and gave Sara a quick kiss before leaving.

"I know that the guys are trying to put together baby furniture, but where is Trent?" I asked as I laid Evelynn in her new bassinet.

"Noah and Liam are taking him down to the gym and I think they are boxing." Sara said with a smile.

Sara walked over to the radio and turned it on. I smiled. There were so many good memories listening to that radio and being in this kitchen. We started to prepare sandwiches as we were discussing wedding details, from colors to types of cake, and Sara looked truly happy.

Evelynn woke up screaming. She had been fussy for the last few days. I held her to my shoulder as I swayed to the music and began to sing softly. I closed my eyes as I remembered dancing with Axel. I gave myself a mental shake. I really needed to steel myself before he and Matt got back. I had to learn to think of him as a friend and only a friend.

"Evelynn is going to look so cute as the flower girl." Sara laughed and I smiled at her.

"She is a little young to be throwing flower petals."

"I was thinking maybe Trent could carry her. She has the thickest hair I have ever seen on a baby. I love it." Sara's smile fell from her face as she looked at me. "Here, I'll take Evelynn for a little bit." She walked around the counter holding onto my mom's arm. "We'll take her to see what her uncles are up to."

I looked at her confused but didn't stop her from lifting Evelynn from my arms. Sara gave me a quick smile before walking past me. I turned to watch her go and my breath caught in my lungs when I saw a stunned Axel and Matt standing in the kitchen doorway. My heart tripped before it picked up speed as my eyes locked with Axel's. Sara and Mom squeezed past them on their way out. Matt, Axel, and I just stood there staring at each other for a long moment before I found my voice.

"I'm so sorry." I managed to say before tears burst from my eyes and I covered my face with my hands. So much for steeling myself for this encounter.

Arms wrapped tightly around me in the next second and my tears came faster. My arms found their way around Axel's neck as I buried my face in his chest. "Trinity? What? How?" he asked as he held me. I tightened my arms around him as I struggled for control. I felt another hand touch my back and I knew Matt was there. Axel buried his face in my neck, and we stood there until I calmed down enough to try to talk but I didn't release him.

"Jason. Shot. Parents. Brother. Evelynn. Attacked. Helicopter." I cried as I held onto him tighter. He began to rub my back slowly until my crying stopped.

"Okay, can you explain again because I didn't quite understand your last explanation?" Matt said with a watery smile.

I stepped away from Axel and gave Matt a tight hug. "I never thought I would miss your ugly mug so much." I whispered and he laughed before pressing a kiss to my forehead.

"Well, Trinity, I missed you too and I am quite confused as to how you made it back here." Matt guided me to the bar, and I sat on a stool. I wiped my eyes on the sleeve of Axel's hoodie. The corner of Axel's mouth tugged up slightly as he watched me. I took a calming breath.

"I wanted to meet with Jason so that I could stop the threat to everyone. I was tired of everyone dying for me. And before you say anything, let me finish." I said, giving them both a pointed look when I saw Matt start to open his mouth. "It was nice having Sara along even though I was nervous that Jason would use her to force me to do whatever he told me to do." Axel moved to sit by me, and I glanced at him. I wanted to lean on him, but I refrained. "Someone shot me just as Trent teleported us to Jason's house."

"I'm so sorry, Trinity. I was aiming for the man chasing you, but he spun and..." Axel said as he looked down with a guilty expression.

"Axel, don't worry about it. I am actually super grateful that you shot me." I said with a smile, and his head jerked up. I leaned against him, and he put his arm around me.

"I don't understand. I could have killed you." Axel whispered.

"I'm not going to sugarcoat it, you almost did. Well, according to Greg, my heart stopped for a few minutes before he did CPR." I said with a shrug. I felt Axel tense behind me. "The bullet barely missed my heart, but it was a direct hit to Jason's. He died within a few minutes. I was bleeding a lot. I don't remember much except for pain and the sound of doors opening and closing as someone carried me." Axel's arm tightened around me. "I was taken to a cell where a very skilled healing magic user was being kept. I was completely fine within a few hours. I was out for a week; I think they said. Lucy and Grace tried to steal my magic but couldn't. I was returned to the cell and found out that the healer was my mother. My father was there too, and I got to meet my brother for the first time."

"Wait? Your parents are alive?" Matt asked, surprised.

"Yes, now let me finish." I glared at him playfully. "After several attempts at trying to strip my magic, I was then forced to clean the house." I continued but was interrupted again when the kitchen door opened.

Sara came back in with an apologetic look. "Evelynn is hungry again." She said as she handed the baby to me. "I'll get the bottle ready."

"Thank you." I said and Axel tensed again behind me. I glanced over at Matt, and he was staring at Evelynn with wide eyes. I could tell that Axel was too. "And then Evelynn here was born. Three days later, Grace and Lucy came to take her away. I passed her to my dad before I was locked in the cell with Lucy and Grace again. They attacked me, of course. One thing led to another, and they both died." I said with a shrug.

"That is a very watered-down version of what you told us yesterday. You didn't mention the fact that they tried to shoot you twice or that stripping your magic was painful." Sara came back around the counter. "I can feed her if you want."

"It's fine. I can do it." I said, accepting the bottle she handed to me before she made her way to the door. "Oh, Sara?" She turned back to me. "Can you remind my dad that we need someone to take the adoption papers to the courts before they close?"

"Sure." Sara left the kitchen with a smile on her face.

Silence fell around the room as Evelynn ate. Axel still had an arm around me, and I laid my head on his shoulder. Being a mom was exhausting and I was ready for a nap. Axel shifted a little behind me and I settled more against him.

Matt cleared his throat. "You're not keeping the baby?" He sounded a bit uncomfortable as he asked.

"Oh, no. This little princess is all mine." I said as I pressed a kiss to her head. "I need to file the adoption papers to make it fully legal."

"I'm confused." Axel said slowly.

"Evelynn's birth mom is a seventeen-year-old victim of Jason's. The trauma of the event made her unable to keep the baby. I guess when she first found out she was pregnant, she tried to end it and almost killed herself in the process. She asked if I would take the baby and I told her I would." I explained. "Everyone keeps saying they thought I was pregnant but what gave you guys that impression? Am I fat or something?" I asked as I bit the inside of my cheek. Sara had said that the guys had overheard some of my conversation with Jason, but I wanted to know what they heard exactly.

"He commented about having you give him a child and you said he was too late." Matt shook his head. "Who is the boy you have been sneaking around with?"

"Wow. We are back to that are we?" I stiffened.

"What else are we supposed to think?" Axel asked. I tried to sit up, but his arm tightened around me, keeping me against him.

"When I said he was too late, I was referring to the fact that I was willing to blow my brains out instead of letting him touch me. If he had come to me while I was living with my aunts and offered me a way out, I might have taken him up on his offer. But not after I had a taste of true freedom."

"So, you weren't pregnant?" Matt clarified. "No boyfriend?"

"Man, you guys really seem to think the worst of me." I shook my head as my frustration grew. This was not how I pictured seeing Matt and Axel going. "Up until a few months ago, I hadn't even been kissed." I stood up and walked around to the sink. I rinsed out the empty bottle before lifting Evelynn to my shoulder as I began to pat her back. I glanced over at them, and I met Axel's eyes briefly before looking away. I felt my cheeks start to heat and I turned my back to them.

"You kissed someone?" Matt growled.

I ignored the men watching me as I moved over to the radio and shut it off. I started to head for the kitchen door. I was not about to tell Matt that I had kissed Axel. I was already mortified. I hadn't meant to tell Axel that he was my first kiss. I walked toward the lounge and took a seat on one of the rocking chairs. Axel came and sat in the chair next to mine. I glanced over and saw him studying me.

"Where is Duncan? Sara said you took him." I was desperate to get him to stop looking at me.

"At the moment, he's out in the barn." Axel answered.

I stood up and moved over to Matt. I placed Evelynn in his arms. I needed space away from Axel to figure out what to do about him. "You get to watch Evelynn while I go see my puppy." I said with a smile.

"But I don't know a single thing about babies." Matt stammered out as he held Evelynn awkwardly.

I maneuvered his arms so that she would be more comfortable, but he was still pretty stiff. "It's easy. Always support her head. She doesn't have the neck muscle to support herself yet. She was just fed and burped, so she should be fine for a while. Oh, if she needs a diaper change, call out for my mom or dad or call Axel's phone, and I'll come back." I turned to Axel and extended my hand. "Can I borrow your phone, please?" I asked.

"Not a chance, Trinity. I'm coming with you." Axel said, getting to his feet and moving towards the door.

I gave a shrug even though I was mentally screaming at him to give me space and followed him out as I ignored Matt's continued protest. I was practically bouncing with excitement as we stepped out onto the back lawn. Almost immediately, a dog started barking and whining from the barn. It sounded panicked and I increased my speed until I was practically running.

I threw open the door and was tackled to the ground by a much bigger Duncan. He was a large nine-month-old puppy instead of the small three-month-old pup I had left. He continued to whine as he licked my face and climbed all over me. I saw Axel lean his shoulder against the barn as he watched us, with a smile on his lips.

Once Duncan calmed down and I was able to get into a sitting position, Axel joined me on the grass. "I don't think he remembers you." He said with a laugh.

I laughed too, as I hugged Duncan. "I really missed you all." I said into the dog's scruff.

"We missed you too, Trin." Axel whispered.

I glanced over at him as I bumped him with my shoulder. "You might retract that once you see what Murphy and my dad have done." Axel lifted his brow in question. "They have turned your room into a space for me and Evelynn." I said with an apologetic look.

"Is that so?" Axel said, but I couldn't tell if he was irritated or pleased with the idea.

"They went out and bought out the whole store, I swear, and are now attempting to set everything up. They have a rocking chair, crib, bedside bassinet, dresser, the works. I told them that that wasn't my room, but Murphy just kept putting together the crib." I couldn't look at Axel, so I focused my attention on Duncan. Would he be angry? I couldn't blame him if he were. "I have a feeling that between Dad and Murphy, Evelynn is going to be the most spoiled little girl on the planet." I laughed as I leaned back on my hands and Duncan laid across my legs.

Duncan lifted his head, and I looked over to see what he was looking at. Dad was walking towards us with a smile on his face. "Hey sweetheart, we need to talk about the adoption forms." He said once he was closer.

Chapter 22

"What about them?" I asked in confusion. "I thought everything was already filled out."

"Everything except for Evelynn's last name." Dad said seriously. "Your mother and I think you need to figure out who the mark belongs to before submitting the paperwork."

"Who's to say he will even want Evelynn and me?" I said in irritation.

"We can ask Murphy to look into it. In order for you to receive the mark, you have had to have met him before. And you said the list is relatively small, right?" Dad pushed.

I pinched the bridge of my nose in an effort to calm myself. "Dad, we have been over this. I am not going to wait weeks just to shift through all my acquaintances, only to be turned away. I want Evelynn's adoption legalized as soon as possible. We only have four days left before we would have to fill it out again."

"I'm sorry, what mark?" Axel asked, confused.

"Trinity has a Bonding Mark. Her magic has affirmed a match for her, but she doesn't want to find the person with the matching mark." Dad explained and I felt my cheeks heat.

"Bonding Mark?" Axel asked.

"When a magic user finds someone that their magic sees as a perfect fit, it will bless the match. Both the magic user and the other person will receive a matching mark on their left shoulder blade. Her mother, Clara, and I have the mark. Clara's symbol is a rose. I have a rose that marks me as her Enforcer, but on the opposite side of that mark is a slightly different rose that is identical to Clara's." Dad continued to explain to Axel about the Bonding Mark. I prayed the earth would open up and swallow me whole.

"Yes, Trinity's mark is a wolf's head." Axel answered a question I must have missed.

"You are one of her Enforcers then?" Dad asked. "She mentioned having four."

"Yes, sir." Axel got to his feet and shook my father's hand. "My name is Axel Brooks."

"Nice to meet you, I'm Adam Sloan, Trinity's father." Dad hesitated before adding. "Can I see your mark?"

"Sir?" Axel asked, surprised.

"I just want to see the Enforcer Mark for Trinity. I haven't seen it yet. Murphy was telling me about it." Dad clarified.

Axel shrugged and pulled his shirt off. He turned to face me, presenting his mark to my dad. My eyes lowered to his chest, and I fought the blush that rose up my neck. I forgot how incredibly fit Axel was. I dropped my gaze to Duncan. I couldn't believe I had been checking Axel out.

Dad continued to study the mark far longer than was necessary. Dad's gaze darted to me before returning to Axel's back. "How long has it looked like this?" My dad asked in a soft tone. I looked back at them.

"Since the day she blessed me, sir." Axel answered without looking away from me.

Dad looked at me with an intensity I hadn't seen before. "What was your blessing, Trinity?" He asked in a no-nonsense tone. "You said that Noah's broke immediately and another one of the four had reacted to it, but you didn't feel anything."

"The blessing was the same for all of them." I said evasively. What was going on?

"What was it?" Dad said again as he walked over to me and grabbed my hand, pulling me to my feet.

"I...uh...I didn't want them to be stuck with me for life. That didn't seem fair. I was a danger magnet and I didn't want anyone to get hurt because of me." I said quickly and my dad raised an eyebrow.

"Trinity Hazel, what was the blessing?" He said more sternly.

Dad never used my middle name unless he was getting irritated with me. I looked down at my hands and willed myself not to blush. "I blessed them that once they fell in love, the Enforcer's Bond with me would break and they would share a similar bond with that person." I said quickly.

It was quiet for a second before my dad started laughing. I looked up at him and his eyes were shining with mirth. He pulled me behind Axel and turned me around. He grabbed my wrist and lifted my hand to a second wolf's head on the Guard's Mark.

I gasped. Axel had the same wolf's head that was on my shoulder. He did not have this the last time I saw his mark. When my fingertips lightly touched it, it shimmered blue, and warmth spread from my left shoulder where my mark was. Axel held perfectly still until my hand lowered to my side. He turned around slowly to face us. I could see the look of surprise and guilt in his eyes.

I didn't know what to say or do. I needed a moment. "Excuse me." I said softly as I walked to the barn and went inside. I took slow deep breaths as I tried to wrap my head around what had just happened. Axel had the same mark that was on me, and according to my dad, that meant my magic approved of him.

I had fallen in love with him sometime during the two months that I had lived at Murphy's. My heart started to beat faster. Oh, how I wanted to just throw my arms around him and not let go. But would he accept me now that I had Evelynn? He seemed to be a bit reserved about her, which is understandable.

The barn door opened slowly behind me, but I didn't turn around. "Trinity?" Axel asked softly. "Look at me, please." I didn't move and his hand touched my arm lightly as he stepped around me. "I would have told you if I knew what it meant. I didn't even know I had it until after you disappeared." His eyes were pleading for me to understand. "I nearly died that day; I thought I killed you. The only thing that kept me going was that Murphy said you were still alive because the Enforcer's Mark was still there. I have been going insane trying to find you." He rested his forehead against mine and took a deep breath.

Axel's phone started to ring but he didn't move to get it. "Axel, what if it's Matt?" I whispered. Axel pulled the phone from his pocket as he slipped his arm around me, keeping me close. I didn't know what to do with this version of Axel. I was feeling a little off balance after what he had just said.

Sure enough, it was Matt. As soon as Axel accepted the call, Evelynn's crying came over the line followed by a panicked Matt. "Poop is everywhere! It's up her back and out her legs! It's all over me!" he cried in horror.

"We will be right there." I said and Axel hung up the phone.

He slipped it into his pocket quickly and looked down at me. I rose up on my toes to press a quick kiss to his cheek, but he turned his head and our lips connected. Axel moved his hand to the back of my neck as he deepened the kiss and I melted against him. His phone dinged with a notification, and Axel let out a frustrated groan. I blushed as I stepped away. Axel began frantically digging in his pockets.

"What are you doing?" I asked curiously.

"Checking for my wallet." He smiled at me. I scoffed and he grabbed my hand before leading me out of the barn.

"I said I was sorry. And you instigated it the first time." I pointed out.

"I had definitely not planned on it. You took me completely by surprise. But I needed money for a ticket, and you seemed distracted, giving me an opportunity to get the wallet."

"So, it was just about the money?"

"I was trying to figure out how to get your wallet when you kissed me. I honestly don't even know why you did but I was able to get the wallet out before you pulled back."

"And the second kiss?"

"I was going to my death, and I didn't want my only kiss to be with me stealing your wallet."

"Was that really your first kiss?" Axel glanced over at me.

"Well...I mean there is this one boy that quickly became a favorite of mine." Axel slowed his steps and his hand tightened around mine. "I used to kiss him all the time before I left. And he was always very enthusiastic to receive them." Axel stopped walking and anger flashed in his eyes. "Duncan can be a bit slobbery at times though."

Axel closed his eyes, squeezed the bridge of his nose, and took a deep breath before he started walking again. I smirked at him when he finally glanced at me. "Careful. Keep doing that and I might just kiss you again." Axel muttered under his breath.

"Is that a threat or a promise?" I said with a lift of my eyebrow.

He stopped just inside the house. He pulled me to him, causing me to gasp in surprise. His lips quickly reclaimed mine. What had gotten into him? Not that I was complaining. I was really enjoying getting kissed by Axel. But he had been so angry when I left. Not to mention the fact that we were usually fighting whenever in close proximity. His phone started to ring again, and he pulled back, clearly frustrated.

"That is a promise, Trinity." He pressed a kiss to my forehead as we continued to the lounge.

"What took you so long?" Matt growled out, holding up Evelynn.

I laughed as I pulled the sweatshirt off before I took her from him. "It isn't even that bad, Matt." Evelynn's crying stopped as I held her close. "Matt is such a drama queen, isn't he?" I whispered loudly to Evelynn. "Come on, little one, let's go get you changed." I said, kissing her little head.

"Drama queen? There is more poop than baby. How did she even have that much in that tiny body?" Matt grumbled as he followed me out of the lounge.

We headed upstairs, and Matt ducked into his room while I went into Axel's. I found a clean outfit and diaper before heading to the bathroom. Axel watched as I carefully bathed Evelynn and got her dressed. It was only her second bath, and I was so new to this. When she was all cleaned up, I turned to find Axel leaning against the door frame.

"Can you watch Evelynn for me so that I can jump in a quick shower?" I asked as I walked up to him.

"Sure." He said as I started to put her into his arms. "Uh...what do I do?" he asked with uncertainty.

"Support her head. Yes, like that." I said softly as I helped Axel settle Evelynn into the crook of his arm.

"What next?" Axel didn't take his eyes off the baby as he asked with an anxious tone in his voice.

"That's it. If you want, you can stand and hold her or find some place to sit. Just as long as you take a step back so I can close the door." I smiled at him. He looked at me with a spark of amusement in his eyes as he took a step farther into the bathroom. I took a step back as he advanced toward me. His strides were bigger, and his free arm caught me around my waist. "Axel, I need a shower." I started to protest just as his lips met mine.

He pulled back with a smile. "Now, you can shower." He stepped out of the bathroom, and I closed the door.

I laughed softly as I turned the shower on. I don't think I would ever get tired of this playful, flirtatious, affectionate Axel. I took a quick shower, not wanting to be away from him or Evelynn for too long. I was drying off when I heard voices in the bedroom. I moved quietly as I continued to dry off as I listened in on the conversation.

"Where's Trinity?" Sara asked.

"She's taking a shower. Why, what's up?" Axel asked softly.

"Alright, where is my brother and what have you done with him?" Sara asked accusingly.

"Ha. Ha. Very funny." Axel said dryly.

"No seriously. For the last six months you have been in a very dark place, Axel. You snapped at everyone. I was beginning to think that I had lost my brother." Sara said, all hints of teasing gone.

"That's because my light was taken from me." Axel said firmly before softening his voice. "I am sorry for worrying you. The day Trinity disappeared, I felt like my soul was ripped from me." I placed a hand over my mouth to cover my gasp. He sounded like he was in pain. "I shot her, Sara. I could have killed her."

"But you didn't. That's one more thing I can thank her for, bringing my brother back." Sara said with a sniffle. It was quiet for a moment, and I started to run a brush through my hair. "She is precious, isn't she?" Sara's voice was soft, and I could hear the smile on her face.

"Honestly, I was a bit hesitant about her. When I first saw her, I thought she was Trinity's and some other guy's baby. That thought made my heart feel like it was ripped in half. Then Trinity told us who Evelynn's parents were, and I was shocked and frustrated. How could she care for that man's child?" Axel took a deep breath and my heart squeezed painfully. I feared he wouldn't be able to accept her. "Then I watched as Trinity acted so caring and loving to the baby. It seems so natural for her. She asked me to watch Evelynn while she showered. The moment she placed the baby in my arms, I couldn't see this little thing as Jason's anymore. Evelynn is Trinity's daughter."

"You seem pretty smitten with her." Sara observed.

"Just like her dang mother, this little girl didn't really give me a choice." Axel let out a soft chuckle and tears burned my eyes. Was he serious? Did he really not care so much that Evelynn was Jason's daughter?

"Well, I just came up here to tell you that dinner will be ready in about…twenty minutes now." Sara sounded like she was headed for the door. I heard the door close, and I wiped my tears.

I pulled my pants and bra back on and reached for my shirt. There was poop all over the side of it. Crap. I didn't have any other clothes up here. I wrapped the towel around my chest and cracked the bathroom door open. Axel turned to look over at me.

"Um…can I borrow one of your shirts? Evelynn left her mark on mine, and I didn't think about getting myself clean clothes before getting into the shower."

"You are welcome to my shirts anytime, Trinity." Axel said with a wink.

I felt a blush heat my cheeks as I pulled the door open and headed for the closet. I could feel his eyes on me as I moved across the room, and I pulled the towel tighter around myself. I stopped once I was inside and looked around. The closet had been rearranged and I wasn't sure where his T-shirts were.

"Trinity?" Axel said softly behind me, and I froze.

I looked over my shoulder and saw him standing in the doorway. "Where is Evelynn?" I asked as I tried to slow my heart rate.

"I put her in her crib." He took a small step towards me. "Can I see your mark?" he asked with uncertainty. I nodded as I turned my head back around as I moved my hair over my other shoulder so he could see it. I felt him move closer. He softly traced the wolf's head and with each touch of his fingers, my heart rate increased. "I can feel it on my mark when I touch yours." He whispered.

"When I touched yours, it shimmered blue." I said softly.

He put his hands on my hips as he pressed a kiss to the mark. Butterflies took flight in my stomach and my breathing hitched. His hands slid all the way around my waist as he stepped closer. I didn't know what to say or do as he continued to hold me with his face in my neck. We stood there for several minutes, and I started to relax back against him. Evelynn started to cry, and Axel pressed another quick kiss to my shoulder before stepping back. He headed for the bedroom.

"Where are all of your shirts?" I asked before he could leave. He took a look around and his brow knit in confusion. He pulled his shirt off before stepping back to me. He pulled it down over my head. "What are you doing?" I laughed. "Now you are without a shirt." I pointed out.

"I much rather have the guys looking at me shirtless than at you." He kissed my forehead before reaching around me and pulling a dress shirt off a hanger. "I can wear this one." He smirked at me when he saw me checking him out.

With his shirt over my head and torso, I allowed the towel to fall to the floor as I put my arms through the sleeves. Axel's eyes followed the towel as it fell. His gaze slowly returned to my face, and I stuck my tongue out at him as I tried to brush past him. He wrapped his arms tightly around me and I squeaked in surprise. I attempted to push away from him, but he only drew me closer.

"Axel, Evelynn is crying." I laughed and he grumbled as he let me go. When I picked her up and turned around, Axel was starting to button up his dark blue shirt that made his eyes pop. He caught me staring again and winked.

"Sara stopped in and said dinner would be ready soon. We should probably head down." Axel finished with his shirt and reached for Evelynn as I approached him. When I didn't hand her over, a pout appeared on his face. He looked like a young boy who was just told he couldn't have a cookie. "You have had her for the last..." His voice trailed off.

"Ten days." I supplied, trying to hide my smile.

"Really? She is only ten days old?" I nodded and he continued. "You have had her for the last ten days, it's my turn to snuggle with her."

"Is that so? I have never heard you say anything about liking kids before." I raised a brow. "You didn't even know how to hold her twenty minutes ago."

"That's because I never really thought about kids before. All the ones I have met are loud and messy and never listen. Then you had to go and put her in my arms. Now all I want is to hold her and..." He cleared his throat and reached for her again. I turned slightly away, blocking him.

"And what?" I asked.

Axel put his arms around me. "I want to hold her and you, Trinity." He pressed a kiss to my temple. "You have no idea how hard it has been not knowing where you were and constantly feeling like you were in danger."

I leaned into him, and his arms tightened. "If it makes you feel any better, I missed you too. But I can't let you have Evelynn during dinner." I stepped away and moved towards the door. "Your sister has already claimed her for that."

We walked into the dining room and mostly everyone was there. We were missing Trent, Liam, and Noah. I gave Evelynn to Sara before I quickly ran to the kitchen to get a bottle. I passed the bottle to Sara when I returned and took my seat between her and Axel. I looked up and gasped.

"What the heck happened to your face, Noah?" I asked as I studied his black eye and fat lip.

"That's what we all want to know." Sara snapped. Clearly Noah was refusing to talk about it.

"He said something he shouldn't have." Liam commented stiffly.

"Liam, why did you hit Noah?" I asked in disbelief. The table fell silent as everyone waited to hear what happened. "Geez, you two are acting like toddlers." I snapped as I stood.

I tried to move to Noah's side, but Liam grabbed my arm, stopping me. "Don't you dare heal him, Trin. Not until he apologizes."

"Apologize? For what?" I looked between them, but they just glared at each other. My frustration with them grew and I felt my magic flowing through me. They both swallowed hard as they tensed.

"Trin, your eyes are glowing again." Matt pointed out. "Don't make her that mad, Trent. She makes you feel like your head is going to explode." He stage-whispered.

"I'm sorry, Trinity. I was frustrated, and I wasn't thinking before speaking." Noah said quickly.

"What is going on?" I asked in frustration. "Just spit it out you two."

"Noah didn't understand how you could adopt the illegitimate child of the man that kidnapped you. He said Evelynn was literally the spawn of an evil man and he didn't want you to have to deal with that kind of darkness anymore. Blah, blah, blah. More words were said. Liam popped Noah once and he fell to the floor. Fists flew a few times. I took them to the castle and locked them in the V.I.P. room. I explained about the chains hanging from the ceiling before giving them the grand tour of the dungeon. I let them see our living conditions and the tortures we were forced to watch each other go through. Especially Tracy's. Then I brought them back here." Trent supplied the story. I was pretty sure it was a watered-down version.

The room was deathly quiet, and Sara was glaring at Noah. My anger instantly cooled, and I started to laugh before I reached out and healed Noah. I moved back to my seat and began eating while everyone watched me with wide eyes.

"Aren't you upset, Trinity?" Liam asked in disbelief.

"How can I be upset when I struggled with the same thoughts, for months, before Evelynn was born?" I asked with a shoulder shrug. "Trent and I had so many conversations about why Mom and Dad would agree to adopt Tracy's baby, given who the father was. We weren't exactly happy about the thought."

"What changed?" Axel asked curiously.

"My dad told me that the baby was innocent. The father was the one who was responsible for his own crimes. The child and its mother had nothing to do with it. That softened me a little, but I still wasn't fully comfortable with the idea of having a sibling that was fathered by that man." I smiled at Mom and Dad.

"Jason was a monster." Trent grumbled. "Lucy and Grace were just as bad."

"The day Evelynn was born; Mom offered the brand-new baby to her mother. Tracy was so traumatized by what Jason had done to her that she literally turned away from her own child and refused to even look at her. Mom then gave the crying baby to me, and I was the one who cleaned her up and fed her. Tracy asked if I would be the one to take care of the baby instead of my parents. I was surprised by the request, and it took me a few hours to decide." I looked over at Evelynn in Sara's arms.

"What made you decide to adopt her instead of having your parents take her?" Noah asked quietly.

"As I held the baby, I couldn't imagine not having her in my life. I felt the need to provide her with a life that she should have had. One with a loving family and a care-free childhood. Her father was a terrible man and was dead, while her mother couldn't even look at her without reliving the trauma she sustained. I couldn't turn her away as well. She has done nothing wrong, and it wouldn't be fair to her to have to grow up with no one to care for her." Sara sniffed as she pressed a kiss to Evelynn's head.

"Trinity, I am so sorry. I shouldn't have questioned you. It was a shock to see you and then you had the baby. I was way out of line." Noah said as he hung his head.

"Noah, it's fine. I promise. All I ask is that you give her a chance. After all, she is only ten days old and hasn't done much." I smiled at him.

"Not much to you maybe. She literally pooped all over me." Matt whined.

Everyone laughed and the tension broke. I glanced at Matt, and he winked at me. Bless him for stepping in. The meal went smoothly after that. I finished my food first and Sara handed Evelynn back to me so that she could finish her meal.

As I walked out of the room, I could feel Axel's eyes on me. I didn't look back and headed to the lounge. I turned on the TV and settled into a rocking chair. Trent popped in a few minutes later with a huge grin on his face.

"That Axel guy is so cool. I have never seen someone eat so fast." Trent laughed. "As soon as you left, he got anxious. His leg kept bouncing under the table and Sara kept telling him to chill. I think he likes you, sis."

"Trent, you are on dish duty tonight with your father! You have two minutes to report to the kitchen, young man!" Mom's voice called down the hall. I laughed at the face Trent pulled before he disappeared.

Matt and Axel walked in a moment later. Axel moved to the chair next to mine. He grabbed the blanket that was draped over the back of his chair and laid it over my lap. I smiled a thank you before passing the remote to him.

Axel and Matt settled on a football game, and I started to doze off. I never did get the nap I wanted, and I was exhausted. My eyes drifted closed but I was still somewhat aware of the game.

"Motherhood looks good on her." Matt commented softly.

"It sure does." Axel murmured. "I should get them up to bed."

"If you pick them up, I can take you up there." Trent's comment was followed by a startled squeak.

"Holy crap kid, stop doing that." Matt scolded. "You're going to give me a heart attack one day."

"You'll get used to it." Trent laughed.

I felt someone, I assumed Axel, pick me up and my arms tightened around Evelynn. He took a wobbly step forward. "That was weird." Axel commented as he laid me down on the bed. Evelynn was gently lifted off my chest and I immediately felt her loss.

"Evelynn doesn't sleep much at night. Trinity goes to great lengths to try to allow the rest of us to get sleep though. Mom said with them up here, it will be easier on Trinity. You seem pretty interested in her." Trent rambled on as he moved around the room.

"Your mother is probably right about Trinity having an easier time up here. The walls are thicker, so she won't need to worry about Evelynn's cries waking anyone." Axel said softly. "And I am interested in her."

"Do you love her?" Trent asked. "Dad and Mom didn't know I heard when they said that it was hard to watch Trinity being so lovesick. Mom told Dad that they needed to find out who he was, so Trinity would eat again. Dad said he wasn't so sure that was the reason Trinity stopped eating much. His theory was that Trinity just didn't want to throw up from the pain she suffered when they took her." *Stop talking Trent.* I wanted to die. I can't believe he was talking to Axel about this.

Chapter 23

"Was she really that bad?" Axel asked curiously.

"The first six weeks she was…well, she spent a lot of time sleeping between sessions. It was really tense. Mom cried a lot and Dad, if he wasn't' comforting Mom, he would pace. Mom had to heal his hand several times after he broke it punching the wall." Trent said sadly.

"Why were things so tense? Was it because of the gunshot?" Axel asked.

"No, that was nothing compared to them trying to pull Trinity's magic. They would drag her out while Mom and Dad begged for them to leave her alone. Within ten minutes we could hear her screams." Trent's voice had dropped to a whisper. "The screams would last for thirty to forty minutes. We would all cry. Mom even threw up a few times." Trent was crying now, and my heart broke. I didn't realize they could hear me. "Once the screaming stopped, Trinity was usually dumped back in with us. Sometimes they left her hanging there for a while before bringing her back. She was barely conscious, and her back would be covered in blood. Mom would immediately start to heal her." He stopped talking as he continued to cry. "I heard Trin telling Mom and Dad that they did that to her every few months for years."

"Trent, I'm so sorry you had to go through that." Axel's voice was soft and it sounded like he was standing next to Trent. "I can't even imagine what you have gone through."

"Every other day for six weeks until they finally gave up." Trent cried. It was quiet for a long time except for Trent's muffled crying. He finally sniffed. "Don't tell Trinity that I heard her. She tried to protect me from seeing the abuse they dealt to her." Trent begged.

"Your secret is safe with me." Axel's voice sounded strained. "Why don't you head off to bed and tomorrow we can go play with Duncan at the lake." Trent thanked Axel and then silence fell around me.

I was too afraid to move. I felt so sick that they had heard all of my screams and had to deal with the resulting trauma. The bed shifted and I felt Axel scoot up behind me. "I know I should go, but I can't leave you just yet." He whispered, his voice sounding so full of pain.

I rolled over to face him as he laid his arm over my waist. "Axel?" I said quietly. He squeezed his eyes shut as he pressed his lips to my forehead. "Axel?" I tried again.

"I just need to hold you for a minute." His voice was thick with emotion. I wrapped my arm around his waist as he pulled me closer to him. He started to shake as he cried silently. After several minutes his shaking stopped, and I snuggled closer to him. "I should have been there. I should have been able to stop it." Axel whispered.

I took his face in my hands and forced him to look at me. "No. If you were there with me, then Jason would still be alive. If he were still alive, I would either be dead or in the same position Tracy was in." I whispered firmly. I didn't want Evelynn to wake up, but I needed Axel to know that everything worked out the way it was supposed to. I pressed a kiss to his lips. "You saved me by taking that shot." I looked into his eyes. They were red from crying and filled with pain. I kissed him again. "And if you hadn't taken that shot when you did, I wouldn't have found my parents, Jason would be alive along with his sisters and I would still be in danger. Not to mention, we wouldn't have Evelynn." I looked into his eyes begging him to not feel guilty.

He pressed his forehead to mine as he closed his eyes. "Never again, Trinity. Promise me you will never leave me again." He whispered.

"I promise. Now, we should probably go to sleep before the night gremlin wakes up." I warned.

"Good night, Trinity." Axel pressed a kiss to my lips before he slowly went to get up.

"Good night, Axel." I whispered as I cuddled up to him and wrapped my arms around his waist.

"What are you doing?" he asked with a little laugh.

"Going to sleep and you should too." I yawned as I closed my eyes.

"Trinity, as much as I would love to stay in bed with you, I don't think I should." He said softly with regret in his voice.

"We can talk about your complaints with our current situation in the morning. But if you get up, I will lock you out of here for days." I smiled to myself at the thought of how angry he would be.

"Your brother likes me; he would bring me up here." Axel retorted.

"Fine." I said and rolled over.

There was a momentary pause before Axel pulled me back to his chest and wrapped his arms around me. He pressed a kiss to my neck. "Just this once, Trinity. Then not again until we have a serious talk." He whispered. I smiled as I closed my eyes.

Evelynn's whimpers that preceded her screaming woke me from a deep sleep. I groaned and sat up. Axel sat up sleepily next to me. "What time is it?" Axel mumbled.

I glanced at the clock and yawned. "It's 1:00am." Evelynn's whimpers picked up and turned into a full-blown cry. I scooted to the edge of the bed and stood up. I picked her up and began bouncing her as I tried to soothe her.

"We came to bed only an hour ago." Axel fell back on the pillows.

I laughed. "I need to make a bottle." I said as I took a step towards the door.

"I will get it. You stay here." Axel got out of bed and headed for the door but paused just before opening it. "How do I make it?"

"One scoop for every two ounces of water. Make four ounces. The water needs to be warm but not hot." I said as I patted Evelynn's back. He nodded and left. I hummed to the little girl as we waited for Axel to get back. It didn't take long for him to return. "Thank you." I reached for the bottle.

"Hand me the night gremlin and you go back to bed." Axel said reaching for Evelynn. He lifted her from my arms and moved to the rocking chair. I stood there and watched him settle in as Evelynn began to eat eagerly. He looked up and saw me still standing there. "Go back to bed, Trin. I've got her this time." I smiled tiredly at him as I crawled back under the covers. I slipped my jeans off to get more comfortable and tossed them on the floor. I fell asleep watching Axel rocking Evelynn.

"Trinity, I'm so sorry to wake you." Axel whispered as he brushed the hair off of my face. "I don't know how to change a diaper."

I slowly sat up and looked around the room, trying to orient myself. Axel was holding a sleeping Evelynn, but he was right, her diaper was close to bursting. I got out of bed and quietly moved to the changing table to collect the wipes and diaper. I moved back to Axel's side.

"Put her in the bassinet." I instructed. He did so softly and thankfully the little girl stayed asleep. I quickly changed her diaper and put a blanket over her before returning to the bed.

Axel settled back down next to me with a tired sigh. "Night gremlin indeed." He whispered and I laughed softly as I laid my head on his shoulder.

"You should sleep while you can because she will be up in about two hours." I whispered back and I heard him groan.

*   *   *

"They look exhausted." Mom said softly.

"What do you expect from new parents." Dad whispered. "Come on, let's take Evelynn downstairs and let them sleep."

"We cannot just let them sleep like this. We know nothing about him." Mom protested. "We should wake them up."

"This is the first time I have seen Trinity sleeping peacefully. She usually is tossing and turning with nightmares. So no, I am not going to wake her up. We can talk to them about rules later today." Dad said as his voice moved closer to the door. There was a soft click as the door closed and then silence.

I opened my eyes and blinked several times as I looked over to find Evelynn's bed empty. I momentarily panicked, even though I heard my parents take her. I sat up quickly and looked around. Strong arms wrapped around me before pulling me back down on the mattress.

"Baby, you heard your parents. They took Evelynn so we could sleep more." Axel mumbled sleepily in my ear. He pressed a kiss to my head, and I relaxed in his arms, allowing myself to fall back to sleep.

I woke a little while later. Axel was still asleep, and I slid off the bed. I glanced at the clock on my way to the bathroom. It was 11:00am. I finished getting dressed and opened the door. Axel was stretching as he sat on the edge of the bed.

"Good morning." I smiled at him.

"Is she like that every night?" Axel asked. I nodded and laughed at Axel's horrified expression. "No wonder you looked so tired yesterday."

"Come on, let's get something to eat and I need to check on Evelynn." I grabbed his hand as I headed out into the hall.

Mom's smile was tight as she greeted us when we walked into the kitchen. "There you two are. Have a rough night?" She asked.

"It was actually better than most. She slept a little more." I said with a yawn.

"Here, eat this really quick and then you need to get ready, Trinity." She handed us each a plate of eggs. "Your father found out that you have to be there to submit the papers."

"What time do the courts close?" I asked.

"They close early today. I think your dad said they close at 1:00pm, but then they are closed for the rest of the week." Mom said looking at the clock. "When you get back, Trinity, your father and I want to talk with you. We understand that you have lived a different life than what we had wanted for you but now that we are a family again, we have some rules."

"Okay, Mom. Talk about rules later, got it." I shoveled two big bites into my mouth before I jumped from my chair and ran down the hall to Sara's and my room. Just in case there were any sort of delay, I needed to leave in the next fifteen minutes in order to get there a little early. I brushed my hair and pulled it into a high ponytail before changing into a clean pair of skinny jeans and blouse. I shoved my feet into a pair of cowgirl boots and left the room.

"Dad!" I called as I moved down the hallway. He peeked his head out of Murphy's office. "I need the adoption papers. I'm heading out to file them." I said, giving him a quick hug. He pulled them out of a drawer in the desk before he passed them to me. He too made a comment about setting rules and Murphy laughed as I left. I headed back to the kitchen and Mom was still there with Evelynn as she cleaned up breakfast. "Can you watch Evelynn while I'm gone?"

"Of course, baby girl. But sweetheart, you need to start eating more." Mom put a hand on her hip. "You have lost too much weight."

"I will, Mom. I promise but I have to leave now in order to get this done. I'll eat something when I get back." I said as I rushed out. I needed to find someone to drive me.

"What's your hurry, Trin?" Matt asked as I bumped into him when I reached the entry hall.

"I have to get to the courthouse as soon as possible. Do you know anyone who can drive me?" I asked as I continued out the front door.

"I'm taking you, Trinity." Axel said as he came down the stairs with his keys in his hand. We jumped into his truck and headed down the road. My leg was bouncing anxiously as we drove in silence. Axel reached across the middle console and held my hand as he drove. With my free hand, I started to play with his fingers that were laced through mine.

Even though Axel parked as close as he could, we still had a longer walk than I wanted. He rounded the hood as I stepped out. He took my hand again and kissed it. "It's okay, Trinity. We got this." Axel said as we walked into the building.

It was just after 12:00pm, yet I still felt pressed for time. Axel pulled me to a stop as he looked to his right. "What is it?" I asked out of breath from our brisk walk from the parking lot. He turned to look at me and I could tell he was thinking over something. "Axel, we need to go." I said, trying to pull him forward.

Instead of following me, he pulled me into an alcove before cupping my face. "Trinity, what if we got married first?" He searched my eyes for something.

"What?" I asked breathlessly.

"I don't want last night to be a one-time thing, Trinity. I want to go to bed with you each night and wake up next to you each morning. I don't want to have to sleep down the hall on a blow-up mattress in Matt's room, wishing I was with you." He looked at me with such desperation. "I told you last night would be the last time, and I meant it. I will not risk putting us in a situation that we might regret later."

I studied his earnest face for several minutes. I would love not to have to be separated from him anymore, but I couldn't be married to a man that didn't love me. I knew he cared for me, but I didn't know the extent of his feelings. I also needed to know what he thought about Evelynn.

"Axel, I…" I closed my eyes and felt a tear slip down my cheek. This was so hard, but I needed to tell him no, until I got my questions answered.

My hesitation made him tense, and I could feel his disappointment. He pressed a kiss to my forehead. "I love you, Trinity. If you need more time, I can wait." He whispered.

"What did you say?" I asked as I stepped back so that I could see his face better.

"If you need more time, I can wait." He said again.

"No, before that." I said scanning his face for any hint that he was lying.

His mouth turned up at one corner. "I love you, Trinity Sloan." He said again as he stared intently into my eyes.

I let out a quick laugh as I threw my arms around his neck. I pressed my lips to his and felt him smile. His arms wrapped around my waist and lifted me off the floor.

A throat cleared and we broke our kiss. Axel slowly put me back on my feet but kept his arms around me. A man in a suit was standing a few feet away watching us with a lifted brow.

"Can I help you kids with something?" he asked with an amused smile.

"Uh…well I had hoped to convince my girl to finally marry me but…" Axel started to say.

My hands were still resting on Axel's shoulders, and I reached behind his neck and tugged on his hair. His eyes snapped back to me in surprise. "We don't have a marriage license." I finished his sentence.

"Actually, I do." Axel reached into his pocket and pulled out his wallet. He withdrew a folded piece of paper and offered it to me. "I've had it since that night." He explained. "It expires next week."

"Follow me." The man gestured for us to follow him as he began to walk down the hall.

"But we need to file adoption papers before the office closes." I said and the man's feet faltered for a step before he continued.

We followed him up a flight of stairs and into an office. He closed the door behind us and gestured for us to take a seat. We hesitated but took the offered chairs, Axel keeping a hold of my hand the whole time. "So, tell me about your situation. It seems quite unique." The man took his seat behind the desk and gave us a kind smile.

"Trinity was asked to adopt the newborn of a friend. We have all the necessary documents. But before we file, I would very much like to make Trinity my wife and sign the adoption papers as well." Axel explained.

"And you are agreeable to this plan?" The man asked. My grip on Axel's hand tightened as I glanced over at him. He was watching me carefully with a whole mix of emotions in his eyes. I looked back at the man and gave him a nod as I fought the tears that threatened to fall. "In that case, you will need a judge to sign off on your changes to the adoption papers. I will be right back. I need to find a couple of witnesses." The man stood with a large smile on his face and left the room, leaving the door ajar.

As soon as he left, Axel was kneeling in front of me cupping my face with questions in his eyes. "What changed? Not that I'm complaining. But I thought you wanted to wait."

"I got my questions answered." I managed to whisper. When he furrowed his brows in confusion, I smiled as a single tear escaped and ran down my cheek. Axel used his thumb to gently brush it away. "I didn't know how you felt about Evelynn or me." My voice was barely louder than a whisper.

Axel gave me a crooked smile. "Is that all?" He leaned forward and gave me a quick kiss before resting his forehead against mine. "I love you and I love our little girl." He whispered.

"I am still nervous though." I whispered back.

"Trinity, we got this." Axel brushed a light kiss to my lips.

"Alright kids, are you ready?" The man returned, followed by a man and a woman. Axel got to his feet and helped me to stand next to him. "My name is Judge Jon Michaels, and this is Donald Renolds, from vital records and Margrete Michaels, head of the adoptions department." My hands began to shake as the judge began to perform the marriage ceremony. Before I knew it both Axel and I answered in the affirmative and we were pronounced husband and wife. I let out a startled squeak as Axel pulled me to him and pressed his lips to mine. I was still trying to process everything and wasn't expecting it. The judge and our two witnesses laughed.

Axel had the biggest smile on his face, and I wrapped my arms around him, needing to feel him close. Margrete stepped up to the desk and smiled at us. "So, the judge here says you have adoption papers?"

"Yes." I pulled the papers out of my handbag. "A friend asked me to adopt her daughter once she was born. She is a minor and her father is her guardian. We got everything signed and filled out just after the baby was born." I explained as I handed the papers to the woman.

She started to look through the papers and Axel placed his hand on my back. "Am I to assume you are wanting to change your last name on this considering...?" I blushed as I nodded. "And there is no last name for the child yet." Margrete pointed out.

"Trinity, before you have any questions, I would love for her to have our last name." Axel whispered into my ear, and I turned to smile at him. "Evelynn's last name will be Brooks." Axel said as he kissed my forehead.

"Sounds great." Margrete handed me a pen. "Just make the corrections and Mr. Brooks, I need you to add your information under the father category." I quickly added Brooks after mine and Evelynn's names. I passed the pen over to Axel and he leaned over the papers as he began filling out his information.

I couldn't believe what was happening. I came today, expecting to just file the paperwork and within thirty minutes I got married and now Axel was filling out the paperwork to adopt Evelynn right alongside me. "I need you to finish signing the marriage certificate and I think that is it." Judge Micheals rubbed his hands together.

When all the paperwork was properly signed, Judge Micheals handed us our marriage certificate and a copy of the adoption papers with a promise that a birth certificate would be mailed to us within a week. "Thank you so much, sir." Axel smiled. We shook everyone's hands before exiting the courthouse.

Axel pulled me to the truck. He put the papers into the back seat before tugging me up against him and claiming my lips. He finally broke the kiss, and I leaned back against the truck breathing hard.

"You do realize, I still need to breathe, right?" I laughed.

"I think you are just going to have to get use to the idea of feeling breathless all the time, Love." Axel smiled at me as he took a step closer.

"Axel, no." I giggled as he tried to kiss me again and I turned my head. "We need to get back home." Axel started to kiss my neck and I pushed on his chest. "Axel, stop." I laughed. "That tickles." I felt him smile as he pressed one more kiss to my neck.

He leaned back with a serious expression on his face as he narrowed his eyes at me. "I just realized something." He paused as he continued to study me. "I told you that I loved you, we got married, and adopted a child together, yet you still haven't told me how you feel about me."

I laughed. He was right, I have never told him that I loved him. "It's not my fault that you can't think logically about these things like I can. I mean, I was prepared to wait until I figured out how you felt about me, and you just strapped yourself to a woman who could totally hate you." I teased him.

Axel went to say something, but his phone started to ring. "This conversation is not over." He said as he answered the phone. "Hello?" He paused. "We got here in time and got everything all squared away." He listened. I inched around the bed of the truck and slipped into my seat and locked my door. "No, we will be back for dinner." He paused again. "Okay, see you later." He hung up the phone and looked around. When he spotted me in the truck, he opened his door and climbed in. "We need to talk about this, Trinity." He glared at me.

"I thought you said we were leaving?" I asked innocently.

Axel started the truck and began to drive without saying another word. We were halfway home when he pulled off the highway and onto a dirt road that led into the forest. He drove for another twenty minutes before putting the truck into park. I wasn't sure where we were. The trees were so dense that I couldn't see through them. When I looked over at Axel, he pulled a lever, and his seat slid all the way back. Axel unclicked my seatbelt as he pulled me across the cab into his lap.

"Trinity." He warned.

"Axel." I said his name in the same way.

"You are going to be the death of me, you know that?" He muttered as he buried his face in my neck.

I snuggled up against him. "You want to know my secret?" I asked him and he nodded but didn't lift his head. I poked his ribs until he raised his head and glared at me. I cupped his face with my hands and kissed him slowly.

His hands moved to the back of my neck. I finally broke the kiss and touched my nose to his. "I left that night because of you." I whispered.

Axel stiffened and leaned back. He looked at me in surprise. "You ran away because of me?"

"Mmhmm." I nodded. "You scared me, Axel." I sat up more and looked across the truck cab. "Jason had taken away my parents. And then he was threatening the only other family I had. I was scared that he would take away everyone I loved. Then you guys came up with that hair brained plan to marry me off and send me away. I panicked the moment you agreed."

"Why?" Axel asked softly.

"Because I saw us as my parents. Getting married and going into hiding didn't save them." I looked back at him. "And I knew that if Jason found us, he would use you to get me to do whatever it was he wanted. That is what he does, Axel; he takes those you love and tortures them in front of you to keep you compliant." I closed my eyes. "And you were my biggest weakness."

Axel stroked my cheek with his thumb until I looked at him. "I love you, Trinity." He said with so much feeling that tears gathered in my eyes again.

"I love you, Axel." I whispered just before his lips pressed to mine.

We stayed there for a while. Tucked away from the world, surrounded by nature. Just me and Axel. I had never felt so at peace. Axel's phone dinged and he looked at it. Matt was asking if they were going to train later today. Axel told him 'no' before tossing his phone in the front seat and pulling me close.

An hour later we were pulling back onto the main road. It was hard to want to return to normal life, but we had been gone for hours and I knew my parents wanted to speak to me about rules.

Axel held tight to my hand as he drove. We were pulling onto the long driveway when I turned to look at him with wide eyes. "What are we going to tell my parents?" I asked in a near panic. They are going to be so upset that I got married without them.

Axel slowed the truck as we continued toward the house. "I didn't think about that. Crap. We can have a ring ceremony or something and just not tell anyone we are actually married yet." Axel suggested.

"How are we going to keep this a secret?" I asked, not seeing how we were going to manage it when we couldn't seem to stop touching in some way since the courthouse.

"I don't think anyone will notice unless we are making out on the couch or something." Axel smiled over at me.

"So, you're planning on sleeping in Matt's room?" I asked with a laugh.

"Okay so we go as long as possible without anyone noticing." Axel amended. "I am sleeping with *my* wife, in *our* bed, in *our* room." Axel stopped the truck and cut the engine. "And I will put our papers in my personal safe."

Axel squeezed my hand before we got out of the truck. We were a few feet apart as we walked side by side into the house. Axel glanced around quickly. A crooked grin spread on his face as he backed me up against the door and kissed me.

"You are going to get us caught." I whispered against his lips as I smiled. Axel's hands went under my shirt as they slipped around my waist and up my back. He looked anything but worried.

"I love you. It's a good thing we spent some time in the woods before we came back home." He whispered before stealing a quick kiss and heading upstairs with the marriage certificate and adoption paperwork. I watched him go with a big smile on my face as I fixed my shirt.

I found everyone in the lounge watching 'Pure Luck'. There were open seats next to Murphy and Matt. I took the seat next to Matt and settled back against the cushion. Mom brought me Evelynn and I pressed a kiss to her head before I snuggled her close.

"How did it go, hun?" Mom asked.

I gave her a smile. "Evelynn Dawn is an official member of the family. They approved it right there and gave me a copy for my records." Everyone congratulated me and was excited.

"You finally chose a last name, then?" Dad asked.

"Yes, Dad, I did." I smiled at him. "And just like I told you before, she has the same last name I do." The disappointment in Dad's eyes made me feel a little guilty.

Just then Axel walked in and paused just inside the door. "Why so glum?" He asked. His eyes scanned the room until they found me. He scowled before moving to sit by Murphy.

"Trinity just told Dad that Evie's last name is the same as hers and he is upset that she didn't wait to find her guy." Trent said while keeping his eyes on the TV.

"Evie?" I said with a laugh. "You finally settled on a nickname, Trenton?" I gave Axel a slight shake of my head, so that he knew that they still didn't know about us.

"I think it fits her best, don't you? Lynn just seems too… calm for her." Trent smiled over at me, and I sent him a wink.

We all settled in to finish the movie. Once it was over, I took Evie up for a nap before dinner. I had just laid her in her crib when hands came around my waist. "Was it really necessary to lean up against Matt?" Axel asked softly.

I turned around and put my arms around his neck. "I fell asleep, Axel. I didn't do it on purpose." I kissed his nose. "What brings you up here?"

"I came to get a power nap with my wife." Axel said as he pulled me towards the bed. I willingly climbed in next to him and snuggled up to his side before I closed my eyes. I was so tired after the long night with Evelyn and then this afternoon. "I'll wake you up when it's time for dinner." Axel pressed a kiss to my head.

Chapter 24

A throat cleared, startling me awake. I sat up quickly when I noticed that Mom, Dad, Liam, Trent, Murphy, Matt, Noah, and Sara were standing at the end of the bed. Axel was still asleep next to me, and I smacked his chest. He jerked awake. "What was that for?" He asked, a little disoriented. I pointed at everyone, and he let out a groan before sitting up slowly.

"What is going on?" Mom asked with barely restrained anger. "I wasn't happy about it this morning, but your father convinced me it was probably a one-time thing." She placed her hands on her hips.

"Axel, I know you were raised better than this." Murphy said softly.

"Better than what? What do you think is going on?" Axel asked, irritated. "Look, Mrs. Sloan, I know you don't know me, but I promise I would never do anything to hurt your daughter." Axel said firmly but softer than how he spoke to Murphy.

"Except shoot her." Liam muttered and I shot him a glare.

"Thanks, Liam." Axel huffed.

"Axel, it looks like you were sleeping with Trinity." Sara said with a straight face, but I could see the glint of humor in her eyes.

"Oh, good because I thought it looked like we were playing Uno or Phase 10." I muttered. Someone snorted.

"Trinity, this is serious. You can't just share a bed with a man." Mom cried. I felt my cheeks heat and I heard Axel cough.

I elbowed him hard. "Hey." He grabbed his ribs.

"Told you." I whispered to him before getting out of bed. It was really awkward sitting there with everyone staring at us. "Mom, calm down. It's not what you think." I said as Axel stood up beside me. And that's when I noticed he didn't have a shirt on. "Really, Axel? No shirt?" I rolled my eyes.

Axel shrugged. "You're like a heater." He said before he wove through everyone and headed for the closet. Matt followed him, while Mom glared at me. When Matt and Axel came back out, Matt was grinning ear to ear. He looked like he was going to burst out laughing at any minute.

Other than Matt's obvious excitement, it was tense in the room, and I glanced back at Axel. I didn't know what to do or say. "Trinity, would you like to show your parents the adoption and other paperwork?" He was leaving the choice to tell them up to me.

"We have already seen it." Mother snapped at Axel. I walked over to Axel and grabbed the papers before turning back to the group. Axel's hand touched my back lightly and I took a deep breath. I put the marriage certificate on the bottom and handed the stack of papers to my mom. She glared at me for a minute before looking down. "Evelynn Dawn Brooks? Whose last name is Brooks?" She asked, confused.

"Keep reading." I pointed back to the papers.

"I thought you said Evelynn's last name and yours are the same?" Dad asked in confusion as he read over Mom's shoulder. Mom's eyes were wide when she looked back up.

"It is." Mom breathed out. "What have you done, Trinity? You said you would not get married unless you found the one with the Bonding Mark." Mom was very upset. Her eyes began to glow softly, and I felt a weight press on me.

"She has." Axel spoke up behind me.

"It's true sweetheart, I have seen the mark on him. But why not wait for us to be there?" Dad looked really hurt.

"Dad, I'm sorry. We needed to get Evelynn's paperwork in as quickly as possible. If we didn't get the papers turned in today, we would have to refill everything out. I didn't want to have to put Tracy through anymore. We didn't plan on it but while we were at the courthouse, it just..." my voice trailed off. I was having trouble explaining exactly what happened because I was still trying to sort it out myself.

Axel's arms circled me from behind. "I was planning on marrying your daughter before she disappeared. I still had the marriage license in my wallet. While at the courthouse, we decided it would be better to get married and then submit the adoption papers so we wouldn't have to change anything afterwards." Axel explained.

"I have a sister!" Sara yelled and Evelynn immediately started to cry.

"Thanks, sis." Axel shot Sara a glare as he walked over and picked up Evelynn, settling her against his shoulder. He patted the little girl's back as he gently bounced her. Evelynn quickly calmed down and Axel placed a kiss on her head before handing her to me. "I had to watch as Trinity disappeared into thin air without any hint of where she had gone. Then I had to spend the next six months going out of my mind trying to locate her while feeling like I was drowning. Call me selfish but I am not ready to go another day without her." he said firmly, crossing his arms over his chest.

Dad and Murphy started to laugh, and Mom smacked Dad's arm as she glared at him. "Clara, Trinity isn't our eight-year-old little girl anymore. While we were in limbo, she grew up and fell in love. You can't be upset with them for doing what we did, minus the adoption part. I recall Murphy being pretty angry we didn't contact him for a wedding." Dad hugged Mom and she wiped her eyes. "And we lived in a tent together for almost a year before we got married."

"Yeah, but you were insufferable, and we fought nonstop." Mom sniffled.

"You should have heard Axel and Trinity for the two months she was here." Murphy chuckled. "I swear I was watching the two of you again."

I looked around the room to see Matt, Liam, Noah, and Sara with huge grins on their faces. All the tension in the room slowly faded. Axel returned to my side and grabbed my left hand. He slipped a ring on my finger before kissing me. Sara squealed and Noah kissed her as he backed out of the room.

We migrated down to the dining room for dinner as Murphy continued telling Mom and Dad about Axel and my many fights. Sara suggested we do a ring ceremony the same day as Noah and her wedding. She was beyond excited that Axel and I were officially married. I did see Matt, Noah, and Liam hand her money in the hall as she did a victory dance.

When I asked her about it, she said they had a bet. She bet that Axel and I would get married before her and Noah did. I asked her when they placed bets, and she said it was after the whole Duncan incident. Axel hadn't been amused by his sister and friend's antics, but I found it hilarious.

As the weeks passed, life settled into a comfortable routine. Axel and I were finally starting to figure out our new relationship. It was strange going from arguing all the time to Axel's constant desire to cuddle and be with me. We were also learning a lot about how to take care of Evelynn.

I had been home for two months when Sara came into my room with a huge smile on her face. "What are your plans for tomorrow?" she asked as she plopped down on the bed.

I finished changing Evie's diaper and turned around to face her. "Evie has an appointment at the pediatrician's around 11:00am. Why?"

"Can you go to town early with me? I have an appointment at the woman doctor, and I don't want to go alone. We can go a little early and pick you up a cell phone too." Sara asked as she gave me puppy dog eyes.

"Sure. What time do you want to leave?" I handed Evelynn over to Sara and we walked out of the room together.

"We can leave at 7:30am so we can get your phone. My appointment isn't until a little later." Sara gave me a grateful smile as we headed into the kitchen to help with dinner.

The night passed normally. Axel and I headed to bed by 9:00pm with Evie. She was getting better at sleeping through the night, thankfully.

Axel woke me up at 6:00am to tell me that he and the guys were heading out to the shooting range with Trent and Dad. He gave me a kiss before he left. His kiss turned to three and then he was late. I wasn't going to be able to go back to sleep after that, so I got up and showered before getting Evelynn ready for our outing with Sara.

We met at the car and Sara smiled nervously at me as she started to drive towards town. "What is this appointment of yours that has you so nervous?" I asked curiously. Sara was normally bubbly and happy. It was strange to see her so out of sorts.

"With the wedding being less than two months away, I need to get on birth control." She said with a blush. I choked on the water I was sipping. Birth control? I had never thought about that.

Sara pulled into a parking spot in front of the phone store, and we got out. We went in and added a phone to Axel's plan. They were giving us the run around until Sara called Axel so he could give his permission. We both were really quiet as we climbed back into the car.

Sara drove to her doctor's office and parked, neither one of us made a move to climb out. "I am so nervous. What was your appointment like?" she asked as she rubbed her palms on her pants.

"I-I never had one." I whispered feeling anxious. "I didn't know I needed to. Do you think I can get seen, too?" I asked as I looked at her and I knew my face was probably pale.

"How did you not know?" She asked me with wide eyes.

"I was eight when my mom was taken, remember? And Lucy and Grace weren't exactly the teaching type." I felt my anxiety increase. I really needed to get on something. Axel and I hadn't talked about kids yet. We were focused on Evie and getting to know each other better. How did this never cross my mind?

Sara's phone began to ring, and she answered it. "Calm down, Axel. Trinity and Evie are with me." She listened and rolled her eyes. "I understand I was with her last time too. We are just out running errands. We picked up Trinity's cell phone, I have an appointment and then we are heading to Evie's appointment. Why don't you meet us at the pediatrician's at 11:00am? I've got to go into the doctor's office now or we will be late. Yeah, yeah, yeah. Trinity loves you too. See you in a bit." Sara hung up the phone and turned to me. "Let's see if they will see us at the same time."

We got Evie out and headed inside. They agreed to add me to the schedule, and they put us in the same room after we left urine samples for them. The doctor came in and talked about several different options for birth control. Sara chose the pills, and the doctor wrote out a prescription for her. The doctor then turned to me with a smile and a sympathetic look on her face.

"We are going to go about this a little different for you, Trinity." She said as she pulled a machine out of the corner. "When was your last cycle?"

"I'm not sure. I have never been regular." I said nervously. "I've been stressed lately, and I heard stress can affect it."

"Can you sit on the table, please." Sara and I changed spots. "Lift your shirt and lay back. This might be a little cold." I did as she asked, and she placed cold gel on my stomach. She put a wand looking thing on the gel and began smearing it around. A whooshing sound came through the speakers and the doctor smiled. "There it is." She pointed to the screen.

My heart was beating so fast that I thought it was going to burst from my chest as I looked at the screen where she pointed. There was a little jellybean like blob moving around. I couldn't seem to find my voice as I tried to calm my breathing.

"What is that?" Sara asked in surprise.

"That is a baby." The doctor sat forward to get a better look at the screen. "Actually, there are two babies." She moved the wand around and pressed a few buttons on the machine. "From the measurements, you are about...eight weeks along. Does that sound about right?" The doctor glanced over at me. "Judging by you coming in for birth control and the look on your face, I'm guessing this wasn't planned."

I shook my head. "No, it wasn't." I finally managed to say as Sara's phone started to ring again. She glanced down at it and ignored the call. It immediately started ringing again. She once again ignored it before she put the phone on silent.

"I know this is a shock for you, but both babies look great. I will have the girls up front get together a bag with all the information for you. If you have any questions, do not hesitate to call. Your next appointment will be in four weeks." The doctor said softly as she patted my leg. "Congratulations, Mrs. Brooks."

Sara, Evie, and I left the office with a bag full of pamphlets and books. I was in a daze as I sat in the passenger seat, staring down at the ultrasound picture. Sara placed Evie's car seat on the base in the back of the car and climbed behind the wheel.

She pulled her phone out of her pocket. "Holy crap! Twenty-four missed calls?" She looked over at me. "I'll text them to meet us at Evie's appointment." She said as she typed out a message and put her phone down before she turned to look at me. "Trinity? How are you feeling?"

"I don't know." I said dumbly. "I didn't even think about it being a possibility."

"Eight weeks? You got married about eight weeks ago!" Sara's surprised expression made me smile a little.

"I'm aware of that Sara." I took a deep breath. "What is Axel going to say?" I asked quietly.

"He is going to meet us at the pediatrician's office. Why don't we head that way? The shock will wear off soon and then I'm sure you will be excited. Because I'm starting to really like the idea of having a few new nieces or nephews." Sara smiled at me, and I attempted a smile, but it was more of a grimace. I twisted around and slipped the pictures into the page I got from the doctor. We drove across town and pulled into a parking spot away from most of the cars already there. "Is that Axel's truck?" Sara asked.

Axel jumped out of the driver's seat and headed for Sara's car. Sara said she would get Evie and I climbed out of the car. I barely had the door closed when Axel wrapped his arms around me protectively and I leaned into him. I held tightly to him, and I could feel how tense he was.

"What happened? Where did you go?" He asked, but I still did not know what to say, so I just buried my face more into his chest. "Trinity?" He asked.

"Shut up, Axel, and just hold your wife. That's what she needs right now. We are all safe and healthy, so relax. Trinity just experienced a little shock." Sara snapped at him, and I laughed. That was one way to describe finding out I was pregnant with twins.

Tires squealed as a jeep whipped into a nearby spot. Matt, Liam, and Noah hopped out. They came running over. "What the heck, Sara? Why didn't you answer our calls?" Noah pulled Sara into his arms. "I swear the Enforcer's Bond turns these guys into mindless war machines. What's wrong with Trinity?"

"I was in an appointment, and it is rude to answer your phone while you are there." She shot back at him. "Speaking of appointments, Trinity, Evie's is in five minutes."

I nodded and stepped out of Axel's embrace. He grabbed Evie's car seat from Sara and held my hand tightly as we headed into the office. Sara kept the other guys out in the parking lot to wait for us.

I could tell that Axel was still worried by how often he kept looking at me. I held his hand and played with his fingers anxiously as we waited for the doctor to come in. Evie was declared completely healthy and received her vaccinations.

Everyone was waiting for us by Axel's truck when we got out. All the guys seemed confused and irritated but Sara was completely at ease. Axel put Evie's car seat in his truck before turning back to me and the gang.

"What's going on?" He finally broke his silence.

"We still need to run to Walmart." I said as I gave Sara a look and she nodded in understanding. "Sara, I have a feeling Axel wants me to ride with him, so I will meet you there." I said as I climbed into the truck. Axel climbed behind the wheel, and I could feel his anger building. "Axel, please give me a few more minutes. I promise I will tell you everything, I just need another minute." He looked at me and worry was written all over his face. He kissed my hand before pulling out of the parking spot.

As we drove to Walmart, I stared out the window as I absentmindedly drew patterns on the back of Axel's hand while I clutched it tightly with my other hand.

When we got there, Axel pulled me into a hug and kissed my head before getting Evie out of the back seat. We met the others inside. Sara walked next to me as she started adding random items into the cart.

When we got towards the back, I spotted the baby clothes. I pointed to them, and Sara smiled. The guys followed us over to them. Axel groaned when we stopped. "Evie has plenty of clothes." He grumbled.

"We need you to stop this negativity and put your numbers into Trin's new phone." Sara said as she handed the phone to the men. They kept a wary eye on us but allowed us to walk through the clothes without saying anything more.

Sara grabbed a purple and blue outfit and showed it to me with a huge grin. The onesie was light purple with blue writing across the front in cursive. It said, 'Big Sister' and there was a matching blue tutu. "This is perfect." She whispered. Her eyes lit up as she grabbed two more shirts. One said 'Copy' and the other said 'Paste'.

"Come on ladies, Evie is getting hungry, and she really doesn't need any more clothes." Axel called as he stood by the cart.

Sara passed me the outfits and walked over to Noah. I stared down at the shirts and my hands began to shake. How would Axel take the news? I glanced back at the group as they watched me.

I folded the clothes with the words on the inside and walked back to the cart before putting them in. Axel raised a brow at me, and I shrugged. We checked out and headed back to the truck. Axel and Matt loaded the truck with our needless purchases. I was holding the bag with the outfits in it because I didn't know if I was ready to say anything yet.

"What's so special about those clothes that you just had to get?" Matt asked as he made a grab for the bag. I was lost in my own thoughts, and he easily snatched it from me. "You are always telling me I can't spoil her with clothes anymore."

"It was too cute to resist." Sara said as she tried to grab it from Matt.

"Matt, please. I'm not in the mood for games." I said as my nervousness grew.

"Matt." Axel said firmly, and Matt tossed the bag to him. "What is going on? You've been pale since the pediatricians and withdrawn. Not to mention the fact that we can sense that you are freaking out about something." he asked with concern. I didn't say anything, and he pulled the purple outfit out. He unfolded it and looked at it and his brows furrowed in confusion. He pulled out the other two onesies before putting them back in the bag. "Uh… Sweetheart. The purple outfit is cute, but did you read what it says? And I don't even know what the two shirts are supposed to mean." Axel looked from the bag in his hand to me.

I nodded my head, as I began to cry. I was in Axel's arms in the next moment. He rubbed his hand up and down my back in a soothing gesture. "I don't understand. Why would you get Evie that if she isn't…" he whispered.

"Axel." Sara said his name as if she was talking to a child.

"Sara, don't." I said as I took a shaky breath. I walked over to Sara's car and pulled out the bag the doctor gave me. I looked through it and found the ultrasound picture. I turned around and walked back to the group. Axel watched me closely. I handed him the picture and held my breath. He stared down at it for several long moments before he slowly lifted his gaze to mine.

"Really?" he asked in a quiet whisper. He sounded just as surprised as I had been. I nodded slowly. He cupped my cheek and pressed a kiss to my lips.

"What is going on?" Liam finally asked in exasperation.

Axel laughed as a smile stretched across his face. He hugged me tight and lifted my feet off the ground before spinning me around in a circle. "So, you're not mad?" I asked anxiously.

"I couldn't be happier, my love." He pressed a kiss to my forehead and relief flooded me. I threw my arms around Axel's neck as he held me tight.

"Seriously, what is happening here?" Noah asked in frustration.

"Looks like you guys are going to have another niece or nephew." Axel said happily as he tossed the bag to Matt. Matt's mouth fell open in shock as he read the shirts. Matt, Liam, and Noah looked at us in surprise while Sara squealed in delight. "Trinity is pregnant." Axel announced proudly.

"That's not all." I said softly, realizing that he had not understood there was more than one baby.

"What do you mean?" Axel asked.

"What do these other two shirts mean?" Matt asked, holding them up.

I swallowed the lump in my throat and glanced over at Sara. She gave me a nod of encouragement and I looked back up at Axel. His smile was gone from his face as he studied me. "We are having twins, Axel." I finally managed to say in a soft voice.

"Copy. Paste. Get it?" Sara laughed.

Axel blinked several times as he processed what I had just said. "Two?" He whispered in disbelief. He looked back at the ultrasound picture and then back at me. Tears gathered in my eyes again. "Trinity? Baby, are you okay?" He asked.

"I'm scared." I whispered and he pulled me to him, wrapping his arms around me. "I don't know how I feel about this."

Sara motioned for the guys to leave and soon Axel and I were standing alone next to the truck. "I know we haven't talked about having kids of our own yet." Axel said, pulling back slightly so he could see my face. "And I know that Evie is still very young but Sweetheart, I couldn't be happier." He pressed a kiss to my lips. "Honestly Trin, I'm scared too. I know it isn't going to be easy, but we can get through it. Especially if they are as amazing as you." He smiled down at me. "Now, why don't we head back home? Evie can spend the rest of the day and tonight with her grandparents." Axel moved one of his hands so that it rested on my stomach. "I think we could both use some time to let this new...development sink in. And we can worry about telling everyone tomorrow."

I leaned into him. "That sounds great. I don't think it's fully hit me yet." Axel's arms tightened around me, and I took a deep breath.

He pressed a kiss to my forehead as he held me close. "I love you, Trinity." He whispered. "But I think we might need to find a place of our own sooner than we thought."

I laughed as I wiped the last of my tears away. "I think you might be right. Three under a year, Axel. That is a lot."

"It's okay, Baby. We got this."

"That is what you told me right before you asked me to marry you." I commented.

"Exactly. And look at how good that turned out." Axel winked at me as he helped me into the truck. Once we made it back to the house he turned to face me. "I hope they are boys. I have a feeling if they are girls, they are going to be just like you. And I don't know if I can handle four of you." I laughed. He had a large grin on his face as he leaned over and kissed me.

THE END

The Hunter Guardian Series

The Hunted Guardian
The Stone's Keeper
The Stone's Secret

Other books by this author:

Left Broken
Embracing Dove

When Worlds Collide Series

When Worlds Collide
Prey of the Corrupted Alpha

Paranormal Books

Enforcer's Mark

Upcoming Books

Hoodwinked
Two Sides of the Same Coin

www.ingramcontent.com/pod-product-compliance
Lightning Source LLC
LaVergne TN
LVHW012014060526
838201LV00061B/4297